SOMETIMES

WE'RE ALWAYS

REAL SAME-SAME

Eric –
It was amazing
to share the
'stage' with
you. Have
a great
summer.
Never
Change!

M S R

SOMETIMES

WE'RE ALWAYS

REAL SAME-SAME

MATTOX ROESCH

UNBRIDLED BOOKS

Unbridled Books
Denver, Colorado

Library of Congress Cataloging-in-Publication Data
Roesch, Mattox, 1977–
Sometimes we're always real same-same/Mattox Roesch.
p. cm.
ISBN 978-1-932961-87-4
1. Eskimos—Alaska—Fiction.   2. Cousins—Fiction.
3. Country life—Alaska—Fiction.   I. Title.
PS3618.O375S66   2009
813'.6—dc22
2009017497

1   3   5   7   9   10   8   6   4   2

Book Design by SH · CV

First Printing

The Eskimo words used in this novel are from the Unalakleet dialect. Unalakleet is the southernmost Iñupiat village, boarding the Central Yup'ik region. Although most of the Eskimo words are Iñupiaq, some are Yup'ik, and some are variations of both. The words used here are by no means authoritative, and their spelling reflets the regional pronunciation.

Dedicated to the memories of

Jason Everhard and Gabriel Towarak

I am grateful for the journals that published the stories that evolved into this novel:

Narrative Magazine, "All the Way Rider"
Redivider, "The Thing in Her Thumb"
AGNI Online, "Humpies"
2007 Best American Nonrequired Reading, "Humpies"
The Missouri Review, "Go at Shaktoolik"
Indiana Review, "Burn the House Down"
The Sun, "Maluksuk"

SOMETIMES

WE'RE ALWAYS

REAL SAME-SAME

ONE

ESKIMO JESUS

I almost ended up with Go-boy's tattoo. I lost the bet and was supposed to get this drawing of an Eskimo Jesus tattooed on my right
forearm. It was the tattoo that Go-boy had inked on his own arm.
The design he had created.

Our bet started when I moved from Los Angeles to Unalakleet,
Alaska. I was seventeen. Mom was sick of my shit and sick of her
own shit, so she gave in and moved us about as far away from LA as
possible—to the place where she'd grown up, the place where she
hadn't been in twenty years. A bunch of family I'd never seen before
welcomed us when we got out of the small plane. My cousin Go-boy
was with them. He was tall, taller than me, and his black hair stood on
end, messy, like a cloud of smoke. Go introduced me to a few people
and then we split, and he gave me a tour of his small village—my
new home. It was only the second time I had met Go, and I told him
I was moving back to California at the end of summer, in three

months, telling him this was just a temporary thing. But for some reason he didn't believe me. He bet I'd stay.

He said, "You'll still be here this time next year."

I laughed at the idea right then. It was strange. I didn't know why he thought he knew me so well or why he didn't want me to leave his town. I'd never known anyone with such confidence—not in other people, not in me. But either way, it turned out he was right—I stayed and lost the bet. I stayed through the summer, through the manic sun of June and July, the ditches full of fireweed, the dusted car windows, the gravel-filled shoes. I stayed into the months of mud puddles and rusted bike chains, and then the forgettable fall. I stayed for my senior year in high school. I stayed for seven months of winter, seven months of blizzards, seven months of east winds and billboard-sized drifts, seven months of short and shorter days. And I stayed through the spring melt and into the next summer. I even stayed during the few times Go himself left.

But I didn't get Go-boy's tattoo.

ALL THE WAY RIDER

We leave the airport and Go throws my bags into his busted hatchback.

He says, "You want the Unalakleet tour? I could ride you around, show you everything."

I assume he means drive.

As we ride, Go only talks about the village. *In the village . . . In the village . . .* He's trying to sell me on this place. I'm not interested. This is the second time I've met Go, but the first was years earlier, back in California, and it feels like I'm meeting him all over again.

"In the village," he says, waving to a group of kids, "everybody's sure always waiting for their shipment." He lists things like house paint, mattresses, rubber boots, even food.

"There's no stores?"

"Well," he says, "there is. But . . ."

He rides me around and we coast over washboard ripples and potholes on the gravel road. The sun is strong. Everything is dry and chalky. The colors, even—dusty beiges and light blues. The dashboard is dirty. An AM station buzzes, and Go waves at everyone he sees. He points out cousins of ours, aunts, family members who weren't at the airport.

"That's your mom's uncle," he says. "Our grandpa lived over there."

He shows me the post office, AC Store, Native Store, Igloo, the lodge, and a bunch of other plywood buildings with tin roofs. There are no signs or advertisements, no trees or grass lawns, and the houses are crowded under empty grids of telephone poles. It's the ugliest place I've ever seen.

Go calls it the real Alaska.

Go says, "In the village, there's no such thing as a family reunion."

As we drive I see a tattoo poking out from under his right cuff. He sees me looking and pulls up his sleeve. Go even smiles a little right then. It's a drawing of an Eskimo Jesus, stretching hand to elbow, wrapping around and blanketing most of Go's forearm. Thin blue strokes shape the Eskimo's face and parka. Facial features are labeled with descriptions. The eyes are *INFINITY*. The ears are *UNITY*. And so on. I want to ask him why he drew Jesus looking that way, but instead I tell him it kind of looks like the guy on the Alaska Airlines logo. Go says it isn't a guy. Go says the returning Jesus will be a woman.

"A Daughter. Daughter of the world."

We pass a playground set in the middle of a dirt lot next to a school. The radio regains reception and I bounce my heel with the song. Go-boy asks if I've graduated. I haven't.

"My pop and me are starting a business together back home, in the fall."

We drive down Beach Road beside the ocean and then back through town on Main Road. Some houses are painted teal and every yard is littered with skeletons of four-wheelers and snowmachines and fishing boats. Sometimes ratty dogs. Sometimes fifty-five-gallon barrels. There are bunches of people out walking around, and I wonder if they have no place to dump all this junk.

Go says, "Yeah, man, in the village there's never any street addresses. No grid. Houses were always just built any old place. Pretty champ, huh?"

A little farther down the road he refers to this place as *Unk*—its airport code.

Go-boy drives us to the edge of town and parks his AMC in the middle of a concrete bridge, blocking the single lane. He shuts the engine off. My side overlooks a slough—a water parking lot of fishing boats lining the shore. In front of us the road splits bare fields of brownish tundra, stretching out and ramping up hills, disappearing into evergreens. With the town in our mirrors and the empty nature through our windshield, we stay in his station wagon, parked on the sun-bleached bridge, waiting for something. At least I think we're waiting.

"Where's this road go?"

"About twelve miles," he says, and laughs.

I ask him if that's it, if it just ends, because I've never heard of a road just ending, but right then a huge jet flies over us and he can't hear me.

Go-boy tells me the plane is Northern Air Cargo. It flies over the village every day at the same time, around three o'clock. The plane is too heavy to take off the runway traveling north like all the other little jets. So at three o'clock it roars over every house and building, roaring over every phone call and TV show, rattling picture frames, interrupting everything. Go says, "If there's something you need, NAC will bring it." He tells me the cargo plane is the town's only connection to the stuff of the world. Mail, groceries, building supplies, everything.

"People sure always phone the airport, ask, 'There a NAC today?' Meaning, 'Did my stuff come?' Village-style shopping, man."

I look through the windshield. "The only road out of town doesn't get anywhere?"

Go-boy nods. "I could show you."

I tell him I'm planning to save money so I can leave Alaska at the end of summer, when I turn eighteen. I say my pop and me are opening a starter and alternator rebuild shop. That it's a respectable gig.

"In three months?" he asks.

I watch that big plane through my passenger window as it tips left and fades behind a wash of distant clouds. We stay parked on the bridge way too long and I wonder what the hell we're doing, but it doesn't matter and I don't even care because I have nothing else to do.

Go is silent. I notice that when he's not talking bullshit, he can be calm. Quiet, even.

Then he says, "I'll make a bet with you, man. I bet you stay for one year."

"A year?"

"Yeah," he says. "You'll stay at least a year. Maybe more. I know you'll do good here."

I laugh because it's ridiculous, because Go has only known me for an hour, and because everything about me—my name and my style—is still back in Los Angeles.

"What are we betting?"

Go looks right to left, through the windshield and out over the nothingness, as if there is anything on the tundra worth wagering. "Does it make a difference?"

It shouldn't, I think. I know I'm leaving. I have to. I know I could never stay in a place like this. But I don't answer.

Five years earlier I met Go-boy in Los Angeles. He'd won a trip to Disneyland for his whole family after making a home movie and entering it in a contest for Native Alaskan high school students—*What are the most important issues facing rural villages in the twenty-first century?* I remember because it was the first time I had ever thought about Alaska. Go-boy brought the tape along and showed us. Mom was silent the whole time, watching. After a while, she asked Go's dad—her brother—"When did they build those snow fences? What happened to General Store?" Go narrated the ten-minute video and ended it by saying, "Unalakleet, like most Alaskan villages and other Native communities, will be a gauge for America's priorities in the twenty-first century."

That was the same month Wicho went to prison. Wicho was my older brother and my only brother, and he had already been locked up for almost a year, in and out of trial, so we were used to him being gone. But it was that month, when Go-boy came to Disneyland, that Wicho was sentenced to life in prison, putting an end to months in limbo.

I remember everything that happened at the time—Wicho's arrest, his trial, his sentencing. I remember how through all the waiting—the string of trials and mistrials, the settlement offers, and the damning evidence—Mom was busing to the courthouse for every meeting and hearing, always convinced of Wicho's innocence, always on time, always optimistic. And I remember when the jury called him guilty and the guards hauled him away (and scolded Mom for trying to talk to him), she managed to stay composed. She led me out of the courtroom, silent, ignoring the PD and the victims' families, not flinching until one of the jurors found us in the hall and tried to apologize. "I'm sorry for your son," he said, jumping in front. I told him to get the hell away, but it was too late. After a year of silent humiliation, Mom broke down. She cried. But when she did, when she walked off through that hall, her arms wrapped around her torso, I wasn't sure if it was for her son or for herself.

What happened was that Wicho gave his life for a gang. A year before any college or army could claim him, he shot two fifteen-year-old kids on a Wednesday afternoon. He shot members of his own gang—Mara Salvatrucha. They had tried to leave the clique, saying they had never represented anybody, but Wicho told me they'd been jumped in and everything, and one even had *MS13* tattooed on his stomach Old English–style. He said they knew what they'd gotten themselves into. Knew being jumped in meant forever.

We lived in West Los Angeles at the time. Every day Go-boy and his family were in LA they'd come by our house in a rental car—Go and his dad and his stepmom—and it was the first time I'd met any of our family from Alaska. Growing up, we'd heard nothing about Mom's side, but there they were in our house. Go-boy looked about the same age as Wicho, but taller, and he spent most of the time trying to find out what we had in common.

Go said, "The Lakers could win the whole thing this year, ah?"

"I like Chicago."

Go told me I should come visit Unalakleet. They were leaving LA, and he said I should come for Bible camp or for silver fishing or even to play on his basketball team in the holiday tournament Jamboree. He said, "Did you know Alaska is so big it stretches from Florida to Minnesota to California? And the whole state only has the population of Milwaukee."

I knew Pop never had any interest in Alaska. When he was around, living with us—which wasn't often—he never talked about Mom's family or where she'd grown up. Never gave her the chance. He'd even change the subject.

Mom's take on her marriage with Pop was this—when she needed him, he was never around, and when she didn't need him, she said, "He eats all our food and tries to get me pregnant." That wasn't true, but this was after she kicked Pop out of the car and left him with the street murals by the Celaya Bakery on Twenty-third. She was trying out this attitude to see how it sounded. I didn't expect she'd turn it into a habit. And that was the last time we saw Pop. Not long after, she started talking about moving to Alaska.

I kept telling her I wanted to stay with Pop, start a business with him, stay in LA. I kept telling her I wanted to stay for Wicho because when I turned eighteen at the end of summer, I would be able to visit him. I told her I wanted to be with my friends.

"Fine, I don't care," she said after a while. "Don't come. Do whatever you want."

That year I was running with a Sureños Thirteen clique—Clicka los Primos. It was a rival gang of Wicho's on the streets, but in prison it was the same. Wicho was Mara Salvatrucha, six years earlier, and maybe even more now that he was in prison.

We both ran with Hispanic gangs even though neither of us had a drop of Hispanic blood. Pop always tried telling us our great-grandma was Mexican and we shouldn't forget that. All Pop's friends were Chicanos and he seemed to think he was Chicano too. He was older than Mom and had grown up in a part of town where being white wasn't cool—that was why he gave his sons Mexican names. Wicho—Luis. Luis Daniel Stone. Me—Cesar. Cesar Silas Stone. He had our names tattooed on his chest, and later I learned that we were named after friends of his who had died. *RIP Wicho. RIP Cesar.* Pop said they were also family names from his grandmother's side. But Wicho said that everybody in LA had a Mexican grandmom and that Pop was just full of shit. And when it came to Pop and his stories and his plans, Wicho tended to side with Mom.

It was just like when Pop beat us, how Wicho—from when he was a little kid all the way up—would throw himself in front of Mom or try to pull Pop away. And it was Wicho who ended up with the purple cheeks and the weeklong limps. Pop would only hit us when he was superdrunk, and I reminded myself of that. Regardless, his punches ended when I was about nine, when Pop threw me backward over an end table, about to pounce because I'd said something about money, and Wicho, at fifteen, stomped in and beat Pop into some kind of mess that surprised both of them. But it was during the years that Pop was raging and we all got beaten that I felt he was raging against us for who we weren't. I felt he was beating me because I wasn't *Cesar* enough and Wicho because he wasn't *Luis* enough.

All through growing up, we didn't see Mom as an Eskimo. Maybe Mom didn't talk about it because she was trying to forget about her family, or maybe Pop tried to ignore the fact that his wife had darker skin than he did. And maybe that was why he thought he could get away with giving us Mexican names—he knew Wicho and me would look just like those pale-skinned Chicanos he'd been running with his whole life. Light, but not pinkish, with black hair, and a day at the beach would tan the shit out of our skin. And he was right. We were those chameleon kids who almost blended in but never quite did—we were too dark to look white with white people and too pale to look anything but white in the streets. I don't know about Wicho, but I always felt like an imposter—Cesar, the white Chicano—like it was a matter of time before my friends called me on it. But they knew our mom wasn't Mexican because she didn't speak Spanish. Not a syllable. And our friends didn't care. Wicho and me weren't the only light-skinned kids running with Sureños or Salvatruchas. We ran with the crews who didn't keep track of where everyone's family was from. And regardless, or maybe as a result, I had forgotten Mom was Native.

Mom said, "It'll be good for you to spend time with your real family." She was trying to convince me that going to Alaska was a good idea. But I'd only met Go-boy and his parents, and the rest were just a bunch of strangers. That wasn't family.

The first step Mom took in leaving Pop was leaving his neighborhood. She moved us out of LA right after Wicho was sentenced. Besides leaving Pop, she thought a better area would be good for us, get us away from the place that landed her son in jail, get us away from the things she related to being poor—the street art and street vendors and tangerine-colored buildings on Pico Boulevard. We moved in with first-generation strip malls. Moved to Santa Ana. And that was where I hooked up with Los Primos.

That was why I didn't want to leave—my friends were in Santa Ana. But more than that, if I moved I could never come back. The thing that had landed Wicho in prison was the same thing that would happen to me if I was ever seen around home again. None of my friends knew I was going to Alaska.

They asked me one night when a dozen of us were at a hotel party. Kids were sitting on beds and tables and the air conditioner under the window, ladies too, smoking and drinking, waiting for me to answer. They were extra suspicious these days because about half our crew was in jail, waiting on a trial, and anyone who disappeared was suspected of pulling some shit and making a deal with police.

I told them we'd bought a house a couple miles up Tustin Ave in Orange. I told them that in spite of moving, nothing would change.

Even though all those kids in the gang would've left if they'd had the chance, disappearing was the worst. Any secrets were the worst. We weren't a real violent clique, like those always out there carjacking or starting shit in other neighborhoods for no reason. Sometimes, if necessary. And we had some enemies. But most of the time we'd just be hanging out, throwing these hotel parties, selling some drugs, getting high, and having sex with girls. School nights, weekends, anytime, it didn't matter. Teachers would flunk us and send us to the non-college-bound part of school. And those teachers would just chuckle when we fell behind and send us down to the technical high or to charter schools—whoever would take us. The teachers spent all their time trying to convince us that we needed to believe our future was important, that we needed to commit our lives to something. They always tried to convince us to get off our butts and work harder when all we wanted to do was have fun. And they were just saying that stuff to make themselves feel good, feel like they were doing the right thing. We knew our future was important. We knew what they didn't believe—that it would work out, somehow.

N ope," Go-boy says. "I bet you never leave, man."

We're still parked on the concrete bridge. Still blocking the road. But it doesn't matter because nobody is coming or leaving. Go adjusts the rearview mirror, nods, says, "You'll sure always find a nice Native girl and get married and have a bunch of real Native kids."

"Tell me what we're betting."

Instead Go-boy tells me more about the village and our family. He tells me he's just gotten back from college in Anchorage, and he's working upriver for the summer on a fish tower. He's not planning to go back to school, though. He's dropping out. And I'm not supposed to say anything about it to anybody because it's still a secret and he doesn't want his sister to find out, but I don't even think twice. Who would I tell? When I ask him what he plans on doing instead of school, Go says he doesn't know yet, but he has lots of ideas and possibilities, maybe jobs, and maybe even a few options that will include me.

"Something's bound to happen around here," he says, still looking through the windshield, as if it's waiting for him. "It already feels like I have a plan, like *we* have a plan."

"My plan is to save cash so I can get back home."

Go says, "She's coming, you know. God." He tells me that humanity has grown from the male essence, the masculine-dominated perspective, and that humanity will become fulfilled in the female, the feminine, the spiritual. When God comes, it won't be the end of the world, but its fulfillment.

I laugh, say, "Grew from the male? Fulfilled in the female?"

He laughs too and tells me the Eskimo word for penis—tunggu.

"So your tattoo is a religious thing?"

"No," he says. "How we love is our religion. Not what we believe."

He's in the driver's seat, looking out at a single row of telephone poles that veer off the road and run up into the hills. Both of his hands are resting at the bottom of the wheel, at six o'clock. He leans back, pulls up his right sleeve again, and shows me the sketch that runs along his forearm. "It isn't real," he says. "I've drawn it on about fifty times with ink-pen." He tells me he's planning to get the permanent kind later that summer.

"I thought about getting some too."

He holds the inside of the wheel at twelve o'clock with that arm, his sleeve hiked to his elbow. He points to parts of the drawing with his left hand. "This will be Native Jesus. She's reaching into the clouds on this side and the sea on that side."

Go-boy tells me his tattoo is why he is dropping out of school, the Bible college. He tells me Jesus died for everybody, not just those who know about him. If people don't believe that, then they're deciding whose life is worth saving and whose isn't.

I say, "I wouldn't give my life for nobody," and that echoes in the cab of the car for a minute. It's awkward. I think about Wicho.

"Well," Go says, "good thing you're not Jesus, then, ah?"

Two kids on a four-wheeler pass us coming into town and squeeze by our wagon. Go-boy waves and they wave back. We stay parked right there, facing the hills and the sky that wrap around on all sides. In the silence, only the occasional village sound from be-

hind us—a barking dog or pickup truck—can remind me that I am
still somewhere.

B efore we left California Mom visited Wicho almost every two
weeks. When she came home from her last visit she said Wicho
didn't want us to leave but told her he'd do his best to behave and
maybe get out on parole. He was optimistic that *life* didn't mean for
life. Mom reported all of this because I was a minor, and minors
weren't allowed to visit guys locked up for murder.

Mom said, "He still believes you'll go to college and find a way
to get him out."

The first year he was jailed I wrote him letters, and sometimes,
when Mom let me, I rode along to the prison and waited in our
Caravan, listened to music. I was twelve, and sometimes we brought
my BMX and Mom dropped me off outside the chain-link fences. I
biked around the little roads, up and down the surrounding hills.
Wicho wrote me letters too, and in the process he'd put this idea
into my head that if I worked hard I could get him out of jail. So I
had a plan. And while I biked around the prison fences I figured out
the time it would take to go to college and become governor so I
could get Wicho free—I'd be twenty-four and Wicho would be
thirty. One time the yard was full of prisoners and from a distance I
could see them watching me, pointing me out to their friends. I kept
riding up and down the roads, with the wind kicking hot dust in my
face and knotting my hair, and I didn't even look at the inmates who
watched. I just whispered to them. Told them to treat their future
governor with respect. Told them if they did that, and if they also
treated Wicho good, then I could get them out someday too. One of

the inmates in the yard whistled—maybe to get my attention, or maybe to get another prisoner's attention. I don't know. Either way, I just kept my eyes on the road. I ignored them. I pretended they weren't there.

Mom seemed sad and defeated after her final visit to the prison, like she was giving up. And when she told me Wicho still believed I would get him out, even though it was a simple nod to our past—a silent understanding of this thing we shared and would always share as brothers—there was a strong part of me that still believed I would someday set him free. I knew my life would always hinge on saving him.

But I moved to Alaska with Mom anyway. We flew from LAX to Anchorage in a jumbo jet and then hopped on a second flight, a Pen-Air twelve-seater, boarding from the tarmac. The small plane had one thin aisle with a single beige seat on either side. Plexiglas windows. Only a little kid could stand up without getting a busted head. In the sky that thing flew on a bungee cord, dipping and bouncing, its twin engines blaring like they were topped out. Mom seemed like a different person once on board. She wouldn't pay attention to anything. It had been twenty years since she'd severed all contact with her home, and I knew she wasn't ready to return. But she had no choice—she was broke.

I'd been asking Mom questions about Alaska since we'd flown out of Anchorage, trying to find something to protest. I asked her if there was running water in the village. If there were cars, TV. I asked about our family. The food. Anything, looking for something that might turn us around and send us home. And in that loud plane, with nobody talking, flying on a string through empty white air, she went along with it all, doing her best not to snap.

"Is there any music in Alaska?" I yelled across the aisle, now less than an hour from Unalakleet.

Mom repeated, "Music in Alaska?" and gave me a dumb look.

"You know, like a sound. Is there such a thing as Alaskan music?"

She mouthed, *Music*, but then something switched in her and she didn't try to answer my question. She turned to the passing clouds. She maybe didn't know. Maybe didn't remember.

The flight was about two hours long. Pale and bright clouds surrounded us the whole trip, jarring us. The two pilots sat up front, shoulder to shoulder, like in a Ford Pinto. The little windshield wipers worked off the rain. A Native guy in the front seat passed back a wire basket filled with complimentary chips and cookies and juice. Occasional beeping sounds could be heard over the engines.

By the end of the trip Mom had closed her eyes in a way that I knew she wasn't sleeping, but thinking, and remembering. Stressing.

Then we saw the ocean with its fingerprint of waves, and the plane banked right as wisps of clouds blew past, and down below us, about the size of a pen cap or cigarette butt, was Unalakleet. Mom opened her eyes and we both looked out our separate windows at the village—stacks of homes on a spit of land between the ocean and a mess of rivers. I looked back at Mom, and we caught each other's nervous glances.

I wondered when she had last seen all this. Later I'd learn that while growing up she'd fly all the time—into Nome for doctors' visits and shots, Anchorage for clothes and groceries. She'd fly on these little planes packed with the girls' basketball team on their way to weekend tournaments. Then at some point she flew on a little plane out of here, got married, had kids, lost her oldest son to prison, then divorced. Never once did she visit. I wondered what drove her to disappear for that long.

The airport was an aluminum building, like a farm shed, next to other aluminum buildings with garage doors for planes. About forty people were inside, standing around, joking and sipping coffee from paper cups. A few sat along the back wall under some windows, watching, waiting to board our same plane and fly back to Anchorage.

Mom walked in behind me, hesitated, then hugged people. Those expecting us looked surprised that we were there, that we hadn't bailed at the last minute. Other people said, "Hey, Lynn," walked up to Mom and stopped three feet away without shaking hands or embracing, and said, "Welcome home!" I met almost everyone in the building. They told me their names and how we were related.

That was when I met Go-boy for the second time. He was even taller than before—his hair adding a couple inches. I could see the tail end of a tattoo poking out from his jacket sleeve. And by the way he weaved through the crowd, smiling and patting shoulders and bringing that same reaction out of everyone, like a hero, I knew he loved this home of his, and this home of his loved him.

Go put his arm around me, said, "Hey, Cousin, here you are," and pointed to a spot on the big map of Alaska that was pinned to the wall.

Out the window a forklift was carrying a pallet stacked with luggage. It wheeled past the building and set the bags next to the parking lot. One of mine was pinched in the middle.

Go kept his arm around me. He said, "Most people think Unalakleet means 'where the east wind blows.' But really it means 'southernmost.'"

"Southern?"

"Yeah," Go-boy said, nodding. "Most."

Go-boy picks me up on my second day in Unk and offers me either a boat ride upriver or another drive up the road. I guess this is what you do here—ride—and there are some things I didn't see yesterday. A couple gravel pits, a dump, a fuel tank field, and a brand-new jail a lot of guys in town are contracted to build. I say okay to the ride. We drive out of town a few miles in Go's wagon. On the way we pass the new jail's work site—a big hole in the ground, bordered with piles of fresh sand and rocks, and I ask why such a small village needs a jail at all.

"It's for the whole region," Go says. "But yeah, I doubt we'll need it much longer. Things have sure been getting better out here."

Go parks at the top of a hill, at the edge of a clearing, and we get out of the car and look around. Below us the town is a small strip of buildings lining the ocean, small and lifeless, like a distant rail yard.

Go points to the right of town, says, "That's Amak Hill. Amak is Eskimo for boob." He traces the perky mound with his finger in the air, then traces a smaller hill right next to it, making a second breast shape. "That used to be the other amak, but they flattened it for the gravel pit. Now we call that one Training Bra." He laughs.

I decide to tell him some shit about LA. Some lies. I say, "Los Angeles was named Los Angeles because those Spanish explorers believed it was a sex paradise of Indian women."

"There's Indians nearby, behind Whaleback Mountains, over at Kaltag."

"Not right here?" I ask.

"No," he says. "Eskimos are a totally different race."

Down the hill I can see guys pouring the concrete foundation for the new jail. It's just a skeleton of the building's structure, an outline, and it's sunk into the side of this hill so it is only visible from where we are standing. You couldn't see it from town yet.

Go-boy tells me we are on Air Force Hill. There was once an army base here, and another at the end of the road. He says the base had a missile detection system they used during the Cold War. "I don't know what the army was so worried about. Eskimos never worry about a Russian invasion."

I spin around and see nothing but little mountains and trees trailing off behind us. The road snakes its way through the hills and valleys, disappearing.

I say, "Maybe they were worried about nuclear bombs."

"Nukes," Go says. "Nukes don't work up here, man. We're too close to the magnetic pole. It messes with the fission or something."

I say, "No way, those bombs work anywhere. They could blow up the moon."

"Yeah, because the moon doesn't have a magnetic pole," Go says. "They don't work in Alaska, though. Lots of stuff doesn't work here. Cold medicine. Airbags. Condoms."

"What?"

"Yeah, man. Why do you think people are always getting sick?"

Go sits on the hood of the car. He's smiling a little, looking toward town. I'm not sure if he's the type of guy to mess with me just because, or if he knows I was messing with him first, or if he believes all that.

"So what do you want to bet?" Go says.

I was hoping he'd forgot.

"Our bet," he says, slapping at a bug on his arm. "From yesterday."

We watch the NAC cargo plane take off again. We are three miles out of town and the jet climbs over Unalakleet, without sound, and then banks toward the interior.

"You still plan on leaving in three months?"

I nod.

"I bet you stay a year, at least. And if you stay, you have to get my tattoo." Go hikes his sleeve to show me the drawing again. It doesn't look as good today. Today it's faded and some of the ink is smudged at the crease where his arm bends.

From on top of the hill—surrounded by the blur of trees and tundra and the bubble of open sky . . . with the strip of an unfamiliar village and all its machinery and junk miles below . . . with this cousin who talks about changing the world from his HUD home—I can't even begin to think about staying in Alaska and not seeing Pop or Wicho for another year, and yet I can't even admit to myself how dangerous it would be for me to go home, so the options are ridiculous. They seem impossible.

"By the time you lose, I'll have the tattoo for real all right. We'll both have it. We'll be real same-same."

"And when I leave before a year?"

"I dunno. Anything. I'll bet whatever you want, man, because I know you'll stay."

"A car?"

He tells me he'll buy me a house if I want. Anything. All I have to do is move in a year. But instead of a car, I think about college. Would he pay for that? And then I think about a lawyer for Wicho, one that's not a public defender and could appeal his case and get him out of prison. Would he pay for that?

"I don't want the tattoo."

We're silent for a while and the mosquitoes start swarming—big, nickel-sized mosquitoes—so Go hops off the hood and we get back in the car.

He says, "I know *the plan* will reveal something."

It wasn't until later that summer that I would understand what he was talking about—his *plan*. It was an idea that everything in his life was part of a world conspiracy—a good conspiracy. It was kind of crazy-sounding. But on my first day in Unalakleet Go was just starting to put these things together. He had always believed everything would work out for everyone. Now he was starting to believe everything would become perfect. Everything would join together to become heaven. Not long after I arrived he said, "People who wait for paradise don't really want it." Go started believing in heaven on earth, believing it was about to happen and believing it was his duty to dedicate his life to the cause. He called it his *strange plan*.

Go-boy was convinced that with the right perspective, anything was possible. This was always evident, even when I'd met him the first time, when we were younger, and the second time, at the airport. He said people walk around most days without feeling alive; people go every moment without paying attention to the quiet life—the life that matters—the voice that can direct a person's destiny away from a world of shame and guilt to a world of meaning and realization. According to Go, the way to live was to listen to your heart. *Intentionality*, he called it. Something about how you've already sketched out your life—joys, sorrows, mistakes, accomplishments—before birth, and it is your conscience that reveals how to live your intended life. The goal is to experience multiple lives, experience everything.

Go drives us out of the hills and back into town, and I start lying again. I say, "Did you know Los Angeles is the religious capital of the world?"

"No," he says. "How?"

The gravel road runs straight downhill and all we see in every direction is miles of open tundra and water. It's strange how small the village seems compared to everything else. I've never been to a city that is so dominated by empty space all around, like a strong wind or wave could just wipe it away.

"LA has the most religions, or is the most religious, or something."

Go parks his car in the middle of the concrete bridge again. This time we are facing the village.

He says, "When I think of LA, I think of Hollywood. And Hollywood projects this America where everything is a product for sale, everything is buyable material—most importantly, identity. Even spiritual identity has gone public. And man, the more we rely on external identity the more detached we become, because the only things of value are earned, and there is never enough to go around, and the travesty is that the valuable and sacred aren't inherent. There's no image of God. No creativity. Only image of image, only replications of replicas."

We watch a lady in a fishing boat pull up to the shore, throw out her front and back anchors, and then hop onto the sand and walk away.

"I've never been to Hollywood," I say, lying.

"LA. New York. Doesn't matter, man. Rural is the new city."

It's my second day here, but it feels like I've already lived in Alaska for too long.

"So this is the only concrete in town?"

Go says, "No, there's the basketball court."

I picture every kid hogged onto that slab, shoulder to shoulder, dribbling basketballs, tre-flipping skateboards, even hopping on pogo sticks. Everyone pushing and shoving for their fair share. And the other kids who aren't into sports sit on benches and watch.

"In the village," Go says, "time is way less important than purpose."

For a minute we see no vehicles. No people are out walking along the roads. No dogs are testing the lengths of their chains. No airplanes are delivering or loading supplies or people. It's as if the village is unpopulated. I never would've imagined something like this being possible in the middle of the day, here or in LA or any-where. For a minute nothing happens.

Then Go says, "I've got it. I've got the bet."

"It won't even matter."

"If you stay here longer than a year, you have to change your first name."

"Change it?"

"To your Eskimo name," Go says.

"But I don't want an Eskimo name."

"You don't have one?"

"No," I say. "I don't want one."

"Man, I'll give you an Eskimo name."

Go-boy starts thinking, and I wonder if Eskimo names can be given to non-Eskimos—this is the first I've ever heard of them. I wonder if they are the kind of thing that Go can just hand out without talking to anyone. It seems like something parents should decide, like something Mom should come up with. But I doubt she's thinking about that on her second day home after twenty years. I can't imagine what she's thinking about. And I can't imagine having something like this—an Eskimo name—without Wicho or Pop having one too. A name is such a permanent thing. A name makes the person almost as much as the person makes the name. And as we sit in Go's car on the bridge, I think about how even though I don't like the name Cesar, it was given to me by Pop, and so I accept it and can't fathom changing it.

He says, "Sure always takes long time to find the right Eskimo name."

Go-boy sits behind the steering wheel of his AMC Eagle for what seems like forever, moving his lips every few seconds and thinking about possible names. And Go keeps on like this—in his car on the bridge . . . and back at his house later that day . . . and even later that summer.

A work truck rolls onto the bridge, maybe heading out of town to the new jail. The guy looks like an engineer from Anchorage. He pulls alongside us, slow, trying to pass, then stops. There are just a few inches between our vehicles. The guy folds in his side mirror. He rolls down his window, and Go, seeing this, rolls down his.

"You got trouble?"

Go-boy says, "No, we're just waiting."

The guy looks up and down the slough for signs of something to wait for. I look with him. He glances around the open fields in front of his truck, then he turns in his seat and looks back at the village. There is nothing happening anywhere. He asks, "For what?"

I am wondering the same thing. Go stares through the windshield, straight down the road and back into town, maybe running through a list of possible names to give me, maybe not. A kid on a bike rolls across the gravel where it curves between two homes. On the left side is a row of dogs who've appeared, sitting on top of their little plywood houses, ugly dogs, watching us.

Go turns back to the guy in his truck, says, "We're waiting to find out."

TWO

BUNNY BOOTS

I told myself that as long as I was living way the hell up here in Alaska, I would have some fun. I would be with this girl—Kiana.

It was her face. She was beautiful, attractive, sexy, all those things, but those weren't what did it. What got me, what hooked me from across the room that night—from the other side of the party—through the beats in the speakers, the smoke in the air, the fight about a crashed four-wheeler, the screams for them to shut the fuck up, the hole punched through a wall—what turned me away from the door and my next shift on the fish-counting tower was Kiana's compelling face. She was mixing rum and diet soda in the kitchen, and instead of leaving I walked over to her.

She was Go-boy's stepsister. She was my stepcousin. I knew I should've forgotten about her and gone back upriver to work my graveyard shift. I knew she had already forgotten about me moving here. But none of that mattered. She had the air. She had the look. I couldn't stop myself. I was walking across the room.

I said, "Kiana?"

Her face was wide and strong, but it wasn't a physical character-istic that gave it gravity. It was the way she looked through every-thing. It was the relationship between her massaged expression and all the hyper kids in the room who were experimenting with all the shit they weren't supposed to. It was something just behind her face. She stood there, looking older than everyone—older than seven-teen, anyway—acting like a woman who had it all, who had already been to this party.

She set the pop can down. I couldn't tell if she was laughing or smiling. Everything seemed to be getting darker, even though the sun outside still refused to set. I noticed Kiana was wearing winter boots—white military boots—bunny boots. It was June.

"We haven't met," I said.

She slid the half-empty can of soda across the counter to me with a mix of boredom and mischievousness. She smiled. I reached past and grabbed the jug of rum.

"Cesar of Los Angeles," she said. "Where's Go?"

She said my name like it meant something. *Cesar*. Like it had purpose, and history, like it was a whole goddamned team to cheer for. *Cesar*. I loved it. She said my name like it had been my destiny. Like *Cesar* wasn't just some of Pop's superficial garbage he dumped on me to somehow fix his own lack of *Cesar*—or his own lack of *Wicho*—but like *Cesar* was me.

"He's at work," I said.

I didn't tell her Go-boy's shift was now over and that I was sup-posed to be there, upriver, on the tower, counting the fish in the river. I didn't tell her he was now covering for me. And I wouldn't tell her that at the moment I didn't care about Go-boy.

"Good," she said. "He needs to save money."

"And Kiana, what about you?"

All along my plan in Unalakleet had been simple—pick up a job, a few paychecks, a plane ticket home. So right after I arrived I started looking around. But jobs weren't available. I tried to get on with the company building the new jail, but I didn't have construction experience, and the crews had already been filled, and something about building a jail seemed wrong. That left the grocery store and the fish-processing plant. The grocery store only had a few employees and all the positions were taken, and I didn't want to work ankle-deep in fish guts and end each day smelling like seafood waste. So I turned to Go-boy. And just like Go-boy—supportive and helpful to a fault—he set me up with a job at the North River counting tower just a few weeks after I arrived, counting fish, making more cash than I would've imagined ever being possible in a place like this.

From the jump, when I moved here, when I got the tour of Unk, Go-boy had been trying to make me feel like a local. And he still was. He stopped by our house every day. He introduced me to his friends. Invited me on boat rides when he and his girlfriend, Valerie, would ride up the coast. He asked Mom if she needed anything from the store or needed help with anything around the house, and asked me if I wanted to check out a movie or ride around in his

AMC. And if I did, if I jumped in the passenger seat of his car, Go would point out people to me on the streets and tell me their stories. He'd tell me who was dating, who was married, and who was part of our extended family. He'd stop and hang out with kids on BMX bikes, introduce me. They'd always ask Go when he wanted to play basketball or softball or bat again, and Go would sometimes make plans to meet them in a day or two, and other times Go would drop everything and we'd all head to the court for a game of bump or tip or three-on-three. And other times, while riding around, Go would warn me about who to avoid—who would steal my stereo, who took basketball too serious, who not to start shit with. Go knew which adults were on probation, and who was smuggling booze and drinking anyway. He even knew who was dealing. And I was grateful he was trying to look out for me and make me feel wanted, but sometimes Go disappeared. Sometimes he was sad and just wanted to be alone. He could spend an entire day or week in his room, writing his girlfriend a thirty-page letter or carving her a miniature wolf head from a caribou antler. So I was bound to hang out with somebody besides Go-boy.

One night I walked over to Go's place in Happy Valley. It was the first—and only—time I saw Kiana before the party. When I was still about a half a block away I saw a girl come out of Go-boy's house, jump on a four-wheeler, and take off. I didn't get a good look. It was raining and she had her hood up. When I got inside I asked Go who the girl was, if it was his girlfriend. He was caught up in a project, trying to melt what he called gillies—sea glass—into some type of creation for his girlfriend.

"I'm making an ulu for Valerie. The handle will be glass."

I didn't know what that was, and I asked him.

"An ulu is an Eskimo knife," he said.

Go pointed to a rounded steel blade—about the size and shape of the bill on a Lakers cap—that had a small handle. He made a motion with one hand, like he was dealing cards, and said, "We always cut fish like this."

There were five or six other ulus, varying in size and shape, lying in the sink. The blade of the new ulu was cut from a Skilsaw blade, the company logo still visible, the teeth ground to a slick edge. In the center was an inscription:

> *The seed of God is in us.*
> *Now*
> *the seed of a pear tree*
> *grows into a pear tree;*
> *and a hazel seed*
> *grows into a hazel tree;*
> *a seed of God*
> *grows into*
> *God.*
>
> . MEISTER ECKHART .

Go said, "Great quote, ah?"

I shrugged.

"Sure always something to live by," he said. *"A seed of God grows into God."*

"Did Valerie just leave?"

"No, Kiana."

I said, "I haven't met her yet."

Go had a torch and leather gloves and had his project splayed all over the kitchen, so I left to find something else to do. I walked back down Main Road, kicking rocks, sometimes picking one up and tossing it into a silver herring boat that was jacked up on pallets in someone's yard. People in trucks passed me, waving. I thought it was odd how so many vehicles didn't have license plates.

A couple guys pulled alongside me in a beat-up Toyota truck. I had met them playing ball with Go. The driver was a guy they called Bum One and he invited me to ride wherever they were riding to. I said okay. They had some beer in the cab and we all squeezed in and rode out of town. Bum One was wearing little earphones, and he asked me about California. About LA. I didn't tell these guys lies like I told Go-boy. We got to a gravel pit and drank more and shot a handgun at the empty bottles. These guys were cool and they loved to just hang out and joke and tell me stories. They told me what it was like in the winter. Told me the sun only shines for a few hours. Said it was the opposite of California. And as they tried to scare me during this night and for nights to come, I wondered where Go-boy was. Bum One told me how it starts snowing in September and doesn't stop till May. He started every sentence with *Did you hear?* He said, "Did you hear we get polar bears?"

"Shit!" I said, acting surprised and worried, but his exaggeration added to Go-boy's mystique—these guys talked as if there were no way I could spend a whole year in Unalakleet, but Go was convinced I'd live here longer than a year, maybe forever, and he'd even bet I would. He seemed more confident that I would stay than I was confident that I would leave, even though I had already started planning my trip home and now was working and saving money.

But there was a part of me that didn't want Go-boy to act so close, like family, so quick, or act like he'd known me for so long. And I didn't know how to say it. And I didn't know if that was even the problem.

It was hard to tell how Kiana and me went from talking in the kitchen over rum and diet soda, to walking down a hall, to messing around in a bedroom. I don't remember much. She was a lot shorter after taking off those bunny boots. She left them by the closed door. Through flashes of nakedness—long thigh, collarbone, brown plains of skin stretching chest to waist—and my hands—my hands and her movements inviting them to explore the soft and the wet and the hot—through it all I kept seeing those enormous white winter boots, each puffy and padded like a volleyball.

Later, at another house, I was passed out between a beanbag and an open window. I felt that swimming sensation as I lay on the gnarled, gritty floor. When I woke the sun was ironing my forehead. It was morning. I was still a little drunk. I couldn't remember specifics, but I knew right away. I knew Kiana and me had had sex. I didn't have any idea of where or how or what, only a handful of images, and that mysterious other feeling—the guilt—the knowledge that I had just jeopardized my friendship with Go.

MALUKSUKS

Go-boy said, "Where you been?"

He wouldn't look at me. He bumped a tin can of peanuts and it fell under the table, spilling open. I could smell the salt. The CB radio was switched off. The pale glow of sunlight through the tent walls gave everything a dead yellow color—the same dead yellow color of old curtains, of bedrooms at two o'clock in the morning.

"I thought the moment is all that exists," I said.

"You saglu, man, you said you'd come back."

I knew it wasn't possible for a normal person to count fish for twelve or sixteen hours straight. It was crazy exhausting, but I also knew that Go-boy would be the type of guy to try something like that.

I said, "You should've just penciled in the numbers."

"If we count wrong—" Go said, but didn't finish.

I tried telling him we couldn't be expected to sit on that tower and count every single fish that swam up or down. I tried telling him it was a give-and-take thing. Shoot for the averages. But he left the kitchen and went back to his sleeping tent, zipping me out. Go-boy had been doing this for a few summers, so questioning his knowledge of the job wasn't a good idea. But neither was telling him why I was late.

Inside his sleeping tent he zipped and unzipped a mummy bag.

"I brought breakfast," I said, lying.

Go-boy told me I should be on the tower, counting. His voice behind the canvas was sluggish. He flipped in his bag, sending a wave along the tent wall. He let out a deep-lung exhale that was so long and full it seemed it would balloon his whole shelter.

Within minutes on the tower the mosquitoes caught up with me, so I lit a coil and balanced it on the empty soup can that was buried under a month's worth of ashes. I overlooked the river, trying to count fish, trying to record their numbers and wondering about Kiana. Wondering why she hadn't stopped us. Wondering why I hadn't stopped us.

Yet when I just thought of Kiana—of the way she looked through me, and of the way she laughed, diverted her flat smile, and slipped her white thumb ring on and off—I allowed myself to remember.

Fish were everywhere in the water. Fish swam past the tower and it was my job to count them, to mark an ink slash under each type that I saw and add up the total every half hour. I had never thought about fish before we'd moved here, before I'd started working this job. But in rural Alaska fish was money. Fish had Natives banking their year's income in a few months and stocking their freezers full for the winter. People woke up in the morning for fish. People stayed up all night for fish. There were jobs catching them and cutting them, jobs weighing them and shipping them. All for fish. Even the people who'd left for college and gotten master's degrees and doctorates—they had nets in the river and vacuum-packed meat in their freezers.

I first learned these kind were salmon. Silvers. Humpies. Kings. Reds. Chums. All salmon. The fish swam upriver to spawn, and they did the same thing every year at about the same time. I figured the rest of the job was simple—tower—clipboard—eyes—count the fish. But from twenty-five feet up, I couldn't tell the humpies from the kings and the silvers. I'd grown up in California. I hadn't spent every summer of my life on the river like most people. And even after the training, with all the instruction about the different colorings and markings and sizes, there was still a built-in skill to recognizing and identifying a fish that was in the water, and I didn't have it.

When Go-boy woke up he sat at the picnic table below the tower. He gulped coffee from a plastic sports bottle, wearing a tight gold t-shirt that said UNITED STATES OF ALASKA around a map of the state.

He was using a black pen to redraw the Jesus tattoo on his right forearm. He'd been telling me that any day now he would fly into Anchorage and get it done for real.

"Jesus needs more hair," I yelled down to him.

He set the pen between flakes of peeling paint on the ragged picnic table and turned to the water.

. . .

We need to scrub the tarp," Go-boy said. He nodded at the white plastic anchored to the bottom of the river, stretching shore to shore like a submerged sidewalk.

Now I was looking for something to snack on in the kitchen tent. Now I was looking for more matches. Now I was grabbing a handful of skipping rocks to toss from the tower. I was doing anything to avoid work.

I asked, "Ain't you tired?"

"It's dirty. And it's low tide."

Go-boy already had green waders and scrub brushes piled on the picnic table.

I said, "I can still see those fish."

I'd watched so many fish since I started this job that when I closed my eyes I'd see them swimming. I'd see fish in town, or while watching TV. I'd dream about fish. Even when I thought about home I saw fish. Fish swimming with the traffic up South Hoover back in West LA. Fish dipping into alleys. Fish hiding in the Earth Crew murals at Pico and Union.

When I thought about home now, the details were blurred—the timeline. I'd never been away from California for so long, and anytime I remembered the place it was as if the events of growing up had happened in no sequential order—the most recent seeming the least real of them all. I remembered Wicho as a fourteen-year-old kid, even on the day when he was sentenced to life in prison. It seemed I could drive back to our place in Westlake and find that kid out there on the street in front of our house, organizing a neighborhood two-on-two football league, each team consisting of a quarterback and a wide receiver. The curbs were the sidelines, meaning you could catch passes that bounced off parked cars, and Wicho would call out that his team's end zone was the silver Plymouth Horizon and the other team's end zone was the telephone pole, one first-down halfway between, three-second blitz, two-hand touch, first team to fifty wins; during the game he'd sometimes yell out, "Car!" not frustrated unless the score was close, and if it was, and he was in the middle of a play that he'd drawn out on the palm of his left hand, and the receiver was down the road, running a route—cutting in and back when he got to the white pickup—Wicho would yell, "Keep play!" and would let that car wait and honk its horn until the ball was caught or dropped.

I wondered if he was playing football in prison.

Go-boy scrubbed the tarp with his hands and arms submerged, holding the long handle of the brush, pushing and pulling against the river. I joined him, waist-deep. The tattoo from his forearm bled off into the water—threads of ink unraveled into the clear water. Upriver, the fish hovered along the bottom.

"Good thing you didn't pay too much for that," I said, pointing at his arm.

It was then—when I was almost up to my chest in water, watching Go work—that this enormous fish swam straight at me. It was slow and ugly and right at the surface, with its back cutting out of the water, and the damn thing was the length of my leg and twice as fat. I said, "Sick!" and swung the scrubber. I nailed it behind the gills, but it wasn't a good hit. It felt like thumping a sandbag with a baseball bat. And the fish wasn't even fazed. It just changed directions.

"This ugly shit swam right at me!"

"Maluksuk?" he asked.

"It looked like it was covered in pus."

Go said, "Yeah, man. Maluksuk."

I looked around, now all thrown off. Go-boy went back to scrubbing like nothing had even happened, but I couldn't. I asked Go what that was.

He stopped working and adjusted an elastic strap on his waders. I asked him again, and he first told me certain types of salmon run at certain times. He went through the list—kings, silvers, and so on. He told me that when they're done running, when they're spawned out, they become half dead.

"Like zombies?" I asked.

He said the Eskimo word for a half-dead fish was maluksuk. A maluksuk became greenish-brown and moldy-looking. It swam around like a normal fish, except way slower. It wasn't conscious or afraid. It had lost its survival instinct of self-awareness. And a lot of times a maluksuk would swim right up and beach itself till it died.

Go-boy said, "You can sometimes see them on the shoreline, their gills opening and closing, still always trying to breathe, their bodies flipping every couple minutes."

I asked if there were always these dying fish around, and he said, "Mostly at the end of summer." He said I should have already known about them because we were supposed to count the maluksuks separate from the healthy fish. But from up on that tower, I couldn't judge which ones were dying and which ones were spawning. I couldn't tell the difference between the living fish.

Later I told Go I was done trying to wash the fish sperm off the white plastic, that the brushes were no good. He was determined to make them work, to make the tarp clean. He kept scrubbing and said, "We need to do this."

"Shouldn't one of us count fish?"

"Man, this is boss's orders."

We both bobbed along in the water. We were buoys. I slapped at a bug on the water's surface and Go-boy leaned into the current, scrubbing at a stain the size of a manhole cover.

Then he asked, "So what did you do in town last night?"

"You know there's nothing to do."

"Can't even try-make something up, ah?"

"Okay," I said. "Truth? I was looking out for your sister."

Go laughed, said, "Man, saglu."

"What?"

"Kiana's the last person who needs anyone looking out for her. Especially you."

"What's *especially you?*"

"Man, she raised herself until she was ten," he said.

I decided that with Go-boy, silence was the best policy. Everyone knew he couldn't hold a grudge past dinnertime, and I reminded myself of that. I told myself that even though Go loved his family more than anything, and even though he treated his stepsister like a blood sister, and even though he would hear about what we'd done,

Go couldn't hold a grudge. At least, this was what I tried telling myself.

Go said, "It doesn't even matter what you did last night. Not to me, anyway."

"What if I was saving the world?"

That same maluksuk I'd hit with the scrubber was paralleling the far shore, cutting its top fin out of the water, almost beaching itself.

I said, "So a seed of God grows into God, but the seed of a salmon grows into a maluksuk?"

Go looked right at me. River water channeled between us in a constant washing. With my scrubber I pointed at the dying fish. It was sloshing itself along the gravel bank, confused, not sure which direction it was supposed to swim.

I got myself into trouble with a girl back in California just a few months before moving to Alaska. I was talking to her at a mall, joking. This girl had an angry, sexy look, a face shaped like an arrowhead and hair pulled back so tight it looked painted on. I was standing around waiting for my friends by the food court. These days I was still gangbanging and I needed to ride it out without drawing too much attention to myself. My clique didn't know I was leaving town. They didn't know I was about to ditch them for Alaska. The girl I was talking to said her name was Lily, and I convinced myself she really was Lily and not the girlfriend of a rival banger. I convinced myself she didn't recognize me.

It was nothing. The girl was telling me that she had left her little brother in the Legos store to play while she shopped, and we were laughing about that, and I was trying to get her number until my friend Kid Cab interrupted us and told me that my ride—him and his pristine old Cadillac—was leaving. The girl recognized Kid Cab. I could see it in her frown. She was holding a small shopping bag full of shampoos and body lotions, and she took a step back, called us assholes, flashed some Eighteenth Street shit, and bolted. I thought it was funny, but Kid Cab reminded me she ran with one of Santa Ana's biggest cliques. One of our rival cliques.

So I forgot about the girl until a month later. I was with my friends in the parking lot of El Curtido. Our stomachs were full and we were just getting into Kid's car. Around the center aisle a small SUV busted a hard left and came at us. I could see the girl riding shotgun, pointing and smiling like she had while she joked about her little brother. The driver wasn't letting up and rocketed right into the grill of Kid's Caddy before we could get out of the parking stall. The impact busted Kid Cab's head on the wheel. The guys in back got thrown onto the seat, pinning me against the dash. When I looked up through the cracked windshield, I saw the SUV steaming, the inflated airbags like a couple clown cheeks. And I saw that girl and her Eighteenth Street boys running off, flashing signs and middle fingers and big-ass grins.

I wanted to tell Kid I should never have tried talking to her, that I was sorry about his car, but he was unconscious, and I was unable to say anything.

I sat on the picnic table and watched for maluksuks, pointing and asking Go-boy if that was one, or if that was one. He was still in the water, scrubbing the tarp. He wasn't amused, and I couldn't seem to find a way to make things right.

"Shouldn't you count fish?" Go asked.

"That's a dead one," I said. "Right? Come on, dude, just tell me."

Go turned away and went back to scrubbing.

This would keep up all summer. Anytime we were near water I'd ask Go if that fish was a maluksuk, or that fish. He'd say, "You should know." And then later that summer I'd point at a seagull and ask if that was a maluksuk. A husky leashed to a steel pole in a dog lot. A Lund fishing boat in the river. A rusted bike. Is that one? He'd be trying to fix his AMC wagon and I'd ask him if it was a maluksuk. He'd laugh, say, "Poor." Say, "For real." What about that girl? That house? Is this village a maluksuk?

It was rare to hear a boat on a weekday morning. It was still out of sight, getting louder and quieter and louder again as it curled around each bend in the river. Go-boy came to the shore, dropping his waders on the ground and ducking into the kitchen to start organizing in case it was someone important. I climbed the tower.

A flatboat with an old guy and two Native girls pulled up to shore. The guy had gray hair that had been disrupted by the boat ride. His glasses were little bull's-eyes and he had too much skin around his neck, like a flat tire. He was Mr. Larsen, our boss. He yelled up to me that he needed Go-boy.

One of the girls was wearing big sunglasses and they both looked college-age, intern-age, and full of confidence and self-respect.

Go came out of the kitchen and the girl without sunglasses said, "Hey, Go." She smiled. She was sitting behind the boat's steering wheel, holding both hands at twelve o'clock. Go smiled. It was Valerie—his girl.

"I have . . . wait," Go said and disappeared.

Mr. Larsen put Go's waders on.

Go-boy came out of the kitchen with the ulu he'd made and walked to the edge of the water, leaned forward over the bow of the boat, and handed it to Valerie. She smiled, said, "For me?"

"I need you in the river," Mr. Larsen said.

The girl with Valerie said the ulu was the coolest ever.

"Quyaana," Valerie said as Go put waders on.

Go-boy and Mr. Larsen went stomping through the river, carrying baby-food jars labeled with strips of magic tape. I watched them from the tower. They were taking samples from the deep water and samples from the shallow water. Go-boy snuck another look at Valerie as she admired her new ulu, reading the inscription.

The two girls stayed in the boat. They laughed, repeating something a little kid had said. Near the motor was an old cooler with no lid, and inside were three fresh salmon. Traces of blood were smeared along the white walls.

I climbed down the tower and from the embankment said hey to the girls.

Low clouds had moved in above us. The water now looked black. Down our same shoreline, evergreens were tipped out over the river, suspended in this position, still alive, waiting to fall.

The girl nearest to me said, "How you like Unk?"

She was wearing those goggle sunglasses and her black hair was pulled back. They both wore jeans and small retro t-shirts under zip-up hoodies, just like girls back in LA.

"Fine," I said. "My mom's an Ayupak. We just moved here from California."

"I know."

"Yeah?"

"For real," she said, and they smiled. "We're cousins, you and me."

Valerie snuck another look at Go-boy as he came out of the river. She was holding the ulu, testing the sharp edge against her fingertips. She looked ready to use it, but Go wasn't catching her glances.

I asked her how he'd gotten the nickname Go-boy.

"He couldn't pronounce J's very good when he was little," Valerie said. "So he couldn't say his name—Joe. He said Go."

From the kitchen tent Go-boy yelled to me. I turned and told him to wait so I could hear the rest of the story, but the girls were already talking about something else, and all I could do was leave.

Mr. Larsen was in the kitchen reading through our fish counts. He said the numbers for kings seemed way too low. He said he'd counted more fish from his boat in five minutes than the logs had recorded in three days. He was exaggerating. The salty peanut smell still hung in the open, and the tin can was still spilled under the table. Go-boy gave me a nervous nod. The yellow air had heated from the sun. It was dense and still.

Mr. Larsen sat in front of us with the fish logs—notebook paper inked blue and black. Go was next to me, on one side of a small card table. He was rubbing the top of his forearm, smearing part of the tattoo that the river hadn't blurred. I was peeling back part of a tear in the table's vinyl covering. Next to it someone had written, BEING BORED. Mr. Larsen's circle glasses reflected the pages in front of him.

Larsen said the river was full of fish, yet some of our shifts had recorded next to nothing. It was affecting the total count, which Fish and Game needed to be accurate in order to open and close the commercial season. Mr. Larsen said we were supposed to sign our names on each separate log. He asked, "And how can there be maluksuks already?"

"I lied!" Go said. "I wrote in guesses! I falsified the counts!"

Go-boy talked fast and loud. He talked about late shifts and exhaustion. He talked and talked, and I didn't think there was any way he could be covering for me—not after I'd skipped a shift—so I was confused.

I said, "Man, there's maluksuks already."

I knew Mr. Larsen was talking about my shifts. And Go knew he was talking about my shifts. It was obvious I didn't know how to count fish, but since neither of us had signed our logs, Mr. Larsen didn't know who to blame. When Go-boy had trained me he'd said he didn't believe in each of us writing our name on the fish logs because he thought we were accountable as a group, not as individuals.

"It was just a mistake," I said to Go, and then again to Mr. Larsen.

Go-boy told him he had been falling asleep and waking up and just writing numbers in. I didn't buy it. Go wouldn't lie about the counts. And if he did, it was only because he was on the tower penning notebooks full of spiritual theories or carving or painting something for Valerie. After a while, his conscience got to him and he felt like he deserved punishment for not doing his job. That was just who he was. Go-boy would let the whole world stroll into heaven for free, but he would make himself pay full price. He took on too much and never gave himself any slack.

"I did it," he said again. "I lied."

. . .

After those kids busted Kid Cab's ride, suspicious cops filled out reports and tow trucks hauled off the stolen SUV and the smashed Cadillac. Later that night we called a friend—Chunky, a kid too nice to run with gangs but who was cool with us—and met him at the indoor valet-parking garage where he worked. Chunky took care of cars for the late-night crowds—the servers and the bartenders and the people who filled the clubs and restaurants. We'd heard those Eighteenth Street fools were at a party over on Booth Street, so we told Chunky what was up, slipped him forty dollars, and he pointed us toward a big-ass dual-cab pickup parked in the lower level. He said there was a stripper who wouldn't miss the truck until three or four in the morning.

Kid Cab drove because he always drove. Kid Cab drove reckless. We laughed when we turned on the stereo and heard some heavy metal. We hollered at girls. And when we came up on the block where the party was, Kid pulled out his .22 pistol and just started banging off shots, pocking the stucco between partygoers.

What we should've done was drive off and have some more fun with the truck before we returned it. Instead Kid Cab turned back around and drove us past the party, hoping the crew who'd busted his car would be out on the front lawn. They were. But this time they came at us hard, firing shots from two or three different guns. Our truck took a couple holes to the rear fender. Kid got us gone, quick, but a minute later the Eighteenth Street crew had caught up and a full-out chase had started. We ran red lights on West First. Kid tried losing them in parking lots. It was real cops-'n'-robbers shit, except robbers-'n'-robbers, and it was then—during the part of the chase where nothing was happening but high speeds and traffic violations—that I wondered what the hell we were doing. This was the result of me talking to a girl at a mall. At worst it was jealousy. At best a rivalry.

Two gunshots cracked the driver's-side door with a denting sound. That girl Lily was next to us, gun in hand, elbow in the open window, that same mean smile on her face, that same mean laugh. Kid Cab ran the truck down a side road, stopped hard, started screaming. His thigh was all blood.

Sometime later we ditched the truck and Kid's sister picked him up and drove him to the hospital. Kid Cab told the police he was at a party over on Booth Street when a big white truck drove by, shooting up the place, and one of the shots got him in the thigh. They took it all in, skeptical.

Kid spent a week in the hospital. His thigh ballooned to the size of a pumpkin, purple and black, and they had to pump him full of morphine to keep him from weeping like a pussy. I thought a leg wound would be nothing, but it was weeks before Kid was back to normal. And with no insurance, Kid's mom was stuck with a stack of hospital bills, the payments scheduled over a decade, all because of some stupid stuff with that girl.

I wanted to hit Mr. Larsen for the way he was talking to Go. I thought about admitting to him that I was the one who'd lied, but contradicting Go-boy didn't seem right. And before I could do either, Mr. Larsen told me to leave, to climb up the tower so he could talk to Go-boy in private. He said, "Count accurately."

Valerie had already cut up two of the fresh salmon with Go-boy's ulu. She was working on the last fish. A square of burlap was stretched across the picnic table, soaked with dark blood.

Valerie first cut down the belly of the fish, unloading strings of guts. Next she hacked off the head, crunching through bones and gills. It was raw—the sounds of fracture. I almost stopped watching, but what came next was different. What happened next was she traced a tender slice along the spine. Her free hand—bare—lay flat along the scales of the salmon, feeling each move she made with the ulu. The blade slid between the pinkish flesh and the branches of white spine—a clean, inaudible slice. She peeled back each fillet, now using the Eskimo knife as a gentle guide. When she was done she held up two rectangular slices of bright red meat, still connected at the tail. There was twice as much fish in her hand as waste on the table. She went to the river and rinsed the meat clean of blood and loose scales. Afterward she rinsed the ulu, the burlap, and her hands. She left a cloud of blood in the clear water—dark red and drifting down the shoreline.

I told them about Go and the fish counts.

"Araa!" my cousin said. "Larsen's sure always bugging about stuff."

I was hoping that as we stood there, Go-boy was telling Mr. Larsen the real reason for the unrealistic fish counts—that I didn't know how to count fish, that I didn't try very hard, that I skipped out and made him work a few shifts straight. I wanted to get caught without turning myself in. I wanted Go-boy to act like he knew me better than I knew myself, like he had the first day I was here.

"Is Go like this?" I asked.

"Like what?"

"Too honest."

She didn't answer, and neither did my cousin.

"He's a good person," Valerie said.

She was picking dried fish scales from the blade of the ulu. She looked up, right at me, and said, "Go-boy hates lies."

The three of us went silent.

Valerie then told me that a friend of Go-boy's had committed suicide the night before. His name was Jay, but everyone called him Trilogy because he was the third brother in the family and all the boys were so similar. Go had known him pretty well. Valerie had come up to the fish tower that morning with Mr. Larsen and my cousin hoping to tell Go. Some people in town were saying that Jay had hung himself; others said he had used a gun. It still wasn't known what had happened. It was still new. Valerie had heard he'd been walking around town, drunk and soaking wet, saying cryptic things to people, and that his dad's boat had been found swamped in the slough.

"I'll let you tell Go," I said.

"And I also wanted to . . ." Valerie said. "You should talk to Kiana."

"Why?"

"About what happened last night, at the party," she said. Valerie wasn't looking at me. She was looking up at the kitchen tent, looking for Go.

"About what?"

"I think you know."

"I don't."

Valerie turned and looked downriver.

My cousin said, "Come on. All night you were telling people you slept with her."

"Poor," Valerie said with half sympathy, half embarrassment.

"She has a boyfriend," my cousin added.

When Kid Cab's stitches were removed and the scabs were all scratched off, he decided it was time to pay back that girl who had shot him. I was feeling like he should drop the whole situation, but this was a month before I was moving to Alaska, and I needed to blend in and ride along with my friends so they didn't get skeptical. The unspoken suspicion of each other's loyalty was always with us. Besides, I was still running by the rules of the game—never snitch, never give, and never ever feel sorry for the shit that happens to people as a result of their own choice.

We found the girl on her walk home from working at Carlo's Market—this made me think Kid had been planning everything for a while. I wondered then if she really was a gangbanger or if it was all a mistake. She looked so harmless in her outfit—blue slacks, yellow apron. I imagined she worked in the bakery or the deli. It had been over a month since she'd shot Kid. It looked like she was now trying to do things right, trying to play it straight. And maybe we all knew that when we grabbed her and locked her in the trunk, but we also knew—including her—how this retaliation shit worked.

At Chunky's valet lot we parked in a corner stall of the basement. The girl was an animal, and it took five of us, at all times, to restrain her. Kid Cab lowered the tailgate of a small pickup. We drug her into the truck bed, each of us kneeling alongside her, pinning her. Kid ordered every move.

Before he started in with the button of her work pants, I wondered what would happen if I let her hand slip free—an accident. If maybe she would be able to gouge out Kid's eyes with her nails, scratch the mania from his face, and manipulate her other arm free so she could punch and kick her way into chaos, out of the trap, into the possibility that she wouldn't be raped, into the possibility that someone, maybe a parking lot maintenance man, would notice suspicious activity before anything happened.

Then there came this point, when the girl was pinned in the back of some stranger's parked pickup and Kid Cab was forcing her pants and panties off, when everyone's mood switched. Before this there had been some laughter at the shit the girl was screaming— angry and aggressive insults. There had been the occasional joke about sexual performance. Sick stuff, of course. But when Kid started in with her pants, everyone's jaw tensed and everyone got quiet like we had all bitten down on a mouthful of sand that we couldn't spit. We were all under each other's microscopes. The girl stopped screaming. The air was dead like we were sealed in a bag, and the only sounds were our breathing and the girl struggling, and we all watched each other, waiting for someone to fail. Waiting for the fake one to give in first.

It was then that I hit the girl in the face. I did it because she started screaming. Or maybe I did it because I thought it would be less painful for her if she were unconscious. Or maybe I was mad at the whole game—the never-ending cycle of attacks and paybacks. I hit her in the temple, and for a second I thought she went unconscious—her shouting stopped and her eyes closed and her head tipped to the side. But instead of nodding off, the girl being raped started to cry.

Valerie told Go-boy to call her later. "Okay?" she said. He didn't answer.

The girls got in the boat and Mr. Larsen pushed off. Valerie still held on to the ulu. After being cleaned in the river it looked new again, almost too bright against her dark fingers.

Go-boy didn't wave or nod or say anything. He was standing on the shore, shoulders slumped. Without looking at me he turned and walked toward the picnic table, stopped halfway, and sat on the embankment between patches of crabgrass.

"He's filing an offense," Go-boy said.

His forehead creased near his nose and his left eye squinted more than his right. He was biting his lower lip, almost chewing. He said, "It's something like a misdemeanor."

"You're in trouble?"

"We both are."

I was right there with him, but not sure what to do. I thought about asking Go why he'd said those things, why he hadn't sold me out and turned me in, why he felt so responsible for me. I wanted to ask if he really had lied about the counts, but in a way I already knew the answer.

After a couple minutes I headed for the tower to finish my shift. Maybe at noon I'd grab a sandwich and start a second shift, give Go some more time off for covering for me. When I was halfway up, Go said, "It's easy not to care."

I stopped.

It seemed like he was about to say something mean or sharp, but he said, "You're not from here. This isn't your home. You're leaving."

I thought about telling him I might not get back to California. Maybe it wouldn't pan out right away. I thought about telling him that, not because I believed it but because it might make him feel better.

I said, "What if I do stay here? Will you still want me on your shift?"

"Man, you won't stay."

"But no, what if I do? What if I stay in Unalakleet?"

I daydreamed different scenarios about that night in the parking-garage basement. In one scenario I convinced Kid Cab and the rest to give up, to just dump her in a random car as a funny joke—the valet bringing someone a vehicle with a girl screaming and kicking from the trunk. In another daydream I stopped it all, I beat everyone—my friends, the girl, even Chunky when he tried getting in my way. And in another daydream the girl was laughing back at us while being raped, laughing the way she was laughing when she shot Kid Cab, mocking him and all of us, mocking me.

But somehow each daydream led to the same finale—I saw the girl being raped, and instead of Kid, it was me on top of her. I was watching myself. At first I saw everything from a detached bird's-eye view. Then I was next to the girl and I knew I was raping her. I noticed how ugly I looked when angry. It was a disgusting and an embarrassing ugly. It was a weak ugly. A fake ugly. And each time I tried to reach out and push my face off the girl, I couldn't. When I walked away, I couldn't get anywhere either. I turned to see if all my friends were still there watching me with the girl. They were. Then I turned again to see if my face got any less ugly.

The fish were running strong, wiggling past the plastic, getting in little fights with other fish for sperming territory. I didn't pay attention to which ones were kings and which ones were chums. I blurred my eyes and watched the river wash one way and the fish swim the other.

Go-boy had walked back into North River, along the white plastic, the scrub brush in his hand. He went all the way to the far shore. His back was now to me. Low tide was over and the water was getting deep—up to Go's waist. With the brush he was working on a dark spot.

I still wasn't counting fish. There were salmon in the river, hundreds of them, but I just stared and bounced between thoughts of the Kiana I'd had sex with and the Kiana who was Go-boy's sister.

The last thing I remembered about my night with Kiana was how she slipped her bare feet back into those bunny boots. I was bent over, searching for my shoes in the dim light, and Kiana's foot—dark with diagonal tan lines—pushed past my face and slipped into a big white winter boot, a bunny boot. The boots were all rubber and were cartoonish in size, and I left the party thinking of how it felt for her beautiful bare feet to be swimming in the oversized boots, walking the dirt roads home. I imagined her removing them in her own bedroom, parallel-parking them next to the door, crawling into bed with her favorite stuffed animal. And that was it, that was the place I wanted to be—in her room, discovering her routine, observing her meaningless actions—rather than the strange room where we had just been.

The smoke from the mosquito coil had my nose aching. Out in the water, the tarp didn't look any better, but Go was still trying to wash it. His forearm was now clean where the ink-pen tattoo had been.

Then Go-boy stopped scrubbing and looked downstream, taking a break. The water wrinkled around his hips as he leaned into the flow. He held the scrub brush above his head, his hands resting on his hair. Go had a squint in his eyes like he still couldn't believe what had just happened, but at the same time, like it was always what happened.

Upstream, about fifteen feet from him, I saw a giant maluksuk. A mammoth. It swam past the spawning fish, slow, and right toward Go-boy. The thing was an easy five feet, maybe six. I was sure it was a maluksuk—I could see its greenish moldy skin and its top fin cutting out of the water. It created its own small wake. And I was sure it was going to swim right into Go-boy.

I grabbed the clipboard to make a mark under *MALUKSUK*. But then I looked again at the dead fish, and something in me switched. I dropped my blue pen and was out of my seat. I was on the ladder, climbing down the tower, then I was on the riverbank. I was running toward the water with the scrub brush high above my head, ready to swing at the dead fish. I yelled, "Maluksuk!" and splashed knee-deep. But I stumbled before I could get to Go. I fell face-first.

For a moment I was underwater, with my eyes shut. The river was ice-cold and it made my muscles feel thick and lethargic. I was numb. I couldn't feel my clothes or the current. I didn't hear anything or touch the gravel. For a moment I stayed underwater like this. Then I opened my eyes. The white tarp inched beneath me. And even though the water was clear, I pretended that Go-boy didn't know where I was, and that he didn't know if I would ever come up out of the river.

REMIND ME, AGAIN

Mom didn't tell me Pop had called until she was already off the phone, on her way out of the house, carrying a square of cardboard and rain pants and an ulu to help Great-Uncle Stanley cut up a seal. She said, "I didn't have time to talk to him." She kicked the door shut behind her.

Anytime I mentioned my plan to move back to LA, Mom reminded me that Pop was a bastard and couldn't be trusted. She reminded me that we didn't have any money and that I'd just gotten suspended from work.

Mom rushed back into the house, grabbed a plastic tub, stopped before leaving again, exhaled, and said, "Nothing's changed. Your father still promises things he can't deliver. He says he's coming up to visit us, but I'm not counting on anything."

But that was the thing. I was still counting on something.

THE THING IN HER THUMB

Kiana and my mom became friends the first time they met. They bonded over something called seal finger. Kiana stopped by our house and walked around the little place, looking at each decoration and family picture, even the stereo, as if everything were exotic. Mom apologized for the mess. She said we hadn't finished unpacking yet. It was Mom who had the seal finger, and Kiana claimed to know a cure.

Kiana pointed to a living room wall, said, "I always wanted a map of the world."

It was the first time I had seen her since we'd had sex, and again I was taken by her striking cheekbones, how high and chiseled they were under her mysterious, almost sad eyes. She had a face with the strength and danger of a hundred-foot cliff.

There was now a well-spread rumor going around town that Kiana had things to say to me, that she was pissed. And I knew it was true. But right here in our living room she acted like she didn't recognize me. Acted like she didn't even know me. Then I worried that maybe she didn't. Maybe my face didn't register. Then I didn't know which would be worse.

Mom held out her hand in the middle of everything, showing her swollen thumb and blocking Kiana's path.

Kiana said, "Real huge, man."

I wanted to leave the room and the house but couldn't. I'd been avoiding the unpacking chores for over a month, but now, with Kiana here, and with the energy of all the rumors surrounding her, I was held captive, and I pulled back the tape on a box labeled PHOTOS. There were four albums and they were in good shape. I flipped through pages. Kiana kept pacing our house, faking curiosity, and I noticed the pictures were all out of order. Pictures of me as a baby were scattered, sometimes right next to the most recent. Others were doubled up or missing.

"Why did it get like this?" Mom said, still displaying her injury in the middle of the room.

The seal finger was ballooning Mom's thumb. She'd been away from Eskimo life for so long that she didn't remember how to use an ulu and sliced her finger open while trying to help Uncle Stanley skin that seal. The little bit of oil that was on the blade had mixed with her blood and cartilage under the skin. When the cut closed up, her thumb swelled like a marble inside a glove.

"Because of the seal oil," Kiana said.

Mom asked, "Can we get rid of it?"

Kiana raised her eyebrows and nodded. But it wasn't very convincing.

I was trying to ignore Mom these days. It had only been a month since we'd moved up and she'd already changed her last name from Pop's back to her family's—Ayupak. She hadn't lived here for twenty years and she was trying to act like she hadn't missed a beat, like she still remembered everything. Overcompensating, it seemed. Like getting a divorce and moving four thousand miles away. Like trying to skin a seal and damn near cutting off her finger.

It was sometime this week that I heard a couple of ladies talking shit about Mom at Native Store. They were standing next to a circular clothes rack, thumbing through outdated Nike t-shirts, using her first name—Lynn. Saying Lynn always showed off by wearing fancy clothes. They said she was trying to act better than the village because she lived in Los Angeles. And they were right. Back home Mom wore tank tops and jeans, and up here she was flapping around with windy black pants and matching v-neck sweaters.

The day we moved here a group of church ladies welcomed Mom by giving her a kuspak they'd made. It was nice, and since Mom had up and left all those years ago and never returned or kept in contact, they could've just ignored her. I would've. The kuspak was a fancy parka cover, like a dress with a hood and pockets, and it was common for ladies to wear them with jeans to church or pie socials or any village event. But Mom would never wear this one. She wanted to be as good an Eskimo as all the other ladies (or so she thought)—she wanted to sew her own.

And I'd just found out that she'd started dating some local dog musher. My only salvation these days was work, and the fact that Pop was coming to visit us sometime soon.

Go-boy and me were working at the fish tower again, but not together. We were sentenced to some kind of probation and separated. I'd heard Go was in a funk because of the whole thing, and I wasn't surprised. He loved that summer job. Always had. And the prospect of losing it had deflated him. Mom tried convincing me Go was depressed, trying to argue it was something deeper than work problems, calling it chemical and genetic. She said he'd had a rough childhood, but she didn't give any specifics to back it up. She just said that Go's biological mom was a disgusting, messed-up woman. "A sick chick," Mom said. Yet I knew Go-boy always strove so hard to do everything right. He was maybe down on himself for messing up at work. That, and a friend had just killed himself. Who wouldn't be depressed?

The whole village loved Go-boy because he was always dependable and energized and smart about how stuff ought to work. He always told me stuff like, *When everyone does better, EVERYONE does better.* Yet I was realizing that since I'd moved here, Go didn't seem to be doing any better. And I didn't want anyone, including Mom, to know I was the reason he'd almost gotten fired.

The day Kiana and my mom met to heal Mom's seal finger, I stopped by Go-boy's house. He was at the kitchen table, reading a note written on a page torn from the Bible. The girl's handwriting was in green marker, her note written on a page from the New Testament. Parts of the text were underlined with red pen. There were arrows and X's connecting and editing things.

"What's that?"

"A letter," he said, drumming one heel on the floor in his reserved excitement.

I was wondering if he had heard anything about me and Kiana. It shouldn't have been that big of a deal, but in a small village, when the word hits the air, it becomes gospel.

"Is that from your girl?"

Go-boy smiled, said, "It's a list."

He was now tapping his heel against the leg of the chair and he leaned out of the way so I could read the title. It was called TEN THINGS I LIKE ABOUT GO-BOY.

"Valerie doesn't believe in heaven," Go said, and it sounded like he wanted to do something about that.

I asked, "What about your sister?"

He didn't look up, said, "Who, Donkey Kong?"

I nodded. I couldn't say her name—*Kiana*—it felt weird. I said, "Yeah, her."

Go-boy had told me about the nickname *Donkey Kong*. He'd given it to her while on a family vacation in South Dakota, in the Black Hills. They were driving a nature loop and parked by a bunch of mules. Kiana was young and she jumped out of the car with slices of bread to feed them, and when the animals started fighting, one bit Kiana on top of her head. She got scared and bled a little, and he'd called her Donkey Kong ever since.

Go said, "Donkey Kong believes in algebra."

Then he laughed, and by the sound of it I knew he hadn't heard anything about me and her. This was the good thing about Go's recent funk—it kept him locked up in his room, away from the rumors and gossip.

"Algebra?" I said.

"Any kind of math."

Go said Kiana was some sort of math prodigy. As a sophomore in high school she'd been taking satellite classes from the university in Anchorage. By the end of her junior year she'd been a quarter done with an undergraduate degree. Go said she could leave the village that coming school year and start college early, but for some reason, she didn't want to. Maybe she was afraid. He said, "She tutors our math teacher." Kiana was a genius, but she did bad in most other classes. She spent too much time on math. Never did anything else.

"My sister thinks that living in the village after high school means failure."

He said this like he was proof she was wrong, or like she was young and dumb and had a lot to learn. But for me, Kiana was speaking the truth. For me, living in the village a year before I finished high school was failure.

"Wanna go potluck?" Go-boy asked.

I said sure, and we left his place.

On the way I asked Go-boy why Kiana liked math. Why not something else—art, or biology?

He said, "She thinks it's simple."

"Math?"

"She likes all the rules and formulas," he said. "She likes the patterns. It's just the way she is."

But I wondered if that was really it. I said, "What if she gets to a level of math that doesn't follow formulas?"

Go-boy and me walked across town to the bowling alley, to the funeral potluck for Jay—Trilogy. Jay had shot himself in the neck with a .22 pistol. He'd bled to death. Go said, "There's been a lot of this stuff this year."

I wanted to ask him about work but didn't. We hadn't talked about what had happened because we didn't need to. At least, that was what I thought.

At the old gym we kicked off our shoes on the worn-out snow-machine track—the village-style doormat—and walked in. Pinsetters were lined up under old basketball hoops. The place was packed, and about half the lanes were filled. This was when I saw Kiana and my mom together for a second time. They sat with Uncle Stanley, tying their laces and sizing up the bowling balls. Mom examined her seal finger. Kiana waved to her brother, not looking at me, and Go walked to the group.

Uncle Stanley held a blue marbled ball and was giving tips on bowling form and the definitions of certain terms. He had a smooth voice that was easy to ignore, and Kiana sat at the scorer's table, humoring him, penciling names and numbers and sneaking sips from her water bottle when he wasn't looking.

Mom said, "Can I have a drink?"

"Oh, I . . ." Kiana murmured, nervous, tracing her fingers down her jaw and kicking the container farther under her chair. She said, "I think I might be sick. I have a cold."

Mom leaned out of her plastic booth, hinting with a type of nod, and said, "I'm sick too." Then she helped herself.

Before we moved here Mom told me that alcoholism was a problem in the village. She said her mom, who was a Scandinavian teacher from Minnesota, had a drinking problem and ended up running back to the lower forty-eight, leaving her dad alone with six kids. She said this place was a *damp* village, meaning booze wasn't illegal, yet they couldn't sell it at stores. But after living here a month I knew more people who never drank a drop—like Go-boy—than I ever did back home. The difference in the village was that there were no secrets. Like at this bowling alley, at this funeral potluck, it was no secret Kiana and my mom were getting drunk, not to us or anyone. It was cheap if you asked me. Disrespectful. And I didn't even know the kid, but I knew that Go-boy knew him and that was enough of a reason to pay respect.

As I stepped up to the lane to bowl, I turned and saw what everyone else at the potluck saw—we were those people, the people on the outside edge of everything, laughing and sneaking booze into some poor kid's funeral. And I could tell this embarrassment was as real as anything to Go-boy, and it was destroying him—this was his family, and would be forever, and he didn't know how to save it. We were his family.

Stanley said, "I heard when you get shot your brain stays alive three minutes before you die."

Go-boy shifted in his seat and looked the room over, trying to ignore Uncle Stanley. I thought about those fifteen-year-olds that Wicho shot.

"Three minutes to think," he said, scratching his bushy gray sideburns. "Pretty long time when you're dead, I guess."

Mom stepped up to the lane for her roll, but she couldn't fit her thumb into the thumbhole. She tried every other ball she could find, but none would fit that seal finger. She already had sort of mannish hands, and her swollen thumb exaggerated it. So first she tried left-handed, and she almost rolled down the wrong lane. Then she went with just the right hand, without using the holes, but the ball slipped and landed by her feet. So Mom settled on using two hands and a shoveling motion from her hip, like she was slamming a car door shut.

"That'll wreck the lane," Stanley said.

Mom didn't respond. She had her back to us and she jackhammered her right leg, nervous, waiting for her ball. She then threw a second roll from her pocket and sat down. Kiana cheered as the ball hit the gutter.

"Sure is a big seal finger all right," Stanley said, laughing with a little wheeze. "Should call it walrus finger. Call it flipper finger."

Mom showed Stanley a little smile, then flipped him off.

Stanley laughed even harder. "Flipper finger," he said again.

It turned out that Go-boy was a dynamite bowler. But you wouldn't have known he was even trying. As we played, he was distracted, looking for Valerie. We were at the far end of the room, against a wall, and Go scanned the crowd nonstop, looked at the clock. People were everywhere. People walked in the door and shook off their logo-embroidered jackets. People dished up seconds from the buffet of Eskimo potluck food—dry fish and seal oil, herring eggs on kelp, black meat. People stood around, watched cousins and nieces knock down pins, consoled mourners, sometimes forced exhausted laughter. Huddled groups of people cried and shared stories. Kids boomeranged around the room like they did anywhere, anytime. There was always someone to look at. And when it was Go's turn he'd roll a strike and then sit back down, look out the door, and sometimes take long walks to the bathroom, searching for his girlfriend. He had something to give her. I'd gotten the impression that tonight was important to him. Go and Valerie hadn't yet kissed, and maybe this was the night he would make his move.

I was bowling pretty good too. Not like Go, but better than Stanley and way better than the girls, who were buzzed, giggling every time someone saw them sipping from the water bottle. Sometime around the fifth frame I leaned over Kiana to see my score. She'd only given me twenty-seven points. I was in last place. She almost laughed when I looked at the card. And I knew she hadn't forgotten about me.

That was when Mom leaned in with her hot breath and said, "Thanks for bringing Go-boy, that's real good of you."

. . .

B y the eighth frame an argument had started. Kiana was doing terrible and getting frustrated. She'd rolled her fourth gutter ball in a row and was ready to storm off, half drunk. It was a one-sided argument about how lame bowling was, and everyone pretended they couldn't hear her.

Go said, "We shouldn't be keeping score. It doesn't matter."

"Gotta keep score," Uncle Stanley claimed. He pulled his dentures from his mouth, licked the gum side, and slipped them back in.

"Stanley, you can keep your own," Go said. "Then compare with the little kids. See who's better."

Stanley said, "I know who's better."

This was when Go saw his girlfriend and smiled like everything before that moment was forgotten. She was at the far end of the room, watching someone bowl, with her baby nephew asleep on her back, held between her jacket and body like a hiking pack, like how all the ladies in town carried babies. She smiled across the room, and the cracking sound of bowling pins wove between them as they shared in each other's sameness. I knew they would kiss tonight.

The dog musher had shown up while Kiana rolled another gutter ball, and he and Mom were flirting, not paying attention to anyone. Stanley stepped up to the lane, getting ready for his turn. This was when Kiana started to argue, not with anyone or anything but just with the state of things, complaining and not noticing that nobody was responding.

"It's so . . . false," she said. "How can I relate to something like it?"

I tried to ignore her like everyone else, but she turned to me and said, "Hateful." It was the first thing she'd said to me since the party.

"We should play Donkey Kong instead," I said, and smiled.

Kiana dialed in an expression like she remembered she was pissed at me. She walked over, stood above me, and grabbed my arm. She started talking about us. Her anger may or may not have been authentic, it may have just been the booze, but I wasn't sure. Maybe both. Her voice was loud enough that Mom and the dog musher could now hear everything, interrupting their bowling-alley moment. Go-boy even turned from smiling at his girlfriend, and Stanley paused before he tried to roll a spare on a seven-ten split. Kiana called me an asshole and kept reinforcing the fact that she had a boyfriend. "Loser," she said. You can imagine a drunk seventeen-year-old mathematician, angry, giving you hell in front of your mom. But it was Go-boy I wanted to protect from hearing this more than anybody. I didn't want to ruin his night. It was Go-boy who would be wounded and haunted for days by the weaknesses of his stepsister and his cousin, the weaknesses of his family.

"Yeah, we had sex," Kiana said. "But it wasn't anything."

Her confessions got so loud that other groups started noticing. I had the feeling of being tried and convicted and sentenced, which I hated because I was a terrible liar. When pressed, I gave in. This was why I hated Wicho's trial because I knew his testimony was a lie, and the whole time I worried the prosecutor would grab me from my seat and ask me if Wicho was guilty. What would I have said?

And this was why I hated the thought of my friends sitting in jail for the rape of that girl. They were waiting to be tried, and how could they not say my name, knowing I was free? I imagined Kid Cab and the others, alone with a couple of cops, being questioned, recorded, pressured. I wondered, under all the stress and fear and intimidation, if Kid Cab was ready to crack, ready to break down, ready to tell them everything that had happened, tell them everyone who was there. I know I would have cracked, and that was why, each day before we'd moved to Alaska, I'd waited for the cops to stop in front of our house—just like they had the day Wicho had been hauled off—but each day passed, no cops, no phone calls, nothing. Even in Alaska I was waiting for it all to catch up to me, like I was expecting it. And I knew if I walked away from the rape without being convicted, it was by luck. I walked away free because I had no priors and because I wasn't well known to our enemies—to the girl—and because my friends still held true to the backward rules of all that gang shit. I walked away free and I wasn't sure that was such a good thing.

Mom stepped in and pulled Kiana away from me, quieting her anger. It was then that I left the potluck.

Late the next day Mom told me the dog musher had proposed—right there in that bowling alley, at the funeral potluck. It happened after I left. In front of a small group of people, including Stanley and Go-boy and Kiana, he stood up on an orange bench seat and said a whole bunch of beautiful things to his drunk bride. He ended the speech with a marriage proposal. They were planning a fall wedding.

As she told me this she was soaking her seal finger, sitting at the kitchen table. It was just the two of us in the quiet house and only her hand agitating water in an ice-cream bucket made any sound. Kiana had told her a mixture of saltwater and boiled stinkweed would shrink the swollen bump. But that wasn't true, and Mom would later realize this. There was no cure for her seal finger.

She said, "You'll like him."

Mom could see me through the doorless frame that separated the living room from the kitchen, but I couldn't see her. I could see a silhouette. I was on the couch, flipping through more photo albums. Sunlight glared through a kitchen window from behind Mom so that everything between me and the window was an over-exposed blur.

"He's a good guy," she said. "He mushes in the Iditarod. He's working construction at the new jail."

Sometimes Mom would pull her thumb from the bucket and hold it up to examine the seal finger. When she did this, her hand was just outside the beam of sunlight, beside the window, and I could see her thumb against the flat background of wood paneling. I watched the water drip off and melt down her forearm. Steam smoked into the path of light as she flipped her hand back and forth—thumb up, thumb down—and her finger was still as bloated as before. She did this every ten minutes or so, sometimes massaging to feel the bump, and I watched with her, and it never got any smaller.

There was a time when I might have said something at that moment. I would've told her not to jump into another marriage so quick. I would've told her I didn't like the idea of this guy—he didn't sound very smart. Who proposes at a funeral?

Mom kept soaking her hand at the kitchen table, holding it up every few minutes to watch if the swelling had gone down. There was a time when she might have said more to me too. She would've used this opportunity to explain herself and try to get any sort of reaction. She would've tried to further sell the idea of her marriage. But now we both stayed silent, waiting and watching her seal finger, not sure what would come next.

HUMPIES

Go-boy asked his girl to marry him.

He had just told me about it, about when he asked her and how—and I couldn't believe it—and that's when we heard his dad, in the living room, freak out.

It was five in the morning. We were in Go-boy's room and I was sitting on his dresser, sideways. My feet dangled over a missing patch of fake wood grain, torn back like a bedsheet, exposing particleboard. I was telling him we needed to get to work because we were late, but he wasn't hearing anything. Go was on his bed. His eyes were wound up like yo-yos ready to drop.

He'd been telling me about Valerie, how he was showing her how to use his boat the night before. He told her the throttle gets stuck sometimes. They drove out to the mouth of the river. I knew this was when he wanted to kiss her and how he wanted it to happen. He shut the engine down and explained that the fuel pump didn't always work right and that you had to pump it by hand. She hopped into the driver's seat. It just felt right, he said. Right then. Before she started the motor. So he asked her to marry him.

I was sitting on that dresser as he told me all this, not believing my ears. Go-boy was superexcited and I wondered if he'd ever had a girlfriend before Valerie. Then we heard his dad in the living room. He was screaming so loud it sounded like someone was cutting metal out there. Go-boy almost didn't even react, like it wasn't weird, and that was when I wanted to leave. But he got up and I followed him down the hall, walking on the little floor rugs with knotted string tassels, into the living room.

Go-boy had been telling me how his girl had said no. He was bummed at first. She didn't even think he was serious, but he was. They were floating out there on the water in a small aluminum fishing boat, around midnight. Daylight was about to drop for a couple hours behind the north end of the ocean, adding that eeriness of a sunset nobody would see. It was graveyard quiet, the occasional slurping sound of a wave hitting the boat. Valerie said she didn't know him very well. She said she was only nineteen, and they had just started dating. But Go said it felt right, that was why he'd asked her.

And then we heard that cutting-metal scream and I followed him into the living room. Then we saw his dad put Go's four-year-old brother in a coma.

That was the morning the humpies came. There were thousands of them. Even more. They were in the river, jumping and splashing like it was raining size-nineteen Chuck Taylors. I was at the shore, sitting in my flatboat, waiting for Go. It was our first shift back working together after the one-week probation, and I was glad to be on his rotation again. We were supposed to motor upriver to the fish tower by five A.M. But the tide went out, and our boat wasn't back-anchored, so it got beached. I tried pushing it alone but the damn thing was heavy.

Down the shoreline, two old guys stood around in rubber boots, heaping a gill net into their boat and talking and watching these fish jump. They stood on the mossy gravel shore, along with the seagulls and the random fish guts where the water had been a couple feet deep not too long ago.

"Lots," one guy said to me, smiling, dropping waders and buckets into his boat.

I just nodded because this shit meant headaches for us up at the tower. It was tough enough counting these salmon from twenty-five feet in the air. It was tougher to know which kind was which. And now it would be a nightmare. It was like babysitting the entire river, keeping tabs on which ones swam upstream and which ones swam down.

The guy asked if I needed help with my boat, and I said no.

"It's like '94," he said, firing up the motor and grinding away.

That was when I gave in and headed for Go's house. I wouldn't have gone there under other circumstances. Kiana hated me now and her boyfriend was threatening to kick my face in, so I was avoiding her. But I thought at five in the morning nobody would be awake. I'd nudge Go, and we'd be on our way. Instead Go-boy wasn't even planning to work. I waited for him, thinking he'd give in and leave, but then we heard his dad and went into the living room, and things went to shit after that.

. . .

We didn't work that day. We didn't radio the tower to let them know what was going on. We didn't call our bosses at IRA or Fish and Game. We didn't do anything. I left Go's place after we saw what we saw and went home and back to sleep.

When a cop showed up at our house, Mom was red in the face. She maybe knew the guy from high school. I was lying in bed, studio headphones blocking out all noise except the music in my ears. She came into the room, her mouth moving, but I couldn't hear.

"Why are the cops asking for you?"

Her black hair was messy and she had a wad of gauze bundled around her seal finger, which if anything had gotten bigger. I wasn't sure if she was embarrassed the cops were looking for her son or if she was embarrassed to be caught looking so disassembled.

"I don't want this shit following you up here," she said. "I'm not gonna put up with another thug living under my roof."

I knew the cops were here to ask me about what happened to Go's little brother, but a part of me couldn't help worrying that maybe my shit really had followed me.

I walked past Mom and out the back door. Even if the cops were here to arrest me, she was still being unreasonable. Up here, where everybody knew everybody, she wasn't concerned about her son ending up dead or losing his freedom for a stupid mistake; she was concerned about her son looking like a thug—getting that reputation. Everybody already knew her oldest son was in prison back in California because of some gang stuff. What if the second son turned out the same way?

She said, "Not under my house," as I passed her and walked outside to tell the cops I didn't know anything about Go's dad and brother. And I didn't know anything. I knew Go-boy a little bit, but not his dad. I didn't know if what I saw was a typical breakfast scene at Go's place or if the whole event was a freak accident.

I later learned that Go-boy's dad was the calm in everyone's life. Go-boy had been living with his dad since he was young, after things had gone bad for his mom. His dad had struggled with a drinking problem the year before Go-boy had moved in, but he'd quit for his son and hadn't had another drop since. Go said his dad was the most stabilizing thing in his life.

A couple years after Go-boy moved in with him, his dad remarried, then adopted Kiana when she was just ten years old. Go's dad was a history teacher in the '80s and '90s at the Unalakleet high school. He won teacher awards. He pushed curriculum to help prepare village kids for college. He became known as the guy who could find funding to help students fly out of Unalakleet for job fairs and college interviews (some parents even thought he used his own money when grants or fund-raising couldn't help).

In the early '80s, Kiana's mom was one of his students, his star student, the type of girl who seemed to understand things before they were taught to her. It was Go's dad who saw her skills and challenged her to work harder and strive for college, and after two years of extra tutoring, essay contests, and scholarship applications, she was accepted to a university in Seattle. At the time Kiana's mom didn't know the impact her teacher had had on her, not until she was into her freshman year, when the cold professors and triple-digit class sizes mocked her distance from Unk. This was around the same time she learned she was pregnant. While home over that Christmas break she decided she wouldn't go back to school. The boy responsible was younger than her by a year and not interested. She had been raised by her grandparents, and they told her to stay in Unalakleet. It was the only choice. So she decided dropping out was what she needed to do, until she spoke with Go-boy's dad. It was after a basketball game in the gym. They sat in the second row of the empty bleachers around half-court. She knew she wasn't ready for a baby because she hadn't yet experienced the world. Go-boy's dad encouraged her not to drop out, and she didn't. She returned to Seattle and gave birth to Kiana the following spring.

Kiana was taken by her great-grandparents in Unalakleet (she called them her parents), and by the time she was nine, her mother had graduated from college and married a man in Seattle and landed a job and a whole new family. Kiana's biological mom and dad had forgotten about her, and when her great-grandma died, she was moved between relatives in Unk and Fairbanks—whoever could take her for a few months. Go-boy's dad maybe felt responsible, or maybe just felt sympathetic, but either way he adopted Kiana when she was ten and gave her a solid home life, with a mother and a father and an older brother, and later, a baby brother she could help raise.

Why are they talking to you?" Mom said after the cop had asked me some questions. She was interested for real now. Word had spread throughout the day that Go's four-year-old brother, Sean, was in a coma. A church group was getting together to pray about it at six o'clock. Mom had cooked meat loaf in an aluminum bread pan for Go and Kiana and their dad. Nobody knew what happened the way me and Go-boy did, and he wasn't saying anything.

"Do you know something?" she asked.

I shrugged and turned away. Mom and me still hadn't been talking to each other, and I didn't plan on changing that.

She said, "There are a few different stories around town. I heard Sean's been staying up past midnight. He walks in his sleep when he's real tired." Mom had removed the bandage from her thumb and was wiping down the counters with a wet rag. These kinds of stressful events, like big news and rumors, gave her a weird energy. "They medevaced him to Anchorage. He's in a coma."

I said, "I don't know. And I haven't talked to Go either."

She told me nobody had talked to Go-boy, they couldn't find him.

"These are the kind of freak accidents Go grew up with," she said. "This one probably sent him off the deep end."

She told me Kiana had discovered Sean lying on the living room floor. Mom added that her brother—Go's dad—had always been a real heavy sleeper and was probably in his bedroom, snoring. It was his guess that Sean sleepwalked, fell, and knocked his head. He was devastated by the accident.

Go-boy wasn't home, or at work, or anywhere.

Early that morning I had knocked on Go-boy's bedroom window. We were supposed to work and the boat was beached and Go was a half hour late—the first time all summer. I knocked again and he parted the curtains and waved me in. The front door was open. I left my shoes in the entryway and walked through the living room into the hall. A kitchen light was on, even though the sun was pretty bright that early. Cheap plastic sports cups were everywhere in the living and dining room—basketball cups with pictures of players and their signatures. Dream Team, from way back, with Michael and Magic. Some football. Barry Sanders. A few commemorative baseball cups.

Go-boy's bedroom smelled like coffee. There were a couple mugs half full on his nightstand. One was steaming. He had a notebook and it looked like he was writing a letter. In about five minutes he would tell me about asking Valerie to marry him and about how she'd said no. But right then his yo-yo eyes glanced up, quick, not even acknowledging I was in the room. Those eyes didn't know what time it was—they hadn't slept. And those eyes, on Go-boy, were unrecognizable.

Before this I hadn't talked to Go for a couple days, not since his sister had bitched me out at the potluck. Go-boy was sitting next to me when Kiana grabbed my forearm and told me she was drunk when we had sex. Since then I had thought about all sorts of things I wanted to tell Go. Some were various forms of apology. Others were about my pop coming to visit and Mom's bloated thumb. It shouldn't have been that hard to talk to him. And what I needed to say didn't even have to be profound, it just needed to be something, anything, but I ignored him, and he ignored me, and I had this feeling that everything would somehow have been different that morning if I had managed to tell Go what I needed to, days earlier.

When I hopped up on Go's dresser, waiting for him to stop scribbling in his legal pad, I squeezed my fist open and closed, still feeling that sensation of Kiana's thin fingers wrapped around my forearm, her nails digging into my long-sleeved shirt. There wasn't a bruise or anything. It was a memory.

"We have to work," I said.

He glanced up like he was surprised I was there. But right away he turned back to the notebook, scribbling a list with his left-handed grip and his elbow high.

I said, "Damn, dude, you don't look good."

"Yeah?"

"Yeah. Maybe you're sick."

There had to be millions of those fish in the river. Those humpies. When they jumped you could see their fleshy bellies, silver and black fading down to pink. Before I went to Go's place, when I was waiting at the shore, I sat in my boat and tried to count every one I could see and hear. But it was impossible. Like counting waves.

I thought about these things swimming in from the Bering Sea—a school of a million darting this way and that, covering thousands of miles. Every single one of them, down to the last one, could change the direction of the whole group. At least, that was how I imagined it. Fish are so nervous all the time. With their unblinking eyes peeled on both sides, any little movement by one freaks them all out. It's a miracle they can end up at a single destination. It's a miracle they don't get so sidetracked that they never find a river to swim up and spawn in and never get to this single most important moment of their lives. It's a miracle they're not all extinct.

After me and Go saw his old man put the little kid in a coma, neither of us moved. His dad stumbled out of the living room, not even noticing we were right there, seeing it all. That was when I left.

That was the way I left. Go-boy frozen. His dad swaying into the kitchen.

They lived in a HUD home on the northeast side of the village. Their house was set up on steel posts, about four feet off the ground—like many homes in town—near a place called Happy Valley. It looked like a neighborhood on an Indian reservation, at least compared to those I'd seen. Rows of lookalike houses. Yards and streets bare of trees or grass. Crooked telephone poles tying everyone together. Behind was a marshy area stretching a mile in both directions to the hills. I headed for Grandpa's old house, where me and Mom stayed, over on the south side, where the river opened to the Norton Sound, to the Bering Sea.

I walked the long way home, down the dirt roads, zigzagging around muddy truck-sized puddles. To my right was the cemetery full of fireweed with white crosses poking above the brush, looking like a picket fence gone wrong. Behind that was the dark gravel runway for the airport. Next to one of the sheds, a forklift spun around, stopped by a plane, and unloaded a shrink-wrapped pallet.

Or maybe the forklift wasn't running that morning. Maybe it was parked.

When Kiana called later that night, I told Mom I didn't want to talk to her.

The cop had been back again around suppertime. He took me out to his truck and sat me in the front seat. Some older kids I recognized from playing ball at open-gym were walking past, and it made me feel weak to be in a patrol truck, to be restrained. The cop started the motor and spun the temperature dial over to red for some heat. He turned on his headlights, stroked his mustache, and asked me the same questions as before. Had I been at Go's place that morning? Had I seen anything happen to Sean? Had I heard from Go-boy since?

Out the window I could see the mouth of the river where Go and Valerie had floated just before he'd asked her to marry him. It was the same place all those humpies were racing through to get upriver, to lay their eggs, and spawn, and make more fish.

The cop told me the seriousness of witnessing a crime. And then, when I still wouldn't say shit, he told me neighbors had seen me leaving Go-boy's house early that morning. But I was cool. I said I was there, but nothing weird happened. Nobody was awake. Go-boy was sick and didn't want to work, so I walked home.

The disjointed events of that morning had been playing over and over in my head, and even though they were as vivid as anything I could remember, I still didn't feel like I knew what had happened. Everything was so surreal. Dreamlike. Everything circled overhead before landing. Everything was still circling.

Truth is, I was waiting for Go to pop up and deal with it all.

The cop was quiet. I asked if I could leave, but he didn't respond. He waited a little longer, then said, "Why didn't you head to work after you left?"

That was easy. I said my boat was high and dry. Then I opened the truck door and went back into the house.

Mom told me I had to let her know what was going on, why the police were bugging me. She had this newfound sense of dominance since we'd moved here—rediscovering her power. I was just a small detail in that plan.

I grabbed a soda from the fridge and she was on my every move, checking right down the list. Did I steal something? Was I doing drugs? Did I get in a fight? Did I tag a building? Her accusations made me feel like she knew everything I had ever done. Her accusations made me not want to care.

"Nothing," I said.

I told her the police were trying to find Go, which wasn't a total lie. They had people out in boats and trucks looking for him. All his uncles had dropped everything and formed a search-and-rescue team. He had only been gone since that morning, but considering what had happened to his little brother, everyone was worried. And the cops even suspected him of hurting Sean. Go wasn't at home or at the fish tower or at the basketball court or anywhere.

And I wouldn't tell Mom the truth anyway. Seeing what I had had given me way too much responsibility. Talking about it would make it worse. I just wanted to forget the whole thing. I just wanted, now more than any other time, to go back to LA.

I went home after Go's dad freaked out. But I didn't sleep at all that morning. I lay in bed. Listened to headphones. I put one of my brother's old tapes in the stereo. It was a blank, recorded for him by some friend. It said *WICHO'S SHIT* in marker. It was old-school rap. Stuff he listened to standing in front of the huge mirrors in our parents' bedroom. He would put the tape in the stereo and dance in front of his reflection, wearing nothing but sweatpants and socks, kicking and jumping all over the mauve carpet, sometimes sparking from the static. This was maybe ten years earlier and I wouldn't join him because I was seven or eight and the last time I tried he thought I was being funny and punched a charcoal bruise on my shoulder. This was serious. This was the place he tried new moves before he showed his friends, before he went to the junior high dances. I felt like I was backstage.

One of the songs on the tape started, *Don't fuck with the mutha-fuckin gangster poppin Glock clip, cuz when the clip is popped I'm gonna make the hit.*

I thought about Wicho, at thirteen, listening to this, four years before he would load his own gun and shoot those kids. I thought of him in prison. I wondered if he was sorry. And I thought of Go-boy's little brother, on the floor, four years old, not knowing what was coming, and Go-boy, seeing this, not knowing what he would do next. I thought about it all and then I imagined what it was like when Wicho shot those kids. Quick. Staccato cracks. The shots. The sun high in the haze. The echo of gunfire off a nearby fast-food restaurant. No other sound or human voices as Wicho ran off. I had never thought of this before. I shut the music off.

When Kiana knocked on our door that night, I knew it was her. People were always coming over to our place and just peeking in and hollering. Nobody knocked. But from my bedroom I could hear a thin little rap on the aluminum door, with thin little fingers. This was fifteen minutes after Mom told me Kiana was on the phone, when I said I didn't want to talk.

Part of me was glad she was here. Not because I wanted to get lectured again or because I wanted her crying and asking me for help but because my muscles had been anxious all day. Because I wanted to get this drama over with.

The padded sound of feet came to my room. There she was. She looked like hell. Her throat was tensed like someone was poking at the undersides of her jaw with pencils. And even though the stress and sadness and all that stuff loomed over everything, I couldn't help being aroused. I couldn't help thinking of the night we had sex. I'd been pretty drunk that night and couldn't remember anything that had happened except her. Those airbrushed forearms and fingertips. Her hipbones and the sides of her neck. That chin and jawbone, somehow smooth but sharp like the curves of an old Eldorado.

"Hey," she said, exhaling.

I nodded her in. She sat on the carpeted floor, and when she did I realized how young she was.

"You okay?" I asked.

She was deep in thought, trying to put together something to say. It looked like she had been doing this all day, this thinking and explaining.

She said, "I know you were there this morning."

I reached to the radio on my dresser, acting like I had something to do.

"Go-boy is missing," she said. "We can't find him." She looked down at the ground next to her hip, her pointer finger twisting a loose string in the carpet, her knees pressed tight side by side. "I know you were there when Sean got hurt."

"Where?" I said.

"I heard you two in his room. I heard my dad."

After that we didn't talk for a while. In my head, that cutting-metal scream sounded different knowing she had heard it. Now it was more a feeling than a sound. I pictured her in a closed room, lying in bed, blankets clenched and knotted around her neck. I imagined her eyes peeled like the eyes of those fish, ready to dart in any direction. And I still wanted nothing to do with this, but now I wanted somebody to snitch on her dad for me, to get some kind of justice.

"Please don't tell anybody," she said. She was looking at the wall behind me. "Don't say anything about what my dad did. He didn't mean to do it. He was drunk. It was an accident."

I didn't believe what she was telling me. Not then anyway. I wouldn't have believed it even if she had told me the whole story of her stepdad—the teacher, the mentor, the recovering alcoholic, the adoptive father to Kiana, and later the man who lost his second wife—Sean's mom—to a heart problem. The memory of what had happened to the little boy early that morning was too sharp. It was too real to be a mistake.

I remember hearing that cutting-metal scream from Go-boy's bedroom as he was telling me about Valerie rejecting his marriage proposal. He didn't say anything, and I didn't either, we were both silent. It was the type of sound that infiltrated all the other senses— we could taste and smell and touch and even see it—and we both experienced this—and it yanked us right to the surface. We got up and walked out to the living room to see what was happening.

Go's brother was on the floor. He was wrapped in an orange blanket, like a stork had left him on the front step but then dragged him into the house. He was half asleep, that tired-little-kid daze in his eyes. The carpet around was matted and full of lint, and the room seemed to tip everything toward him. The room smelled like old bananas. A New York Knicks cup, caked with soda syrup, was leaning sideways, tucked under the couch.

That was when Go's dad appeared from the kitchen at the far end of the room. He was a terror. He raged under his breath, swaying side to side like he was on a boat, and he felt so close to us at that moment, like we could taste the moisture in his panting breath. He came swinging, throwing a glass ashtray straight at the little boy on the floor, hitting him in the head. And then he kept throwing more stuff. The ashtray knocked the kid out. It was a lucky shot because when he threw a wooden napkin holder and the remote control, at random, one ricocheted off the opposite wall and the other flew back into the kitchen. He wasn't aiming at Sean or at anything, he was just throwing things for the sake of throwing.

But the messed-up part was that Go didn't do anything and I didn't either. In my memory, the distance between us and Sean—the fifteen feet—seemed close enough for one of us to reach out and block the ashtray. But we didn't. We just watched it happen.

Kiana and me left the house. On our way out Mom gave me one of those looks. I don't know what it meant, it was just one of those looks.

We walked down the road to the point. Kiana was a half step in front of me and I looked at the ground and watched the backs of her jeans drag on the gravel. We sat on an old telephone pole lying sideways that overlooked the mouth of the river and the ocean. I wanted to tell her it was just out there, not even a day ago, that her brother Go had floated in a boat and asked a girl to marry him. But I wasn't the type of guy to be yapping. Pop was always telling me not to mess around in other families' business.

She told me that when Go was little he used to run around the house naked with his arms raised above his head. He'd wear a fireman's hat. She laughed when she said this, even though she hadn't

been a part of the family then—when Go had lived with his mom—
she'd just seen pictures. "He was so cute," she said.

And I thought about how tomorrow would come, and how
Go might still be missing, and I'd still be the only one who knew
what happened, what almost killed that little kid. Go-boy would be
gone and Sean would be half dead and their dad wouldn't even remember why.

The humpies were still jumping in the river, maybe not as strong
as they were that morning, but close. I told Kiana I had watched
them swim in. I told her that in thirty minutes the river had gone
from calm to crazy. I was lying, but it didn't matter because she
didn't care.

"Man," I said, "where do they all come from?"

She didn't answer.

"I wonder if they swim in from Russia, or Hawaii?"

Then we were silent again.

Kiana's thin hand was sideways on her knee. She was wearing a
white ring on her thumb, rotating it around and around with her
index finger from the same hand. In the dim light, it almost glowed,
looking to be made from some type of bone. The band was smooth
and had a small, almost invisible hole carved through the thickest
part, with two black dots on either side.

"Is that ivory?" I asked, pointing at her thumb.

She didn't answer.

Upriver a boat stopped along the far shore and a lady hopped
out, carrying ten-gallon buckets, and walked up to her drying racks.
Underneath her miniature gazebo, fifty or sixty salmon fillets hung.

"Sorry about yelling at you," Kiana said, shifting, and pulling
her knee to her chest and then dropping it back down. I could tell it

wasn't easy for her to say that. If she hadn't had a boyfriend, that would have been the moment to grab her hand or her thigh or something.

We sat a little longer, and I bet her she couldn't count every single humpy that jumped. She didn't try.

"I wasn't really drunk," she told me. "I lied. I wasn't drunk at that party."

I picked up a gilly—a broken chunk of glass that had been polished by the ocean—and massaged it between my fingers. Kiana was sitting on my right side, and I hoped she'd grab at that gilly and pretend she wanted it. But instead of taking it from me, she would hold my fingers, and our hands would drop between us, still locked. Then we'd weave them all together like a zipper and I'd set them on her lap. Maybe we'd kiss in a few minutes. Maybe not. I didn't care. We could wait. We could just sit there like that, hold hands. Either way it would erase everything that had happened.

"So," she said, "you promise you won't say anything about my dad?"

I leaned forward, confused, dropping my elbows on my knees. Then I dropped that gilly and pulled my jeans legs up to keep them from touching the ground.

"Please."

I would later understand how stressful this was for Kiana, how keeping the family together was her main priority, how it was more important to her than to anyone else. But while sitting on the telephone pole I couldn't see that. I felt used. I felt she was messing with me. Maybe she was being honest—maybe she'd been sober at that party and was now sorry. I didn't feel that way. Now I didn't believe her.

I said, "I already told you, I wasn't there."

"Thank you."

Then she got up and left me sitting.

The ashtray hit Sean's head just above his ear and then rolled in a short half moon, bumping against the leg of the couch. It was emerald green with floating sparkles and caked with muddy ash residue. Where it hit Sean's head it looked like it left a divot the size of a watch battery, for just a split second, before the swelling flared. Go-boy was standing in front of me. I saw it happen around his shoulder. To my right were the entryway and the door.

But we didn't move. Go-boy's dad threw that napkin holder and remote control, still screaming, then tripped a bit and caught himself on a lamp. Then he looked around like he'd forgotten what he was doing.

That was when I left. I grabbed my shoes and went out the door without even putting them on. The front step was muddy and my right sock got wet from my big toe to my arch.

After Kiana left me sitting on that telephone pole, I watched the humpies jump some more. In a week or two, all of these flapping and wiggling things would be dead. They'd become maluksuks, and they'd wash up on the beaches and sandbars like all of them before. Go-boy told me that when the humpies swim into the river from the ocean to spawn, they stop eating. He said the freshwater messes with them more than any other salmon. After a couple weeks, after they've dropped their eggs and sperm in all the right places, they become maluksuks, then die. Just like that. These things cruise around the ocean for years, healthy and alive, and then when they're ready, when they group up and find their way to some river, they swim right in and die.

I figured I'd sit there on that telephone pole and watch them a little longer. They were right at the mouth of the river. They had swam some long-ass distance and were just happy to flip around. They didn't know what was ahead of them. They didn't know that all of this led to their death. But I imagined it didn't even matter. They'd still swim up this river if they knew what it meant, because it was the only thing they knew how to do.

LEGEND OF WHITE ALICE

Go-boy had been missing for two weeks when I decided to ride his BMX bike to the end of the road—thirteen miles to a hill called White Alice. Every day for a week I pedaled out of town as far as I could. I thought on one of these bike rides I'd maybe find Go. I wasn't searching the way his uncles had been—along with all the rescue workers in the state of Alaska, who were getting more and more discouraged—but I wasn't not looking. I rode Go's BMX because I didn't have a car and because Go-boy's AMC wagon was broken again.

Each day of the week I pedaled that BMX down the single-lane dirt road—over the bridge, past the new jail, past the landfill, and into the empty hills, getting closer to the end every time before I turned back.

Pop was coming to visit at the end of the week. He had only called twice since we'd moved to Alaska—the first time a month ago to say he would visit us soon, the second last week to say he was coming. He talked to Mom. He told her he had some stuff about Wicho that he wanted to tell me. He was coming on Friday.

Monday was when Mom started erasing scuff marks off the kitchen floor. She used a paintbrush to dust Grandpa's old family pictures that covered every square inch of every wall. She said she didn't care if Pop came to visit us or not. Said we shouldn't get our hopes up. He probably wouldn't show—being the liar he was—but if he did come, she said he wouldn't be staying with us. He'd sleep at Uncle Stanley's house. She said she'd had enough stress these past couple weeks to last her a year.

"If he stays here he's gonna want sex," she said, moving the couch. "And I'm engaged."

"Maybe he just wants to stay with his family?"

She said, "We don't have any room. It's already too crowded."

I'd been thinking about where the road ended. Go-boy told me it was at an abandoned Air Force base, but that it had been named White Alice long before the military had come. Go called it a legend. I wasn't sure if he was just making up the story to mess with me, like he sometimes did, but Go said there were a few different versions of the legend and they were all about this Eskimo woman named Alice. The main story was that Alice had discovered a community of *little people* living in miniature sod houses on the back side of this hill. When I asked him how small, he said, "About a foot tall," and leveled his hand at knee height. They were little Eskimos who lived traditional lives and spoke Iñupiaq and were smart enough to avoid people. Even though they were tiny, they had full-sized human strength and intelligence. The story was they had lived alongside the Natives in town when everybody had stayed on the south side of the river. One day, maybe a couple of hundred years ago, a dog had mistaken one of their children for a rodent and eaten him, and after that, the little people had gone into hiding—they had disappeared. Sometime in the early 1900s this Eskimo woman named Alice found a group of them living on the side of a hill. She was a sad woman who didn't have any family and who was cursed by the village shaman because of it. She wandered as far from town as she could in order to kill herself. That was when she found the little people. Although she couldn't catch any of them to bring back to Unalakleet, she stole a small parka from one of the little women and became blessed by it. After that her life changed—she became pregnant, she became a better hunter than all the men combined, and she even shunned the shaman and drove him to his own suicide.

"What happened to that little parka?" I asked.

Go said nobody was ever allowed to see it because Alice knew that if she showed anyone, her fortunes would reverse.

I asked Go if he believed in the little people, and he said, "No, I've never seen one. But I know I'll never see one because I don't believe."

I was supposed to go to the police station. They had called to say some paperwork was missing. They needed to interview me again. I said I'd stop by on Monday, but instead I jumped on Go's BMX bike and pedaled out of town.

The cops still didn't know I had witnessed Go's little brother getting knocked into a coma. They knew I had been at the house that morning, and nothing else. They had interviewed Kiana, but she kept denying everything—lying—saying she was asleep and that she didn't hear anything. I'd just talked to Kiana the day before Monday, and she hadn't asked me again to *saglu* about the incident. She wasn't asking me to forget about it. She didn't even try excusing what her pop had done. She just told me she planned on breaking up with her boyfriend sometime before the end of the week. And that was all she said.

I rode that BMX down Main Road. It was a bright, dusty day, and I passed women watering the gravel streets in front of their homes. I learned fast to bike on the upwind side of the road—to avoid the fog of dirt from four-wheelers and trucks—and realized this was why everybody in town always walked on the same shoulder, west side or east side, on any given day.

Unk sat right on the ocean, so it was flat for a mile in every direction, an easy ride before the hills. To avoid Kiana's boyfriend I cut down to the river, past the rusted old barge that now served as a beached playground, and followed the shoreline to the bridge. That guy had been telling people he was going to kick my ass into something terrible. His red-and-white Ford Bronco would pass by Grandpa's house a few times a day. You could hear its rusted muffler rumbling the light fixtures in every room. That was all this guy did—drive around the little village. All day. He was supposed to be working at the new jail this summer, but I always saw him driving around.

I rode to an old musk-ox farm on this first day. To get there I pedaled eight miles and turned left off the road onto a skinny dirt path, ducking under overgrown willows, and then walked when the path started to climb. I figured I was there when the trail ended. Mom had told me about the farm. She said when she was in high school they'd come out here and watch the big things mill around and eat grass. They seemed prehistoric. It was like seeing the world a hundred thousand years earlier. She said it was almost magical. These musk oxen were slow, and enormous, and had soft, dense underhair that Native ladies knitted into hats and scarves and mittens and sold to tourists in Anchorage.

Before I'd left town I thought I might find a nice place to smoke some weed, maybe at the musk-ox farm, maybe someplace else, so I bought enough for three or four days and zipped the baggie in my coat pocket. Each day I brought it along. I hadn't smoked for a couple months, not since California, so I was looking forward to it. I was looking for a little escape. But on this first day I wasn't even sure if I was at the musk-ox farm. And after all the pedaling, my rusty lungs couldn't handle smoke.

Up in the hills I could see what was left of a ten-foot fence that had bordered the farm—a few patches here and there of twisted and trampled steel, pulled to the ground in places like a breaking wave. Nothing else made it look like a musk-ox farm used to be here. No dirt paths worn into the ground. No skeletons of animals that had died. Nothing.

Everywhere I looked I thought I might see Go-boy. I imagined I'd see him just lounging under a tree, scribbling in his journal, looking like a natural part of the scene.

The next morning I went to the store with a bunch of quarters in my pocket to buy a corndog from the deli. When I got home there was a half-burned cigarette smoking on the front step, orange lipstick stains on the filter. A tall red-headed lady with huge feet was sitting at our kitchen table, drinking coffee, twisting her wedding band on and off while listening to Mom talk about her seal finger. The lady wore her shoes in the house.

"It's gone down a little," Mom said. "But what if it never goes away?"

This woman was a social worker from Nome and knew Mom from way back. She asked me some of the same stuff the cops had about Go and Kiana. I knew there was nothing official about her visit—it was just talk, gossip.

"Has Joseph ever showed signs of this kind of behavior?" she said in a deep voice. I hadn't heard Go-boy's real name—Joseph—or Joe—since I'd moved up, so I had to think a minute.

She said, "Does he act spontaneously? Does he have mental health issues?"

I was beginning to feel as if this was all my fault; I mean, no, I hadn't put that kid in a coma, but I also didn't feel like my being in Unalakleet was helping Go.

Mom told her old friend that Go-boy was clinically depressed. She said things to the lady that she wouldn't have said to anyone else. It was embarrassing and awkward. And frustrating. I had only known Go for a couple months, so I didn't know if he was depressed. Go-boy got bummed like any other guy in the village, like any other guy at college. Was that clinical? Everyone wanted to read into everything. Everyone wanted concrete reasons. So I convinced myself that sometimes it was just too complicated for that. Go needed to get away for a bit, that was all.

Instead of answering her questions I hopped on Go's BMX and pedaled out of town, past the turnoff for the abandoned musk-ox farm to the North River swimming hole. A couple kids were jumping into the water, giggling and hugging their shivering bodies. Even now, in August, that shit was ice-cold.

I turned off the road and pedaled down a trail to the fish tower. Uncle Stanley had a cabin somewhere around there that I thought about checking out, taking a break in, maybe smoking my weed there.

I pedaled past a guy who was fishing from his boat, jigging his rod and letting the current take his lure. He was anchored by a bend, floating just in front of a sandbar and casting across the river into the deep channel. It was there, on the beach next to him, that I saw the skeleton of an old VW bug, rusting and stripped clean of everything. It was just the body of the car, and it seemed mysterious. No roads led to that shore. And more than that, I wondered who would need to strip parts from it. There weren't many cars in town, and none like this.

The old guy waved and smiled from his boat. The silver salmon had started to run thick this week, with all the humpies dead or dying. If Go had been with me he would've known the guy. Go-boy would have asked how he was doing and the guy would have shrugged, said something like, "Pretty okay, I guess," and counted the fish with his pointer finger tapping at the air just above his feet.

I didn't say anything and kept pedaling.

Valerie was on the fish tower. She was wearing an old royal-blue t-shirt that said *RIPPER* in red print. Ripper was her nickname. Some little kid at some point had thought that was what he was supposed to call her, and the name had caught on. That was how lots of nicknames and catch phrases got started in the village—a little kid said something funny and it stuck.

When I pedaled up she looked down at me, frightened, hopeful, anticipating that I had news. I shook my head, no, and she slouched back. She looked out over the river. Valerie had been hired to work the rest of the summer to fill in for Go-boy.

"Larsen's looking for you," she said, twenty-five feet in the air.

Valerie was feeling guilty about Go's disappearance. She thought he'd left because she'd turned down his marriage proposal. I tried to convince her that wasn't the case. She'd call me, wondering if I'd heard anything. And when I said no she would start to cry, then talk hysterical about how sorry she was and how she hadn't known what else to do. I told her that what happened to Go's little brother was what had made him disappear, not the proposal. But I didn't know.

Mr. Larsen came out of the white tent and asked me to sit at the picnic table.

He asked, "Have you heard from Go?"

"Nobody has," I said.

"Yeah, well," he said, but he didn't need to go on. We were getting fired.

I was starting to understand why Go had disappeared. It was just like the little people who no longer trusted humans. And as I pedaled the nine miles back to town, I smiled from time to time, thinking about Go sitting next to a miniature sod hut, with doll-sized Eskimos chopping small pieces of wood and sewing tiny pants.

Mom told me she needed my help moving a sofa bed to Uncle Stanley's place. I told her Pop could sleep in my room and I'd crash on the couch in the living room, but she repeated that he wasn't going to stay at our house. He might want to, but he wouldn't. She wanted Pop to see what he was missing. What he couldn't have. It was Wednesday and Pop would be here Friday and I didn't understand why something like a visit had to be so complicated.

I was wondering what Pop had to tell me about Wicho. Something specific? It seemed weird for Wicho to communicate this way. If he ever said anything, it was direct, sometimes too direct. And besides, Pop never visited Wicho. Pop talked to Wicho less than we did.

I rode Go-boy's BMX farther out of town that afternoon, past the vacant musk-ox farm and the North River swimming hole to the old potato field, which was now just an overgrown space with fireweed and mosquitoes. Every direction looked the same. If the trail and the river hadn't been there, everything would've blended together—a panoramic sweep of one repeating image—trees and sky, trees and sky, blurring, losing definition. Trees and sky.

Sitting by the river, I started hearing something. It wasn't anything dangerous like a bear. But like beats. Rhythm. An echo of clanging and thumping. It came from downriver. It was drums.

I pedaled a trail, following the drumbeats to a cabin. I thought it might be Go-boy messing around, but instead it was this lady. She was sitting at a pearl-gray drum set beating away. Her back was to me. The cymbals echoed off the bare walls like stuff was falling from the ceiling, and I could tell she was good—she kept the beat and did some stuff that was pretty fast, so I stood there a minute or two and watched.

"Hey," I said when she stopped.

She was a lot older than me, yet still in good shape. She must've been in her late forties. About the same age as Mom.

"You need something?" she asked.

"I heard the drums."

She had a red bandana holding her hair back, and had a flat, smooth face.

She said, "This is my summer retreat. I haul these up from town."

"I thought you might be someone else."

She nodded and stayed sitting at the kit, holding both drumsticks in her left hand and monkeying with the hi-hats.

Then she held out the sticks like they were an invitation for me to play. I said no thanks, meaning, not at that moment, even though I wanted to sit down and get funky all over that drum set.

If Pop isn't staying here, why does everything have to be so clean?"

Mom dumped a pile of my jackets and magazines and work clothes between me and the TV and said, "This isn't about him."

I didn't believe her, this seemed to be all about Pop. But I didn't realize how nervous she was for her brother and for Sean and for Go-boy. Most people around town didn't suspect Go's dad for what happened to Sean. Most people knew him as the Parent of the Year—an award he'd won three years earlier, after his wife had died. Most people had been dropping off pasta dishes and salads and pizza for him and Kiana to eat, even though he had spent most of the past couple weeks in Anchorage, at the hospital with Sean. But there were a few people—the health care workers—who were suspicious of such a traumatic head wound. They knew it took real force to put a person in a coma, and busting your head on the wall or floor shouldn't do it.

I still hadn't gone to the police. They were calling and stopping by every day. They expected me to repeat my story because I slipped in one version and said I saw Sean in the living room that morning. They ran with this because they had nothing else to go on. *Was he awake? Who else was there?* But I couldn't tell them the truth. How could I put Go's dad in jail when I had dodged my own conviction by stupid luck?

After we hauled a sofa bed next door to Uncle Stanley's place, I stayed there, not wanting to go home. He had a dresser he needed me to move, so I helped him. With all the lifting and bending I was feeling how sore the bike rides were making me. Legs and back. I was as stiff as Stanley looked.

He said, "You ride to pump house yet?" His voice was breathy, almost a whisper, and sometimes it was tough to follow him because he left out words. His hearing aids were almost invisible behind his kinky sideburns.

I asked him where pump house was.

"Up the coast," he said, waving a hand.

There was a short road that ran along the beach, up the ocean about four miles to a little creek where the town got its water. I wanted to ask Stanley about White Alice, but I was afraid the story was a joke.

Stanley motioned again with his hand and said, "We used to stay there during summer, where pump house is. That was our fish camp back then. Your grandpa and your mom and her brothers, and my kids and my wife. Men go out in the ocean with seine nets. Catch fish, cut them, dry them on racks, smoke them, everything. The women pick the berries and cut the fish, but your mom was only girl in her family, after your grandmother went back to wherever she came from. Minnesota, I think. She never liked me, and that's okay because she was real different. Sure made your grandpa nervous all right. I was glad when she moved.

"One time, when your mom was real little, I took the ladies berry-picking. It was me, your mom, Gram, Quvluk, Aunty Striptease, Bake Sale, Aunty Lois, and I don't remember who else. The ladies were up on those hills by pump house and I was on the beach working on the boat. The ladies see big brown bear walking down the hill right at them. They all start yelling and screaming, but that bear sure keep on coming. Aunty Striptease yelled, 'Show it your amaks!' There was this idea if you show your boobs the bear will think you're a nursing mother and go away all right. So the ladies pull up their shirts and jump around, their amaks flapping like seal flippers."

Stanley laughed.

I asked, "Did it work?"

"I don't know," he said. "I heard screaming and ran to them and shot that bear. Sure never saw so many boobs my whole life all right. And that was when we started calling her Aunty Striptease."

Stanley laughed again. He said, "But your mom had to do a lot more work when your gram left. She take care of your grandpa all the time. She always cook and raise little brothers. And you know, your grandpa and me lost all our brothers and sisters. It was just the two of us left. Most of them got tuberculosis. Our brother Harold got lost hunting and froze, and the other, Daniel, he was a lot like Go-boy. That's why I give Go the Eskimo name Isumatturuq—Daniel's Eskimo name. Even when Go was little he sure always was just like him. Those two have the ideas and energy, always want to help everyone.

"But your mom was a strong young girl to take care of your grandpa and all the boys like she did. I remember your mom always never even say anything about what she want, like go to college or anything, just make food and clean, mend parkas and clothes, go school and study. And you know, back then it sure was a lot more work all right. Yup. He miss your grandmother and miss your mom when she left. He died probably before you were born. I think same time. He was quiet and didn't always say what he needed. Not to

anyone. But he knew a lot. I guess maybe there just too many Ayupak boys, and it wore him out. Maybe I should Eskimo-name you
after him."

I left Stanley's place and grabbed Go's BMX and headed out of
town. On my way I saw Kiana at the edge of town by the Kuuk
Bridge. She was walking alone, lingering with each step, and I slowed
and pedaled alongside.

"The cops keep bugging me," I said.

She asked, "Have you heard from Go?"

"He's back?"

"No," she said. "No."

Her heels scuffed the gravel. The sound of rolling bike tires next
to the constant beat of her feet was like a song we were creating. Her
face was flushed as she watched the ground. I could see she had been
drinking.

I heard a truck and turned to look. It wasn't her boyfriend. I
said, "Maybe I shouldn't be seen with you."

She laughed but didn't speak. I kept rolling alongside, looking
forward and waiting. Then she stopped. Her hair was pulled back,
but loose, and messy, like she had just gotten out of bed. She sat on
the railing of the bridge where the road narrowed from two lanes to
one. There was nothing behind her, only air, and the water twenty
feet below.

"Be careful."

"You know," she said, looking at my chin, "try-understand my
situation."

I was confused, and right then I could see how drunk she was.
The sight of this beautiful seventeen-year-old, trashed in the middle
of a Thursday, was one of the worst things.

She said, "You don't even know what you're asking me to do."

"Do you?"

"I wanted something meaningful, but you just want drama."

I waited a second to see if she would calm down, but she didn't. I could feel the baggie of weed in my inside jacket pocket, against my rib cage. She could have used some smoke. She was an angry drunk and wanted a fight so she started sobbing some more non-sense, and I pedaled off, across fifty yards of the concrete bridge, with her yelling behind me, "Run away! Just like every time."

When I was a mile down the road I knew I should've turned around—I shouldn't have left her that way. She was picking a fight because she was stressed, but I wasn't strong enough to deal with her. I didn't know how.

White Alice was thirteen miles from where I left Kiana, but it was tough work just getting to North River. The first hill outside town was a mile climb, and after that were at least three or four more real hills. I guessed it was a total of ten miles to the potato field. By then my hands and wrists were tingling from the constant vibra-tions. To avoid the rush of mosquitoes, I had to either ride hard or reapply bug dope every half hour. Both got old. The plastic seat was numbing the bones in my ass, and I was getting sick of that paper-crumpling sound of bike tires on the gravel road. But regardless, I wanted to see the end. Go-boy had told me that the old Air Force base on White Alice had been used during the Cold War for a missile-detection system. He said there was a huge white panel, the size of a drive-in movie theater screen, dished and tipped at an angle, facing the horizon and Russia. It stood out from the top of the hill, like its own skyscraper, surrounded by nothing but dark evergreens. He wasn't sure how the panel worked.

He said, "When I was in seventh grade I went out there with some friends and we climbed it and spray-painted *HI MOM* across the whole thing."

The road got straight and boring after the potato field. Trees crowded from both sides, and the farther I rode, the tighter they squeezed, and the more I started to worry about bears. Every once in a while there would be a little stream that had washed a dip in the road. I'd stand up and pedal fast, and try to jump.

Pop hadn't yet confirmed that he was coming. He'd said he was flying in on Friday, the next day, and there was only one flight from Anchorage that came every afternoon, so we didn't need to know flight numbers or gates or any of that stuff, but he hadn't called to let us know for sure.

On my way back to town I pulled off the main road to look for that cabin with the drums. Instead I found the Unalakleet Bible Camp. I rode from cabin to cabin, thinking Go might be squatting here. He'd grown up going to camp, had become a devout young Christian at camp, and had been a counselor at camp, so he knew the area. But this past summer, during the senior high session, Go had been asked to leave. He said, "I got fired." He laughed about it afterward.

Go said, "I taught my campers that it was a sin to desire God."

He claimed that human desire predetermined its object—you put God in a box when you desired God. The act itself minimized and reduced possibility. It killed spontaneity. And spontaneity, Go claimed, was the only human state of true freedom and true enlightenment—attachment to nothing. Go-boy said that in order to experience God with all of our human capacity, we had to dispel all of our definitions. Any real disciple, real prophet, or real mystic had to travel from theist to atheist in order to appreciate and accept God into his or her life. And even then, the disciple would not know God in the conventional way but would participate with God in everyday existence, without awareness.

Go told his campers that Jesus taught this in everything he said and did. When, out of confusion and skepticism, one kid asked for proof, Go said, "The proof is everywhere, man. Jesus never made sense. Jesus was the king of nonsense and contradiction. Jesus was the king of bullshit. This is why. This is what he was saying."

I had never heard Go swear before.

Farther down the road I found the cabin with those drums. It was silent. When I went inside the kit was still there, in the middle of the room.

I stood over the drums, mapping the way the cymbals and toms all hugged around the kick drum. I sat at them. All my life I'd heard beats in my head. I remember being in the backseat of Mom's silver Pinto when I was a little kid. She had the radio on and I was tapping my feet and hands with the rhythm of the song. She yelled and said to quit kicking her. I was trying to drum along with the stereo. And since then, drumming along to music had been a habit. I drummed along to Wicho's old-school rap as he practiced his dance moves in front of the mirror. Drummed along to songs in my head while in school, ignoring the lesson. Drummed along to anything, even the AM station buzzing in Go-boy's car. It didn't matter what kind of tune was playing, there were always beats in the air, somewhere.

The sticks were angled across the snare, side by side, like they were pointing at eleven o'clock. I rested my right foot on the bass pedal. It squeaked a little, but I didn't kick it. I didn't pick up the sticks or hit any of the drums. I just sat there about a minute and let the idea of playing a solid beat roll through my head. I didn't want to spoil that by making real noise, because trying to play would remind me how much I didn't know.

P op never showed up. Mom tried calling him, but nobody answered. The two of us walked down to the airport early in the afternoon and waited. Mom wore some good clothes, which she tried hiding under a leather coat, but everyone could see she wanted to look nice. She'd put her engagement ring on her right hand.

Mom checked with the ticket agent to see if Pop was on the flight.

"Last name is Stone?" the agent said.

She took a little extra time, trying to be polite and not deflate our hopes too quick. She then said nobody by that name had a ticket, but we waited anyway. When the Pen-Air flight landed we stood side by side looking out the window. Next to me, Mom seemed shorter than usual. People climbed out of the little plane, ducking through the door and walking down the ladder to the runway and it seemed like years had passed since that was us, arriving at the beginning of summer. The passengers filed into the building. People hugged and shook hands, and when everyone was off the plane and none of them were Pop, Mom turned around, said, "I knew it," and walked out the door. This was the first time all summer that I realized I maybe wouldn't move back home.

Before I left I sat with Bum One. He was working at the airport, wearing an orange vest, Carhartts, boots. Two earphones hung from the neck of his jacket. Now he was taking a break, talking to his younger brother, who was leaving town for the weekend. The two were talking about Kiana.

Bum One said, "Did you hear?"

Two nights ago his little brother had caught Kiana having sex with an older guy. Bum One's little brother was smirking. And it was then that the mystique of Kiana's attractiveness faded.

I said, "Kiana? Really?"

Bum One nodded, but he must have seen something on my face, and his smile disappeared. He got up and went back to work. The only image of Kiana I had right then was of that angry drunk girl I'd left sitting at the edge of the bridge.

It wasn't until a week later that I rode Go-boy's BMX all the way to the end of the road.

When I was leaving town, pedaling away from AC Store and eating a breakfast burrito, Kiana's boyfriend drove past with his buddies. The red Bronco rumbled as he pulled up behind me. I didn't veer off the road—I didn't want to give him an inch, and when he pulled alongside, he pointed. I nodded. His buddy rolled down the window and said, "Yeah, look, a real fuckin' BMX-ican!"

I almost laughed with them because it was funny—funny he was still mad at me—funny to think that this was how they saw me. But it was also a reminder that I didn't have a single hair—not a single drop of blood or sweat or sperm—not a single joy or frustration in my skin that was Mexican. All I had was a name. Cesar. And a brother with a name. Wicho.

The road had become monotonous. The hills and curves were old to me now, even after sitting at home for a week and doing nothing. The washboard ripples and mud puddles were all in the same places. It was way too far to ride on a BMX, but I kept going anyway because there was nothing I wanted to do more than go all the way to the end of the road, to see White Alice.

And when I got to the end, there wasn't anything. It was a small clearing on the top of a hill, about twice the size of a fast-food parking lot. There were some ashes from campfires with burned soda bottles and melted jugs of peppermint schnapps. There were a couple of four-wheeler trails going off into the tundra in random directions. I had expected a shelter or a bunker. I figured that at least a deserted Air Force base would be something. I wanted to see the big white panel. But it was just like everything else. Just an empty space. I biked around three or four times, looking, trying to imagine what it had felt like when this was an active military base, but there wasn't anything to see. All I could imagine was a similar version of what it was now. No missile-detection systems. No purpose of national security. No little people.

When Go had told me he didn't believe in the story about White Alice and the little people, I asked, "Why?"

He said, "I think the legend started around the same time that white people were moving into western Alaska. There was this sudden quick change for Eskimos that they knew was coming— missionaries were teaching different religions, gold-hungry people were coming with boats and guns. I think the little people represented what some of the Eskimos wanted to be, or stay—invisible but powerful, simple, and traditional."

He said, "But I sure always think about how huge Alaska is. It's still so undeveloped. When I think about that, I can't help but feel that maybe the little people really do exist. And, man, if they are out there, I want to give the idea a chance. I want to see them."

That was the opposite of how I felt. I didn't want to see or be seen. I felt everyone was already watching me, knowing that I knew what happened to Go-boy's brother. I felt them blaming me. And yet, I couldn't heal the kid or bring Go back, I couldn't even run away. I was stuck. Like Wicho. Except in prison you could stay invisible. Nobody expected anything from a felon. Nobody knew when you were wounded or hurt because you were a ghost to your family and the world. Nobody relied on you when you were locked up. You were a memory. You were no longer part of society. And yet, if I told Go-boy my wish to be invisible, he would argue, "What good is that?" Even though he'd run away to deal with his problems, Go was the only person I'd ever known who could take a good perspective on anything, and the only person I knew who assumed I could and would do the right thing, the good thing. It was obvious that when Wicho told me he believed I would go to college and get him out of jail, he was just messing with a little kid, trying to cheer up his sorry- and lonely-ass little brother. But when Go-boy bet me I'd stay in Alaska, and when Go-boy encouraged me to pursue a hundred other interests and plans, even invited me to help him, it felt authentic. All of it. It was real. And I liked the version of myself that Go-boy saw.

On the way back to town I decided I would tell the police what had happened to Sean. Even though I had the lingering fear that all cops were waiting to arrest me, and even though I had no right to send someone to prison—someone as good as Go's dad—my mind was set that I was going to do this, I was going to tell them what I knew. I didn't know why I'd decided so quick, but I had to. I had to do this for Go-boy. I had to do this before anything good could happen.

For most of the two-hour bike ride I replayed what I thought I'd seen when Go's little brother had ended up in a coma, and how I would describe it. It didn't seem intentional, I'd tell them that. But, yeah, his dad had hurt Sean.

Halfway home I stopped by the river and hid my weed in Uncle Stanley's cabin to avoid any extra trouble from the cops. Save it for my next ride out here, I thought.

I had found out that there was no Eskimo lady named Alice. The legend was just that—a legend. White Alice was the name of the missile-detection systems, not the hill or the Eskimo lady. There were White Alice sites all over rural Alaska. White Alice Hill was nothing before it was a military base.

Go-boy's legend of White Alice ended as a sad story anyway. So I was glad it wasn't true. He said just a few months after Alice found the little people and took the coat and became pregnant, the blessing wore off. She almost froze to death trying to walk across a hundred miles of sea ice to Nome, and in the process miscarried her child and lost most of her fingers to frostbite. Then, after months of physical and mental instability in a Nome hospital, far from her village, she gained enough strength to return, but instead of going home, she walked down a busy Front Street during the peak of the gold rush, past rows of trading stores and taverns and hotels, and threw herself into the Bering Sea, and drowned.

It didn't matter that the legend wasn't true. While sitting at the deserted military base and looking around into the nothingness— into the empty land and air that seemed removed from everything— I wondered if this was what Go-boy did when he disappeared. I wondered if he came all the way to the end of the road, stood at the edge, and looked around, standing where everything that touched the village and the rest of humanity came to an end, and then decided to jump. I wondered if Go-boy could look at all the open and empty space and see something real. Something worth giving himself to. Something with possibility. I didn't know much about Alaska, but in every direction I looked there were only hills and trees. And I figured those all kept going farther than I could, farther than most people could. I figured those kept going farther than Go-boy could, with or without his BMX.

THREE

ATAUSIQ

"Your Eskimo name will be Atausiq," Go-boy tells me. He comes back after disappearing for almost a month, and that's the first thing he says.

Well, no. The first thing he says is "Let's take a ride." So we jump in his AMC and tour the whole village about eight times in fifteen minutes. He talks nonstop while he drives and waves to people, but he isn't talking to me. He's wound up. I wonder when he's had time to fix his wagon.

I say, "Nothing's changed," but it isn't very convincing.

And that's when we end up on the bridge at the edge of town, when he tells me my Eskimo name. He's driven three miles out on the road to see how construction of the new jail is coming along and then has turned back around. The car dies as we roll onto concrete, leaving us in the middle of the single-lane bridge. Go-boy holds the wheel with three fingers of his right hand as the car crunches rogue pieces of gravel on the pavement. We stop halfway. Steel railing on either side. A light on the dash blinks red and a smell like melting rubber is right there with us. Go keeps holding the wheel. His nails are cut short like a farmer's, or a mechanic's.

He says, "Yeah, man. Atausiq. Just in time."

He tells me everyone in the village has an Eskimo name, but most of the time it isn't official. It isn't on a person's driver's license or birth certificate—an Eskimo name is like a fancy nickname. I'm not sure where Eskimo names come from—ancestors or mountains or rivers, or if they're just made up—so I ask Go.

"Atausiq?"

"Yeah," I say. "Does it mean something? Like whale-fighter or seal-clubber?"

"Atausiq doesn't mean anything," he says, smirking. "It's just a name."

It has been three months since he came up with his plan to give me an Eskimo name, right here on this same bridge, on my second day in town. Go reminds me of this. He mentions our bet and I tell him I had forgotten all about it.

"So what do I do with an Eskimo name?" I ask, but I'd rather know where he's been for the past month.

He rolls down his window and hangs his elbow into the breeze, smiles. He hasn't stopped smiling since coming back. And he hasn't taken his hand off the wheel. "It's part of the new beginning, the reason I came back."

"Where were you?"

"I was preparing for exactly this," he says, waving his hand at the village. "Heaven on earth."

The town in front of us stretches out all soft blue and rust-colored to the left. Snow fences line the slough's edge, bordering the town from tundra. To our right a small passenger plane is landing on top of the horizon, kicking a trail of dust that crescendos and blurs across the landscape and circles around behind us to where dump trucks are kicking up their own puffs, running down our same road, pulling onto the bridge behind us.

I turn around in my seat and look behind us. I say, "We better do something."

Go-boy wipes the Plexiglas dash panel with his index finger, smearing dirt film, as if a diagnosis could be found in that blinking red light. He says, "Everybody's sure always in some kinda rush." Then he laughs.

I say, "I need to get back to school. Lunch break is over."

"You need to experience something phenomenal. We all do. We all have an idea of what we want but we're too afraid to express it."

Then Go sticks his head out the window and yells, "Heaven is a dead car stuck on a bridge!"

"We're in the way."

I hurry out of the wagon and start pushing us toward town—leaning into the trunk, my feet slipping on loose rocks—to at least get us off the bridge so the trucks can pass. It's better than trying to tell Go that our boss has fired us and that I put his dad in jail by ratting him out to the police.

A dump truck inches up behind me, close enough that I can smell its sulfuric exhaust. He's losing money the longer his load takes, but now I don't care. I ease up. The AMC slows down. I turn around and look at the driver, smile, shrug. It feels good to have Go-boy back. And by the time Go steers off the bridge and onto the shoulder, and the train of diesel rigs blow past while I hop into the passenger seat, I'm no longer ready to find out where he's been, what he's done, and why the hell he ditched us for a month, but I am ready to become Atausiq.

HER BEDROOM

Kiana's bedroom was now mine. We switched. After her dad went to jail Kiana moved in with my mom and I moved over to Go-boy's place. Mom and Kiana didn't want Go living alone. They were worried about him—about why he'd disappeared for so long and why he wouldn't tell anyone where he'd been—and Go refused to live anywhere but his own house. So the end result was me moving over to his place. To keep an eye on him. At least, that was how Mom and Kiana saw it.

After I told the police what had happened to Sean, Go-boy's dad didn't protest. He said if that was what I'd seen, he believed me. He knew he'd blacked out that morning. He didn't remember anything and was devastated to learn he'd hurt Sean. He told me I'd done right by telling the truth—even though Kiana was now furious with me—and he went to jail just a few days before Go came back to town.

Her bedroom was green. Green walls. Green curtains. Green bits of fabric covering her dresser and bedside table. All the greens were different—from olive to pine—and in a few places she had something orange that stood out—a lampshade, a woven rug. I knew I wouldn't touch or rearrange anything. I would set my duffel bag in the corner. Pull clothes out when I needed them. Maybe clear a space on an end table for my wallet. It would still be her bedroom.

There was a mirror on top of the dresser, framed by pictures of Kiana and her girlfriends, arranged between magazine cutouts of the famous skyscrapers she hoped to someday visit. I saw myself there, in the mirror, with Kiana looking back at me and Kiana's room all around me. And every morning, for the rest of the year and into the next, this would be the first thing I'd see.

"Well, what do you think?" Go said, standing in the doorframe behind me. "Bring out your feminine side?"

I thought it was better than sleeping in his dad's room.

Kiana was now doing the same thing at Mom's place—standing in my room, looking around at her new digs. But her first reaction wasn't to set her bag in the corner and rearrange an end table so she could have space for a book or two. Her first reaction was to get a box and clear out my dresser. She packed my magazines, old CDs and tapes, notebooks, anything I'd left lying around, and stashed them in a closet. She ripped posters off the walls. She hauled a pile of my shoes to the porch. She changed the blankets. And then, a day or two later, as if that shit wasn't good enough, she pulled everything else from the room and repainted the walls a light color. A green-beige.

Kiana now had two bedrooms.

In her original bedroom, I sat on the mattress. Go had left me alone. He had just started a new project—putting together a proposal he said would change the world. He was working in the living room. The whole house had now become a studio for his endless projects.

The one thing I didn't leave in my old room was a picture frame that had two photos of Wicho and me. Mom had given it to me for a birthday present five years earlier, right after Wicho had gone to prison. The first was a photo of us bathing together as little kids. Wicho must've been six and he was laughing, trying to stay out of the water by putting his feet and hands on the edge of the tub, elevating his body. I was in the water, laughing because Wicho was laughing. The other picture had been taken a month before Wicho had gone to jail, at my elementary school graduation. The school I was attending at the time made a big deal out of our leaving for middle school. They dressed us up in gowns and put us through a ceremony. In the photo Wicho was in a nice button-up shirt and tie. It was a typical grad photo. Big brother with his arm around little brother. Sunny day. Grassy field. Scatters of people behind. But this photo was weird because Wicho and I weren't looking at the camera. He was glancing past, as if he were watching a movie he'd seen before and was anticipating what was next. I had turned my eyes without moving my head, like I was trying to look at him.

I put the picture frame on Kiana's dresser. So when I looked in the mirror and saw only her and her images and her room all around, I could look down and at least see Wicho.

I thought about my old room. I remembered sitting on the bed while Kiana sat on the floor, just a couple months before all of this. It was the day after Sean was knocked into a coma. Go was missing. Kiana was getting ready to ask me to lie about what her dad had done. She was twisting a loose string in the carpet. I remember feeling a jolt, like a small electrical wave, when she told me she had heard everything that had happened that morning. She knew her dad had been drinking. She was lying in bed, wide awake, nervous, almost panicking, not quite sure what to do. She heard Go and me talking in his bedroom. She heard her dad scream. I remember feeling connected to Kiana when she told me this—she could be vulnerable. And by telling me she let me into her life just a little more. It was the place where I wanted to be, and the place where I needed not to be. I remember feeling good about the talk, glad that Kiana and me could talk. And yet, I was afraid. Kiana was a dangerous person. Kiana wasn't a passive observer. Kiana was the type of girl who could change everything.

I remember sitting on my bed in my old room, watching Kiana twist the loose string with her index finger, with the tension of all the things that had happened and the tension of things yet to come, and I remember feeling ready to try. I was ready to let Kiana be Kiana. I was ready to let myself be me.

'63 ROGERS

The day I got suspended from school, Go-boy was at home design-
ing some crazy envelope that he claimed was our *ticket to heaven*. He
was in the living room with colored chalk and markers and a roll of
duct tape, and he was getting creative all over a manila package.
Music echoed from his bedroom down the hall—music from the
stereo that never stopped—music in the morning, so loud he could
hear it in the shower—music at lunch, echoing off the angled door
so he could hear it in the kitchen. Even while he slept, music still
hummed. I was now almost used to it. Almost.

Go-boy looked up from the floor, said, "I'm feeling like Jesus
today."

He slid a stack of yellow legal paper inside a painted package.
His face was superboyish right now, smooth, clear of all the facial
hair that grew only in patches at his jaw and chin. He never needed
to shave. And when he did shave, like today, he looked even
younger.

Go said, "Pick a hand," and held both of his arms behind his back. I pointed to his left and he stuffed something else into the envelope. He wasn't even curious why I was home this early on a school day.

"I got suspended," I said.

"From school?"

I nodded.

"Perfect, man! Real awesome."

He had been talking like this since I'd moved in—all positives, as if nothing had happened to his family over the past month.

He said, "The timing is uncanny."

I still felt weird and guilty for not clearing the air between us before he'd disappeared. And we still hadn't talked about anything—about what he'd done and what his dad had done and what had happened between me and his sister. All I needed to do was give him a simple nod. A gesture, maybe. Something to signify what we both knew. I felt if I had done that, maybe he wouldn't have disappeared in the first place.

Go said, "Your subconscious planned it this way."

I got suspended over an assignment. I told Go I wrote a paper about Wicho instead of following the teacher's guidelines. We were supposed to write about a U.S. president. The teacher claimed everyone should have a favorite, like a sports team, and if we didn't he was happy to suggest a few.

Go said, "We should fly down to LA and visit Wicho."

He had never said anything about my brother, and this was like a dropkick. I felt my gut cave. Go-boy had never even known Wicho, never even met him. I wondered what he thought about Wicho's situation—about why he was in jail, and for how long. It had been five years since Wicho was sent to prison and that was why I wrote a paper about him. I felt I needed to do everything I could just to re-member him. And the longer I stayed in Alaska, the farther away from him I felt.

Go said, "We could probably learn a lot from Wicho."

I told Go the suspension would turn into expulsion if I didn't apologize to my teacher and the principal.

"Can I read your paper?" Go asked. "I'll include it in my proposal."

I didn't think Go-boy would like it, or even agree with it, so in-stead I told him what it said—

I wrote that if my brother had killed two kids in the village in-stead of in LA, there wouldn't have been stone monuments. Just white wooden crosses. An empty field. Their fifteen-year-old bodies hiding below fireweed.

I wrote that if we had grown up here, Wicho wouldn't have shot anybody. There were no gangs on the tundra. Nobody was shooting to claim shoreline. Nobody was walking around town flashing any-thing but a wave.

I wrote that the river rose and fell with the ocean. It got so low every day that the fish swam sideways. When it was shallow back home in California and Pop could see the wet sand uncovered by the sea, stretching out smooth and flat like fresh concrete, then it was deep up here. And when it was deep up here our boats didn't get stuck, and when all of life's shit landed on a single day, when the moment arose that we wanted to reach for our guns and spray a bul-let or two through a couple people, instead we could drive up North River till we ran out of gas, sit on the shore, skip some rocks, and never see another person. Time was everywhere. We could wait any-thing out.

I wrote that Wicho might like this place.

Go said, "Our ticket to heaven starts by getting Wicho out of prison."

I no longer visited Mom's place. Not for lunch or dinners. Nothing. Kiana seemed to be putting all the blame on me for what had happened to Sean and Go-boy and their dad and I just couldn't be around her. It went both ways.

I convinced myself that this was okay because even though she was treating me like shit, I was feeling—as Go-boy put it right after he'd returned—like there was a newness. The Eskimo name started something in me. It was strange. It was this thing that only Go-boy knew about—our secret—and I was left with the anticipation of whether he would tell anyone.

That, and I was now playing drums. I was now a drummer.

I took my first lesson on an old 1963 Rogers drum set the week school started. Every couple days I met Flo—the school's principal—and she sat me down at the kit and told me to kick this and hit that. It was the same set she'd had at her cabin that summer when I'd ridden Go's BMX up the road, and it was tough learning how, on this set or any set. I always knew I could play if I tried. I just didn't know how hard it was to make each leg and arm do its own thing with every different piece of the set, in rhythm. But I was right there, picking it up fast enough to feel progression. Go-boy said we could start a band. He would sing and the postmaster would play guitar. I thought he was joking, but that was the thing about Go-boy—it sounded like he was always saying shit just to be funny. But he wasn't. He was serious.

This was the real problem with getting kicked out of school. Flo told me that as long as I was suspended I couldn't play drums or get any lessons. She had the only drum set in town. And her set was at the school. Flo said I needed to make things right with my teacher. An apology. But I wasn't sorry. I knew the teacher owed me the forgiveness.

So my drum set had become a couch cushion, or one of Go's philosophy textbooks, or even a piece of plywood. The day I was suspended from school I left Go-boy alone in the living room with his elaborate envelope and went into Kiana's bedroom, looking for something to drum on. It just needed to be something firm enough to feel kickback—somewhat like an actual drum. I found an old shoebox, black with a single green vine, full of letters and notes. I didn't read anything. I didn't need Kiana to be more pissed. I just shut the lid and practiced drum techniques. Flo had taught me something called a paradiddle. I wasn't sure if I had it right and I could only hold my attention on each exercise for a few minutes, but I tried anyway because I wanted to know drums and beats. I wanted a real set. I wanted the skills to play. I wanted Kiana's box of letters to become a drum set so I could hit it as hard as I could while still keeping beat. I wanted the ability to get lost in the rhythms and the fills. The ability to shut my mind down and watch my arms and legs and whole body act as an extension of something bigger. And for a minute it happened, right there in her bedroom. For a minute my arms found a consistent rhythm and I closed my eyes and hummed a melody while throwing emphasis on a beat here and there for accent. For a minute I disappeared in Kiana's room, and the flat thuds of a beat on a shoebox were all that existed.

Then I lost it.

I heard Go-boy tear strips of duct tape in the living room, then snap open a pop can. Although I waited a moment in silence, on the floor, still holding the sticks, with the echoes and chaos of Go's unknown music filling every room in the house, I knew at some point I would join Go and listen to him talk about who he was sending the envelope to, and why.

Mom had told me to keep an eye on Go-boy. She said he hadn't been reacting in a healthy way to their family troubles. She said, "*Our* family troubles." She was trying to make the case that Go's apathy was because of an illness rather than the possibility that he just didn't give a fuck that his dad was in jail—or the other possibility, that he was glad for it.

"Some of us are worried," she said, meaning her and Kiana.

The thing I noticed about Go-boy was that he was feeling good. He was full of energy and ideas. And I didn't want to get in his way.

Mom said, "He dropped out of college for no reason. And you know we had an uncle who killed himself."

"He has reasons," I told her.

Go-boy believed people already had everything they needed to know inside themselves. School was redundant. But he couldn't tell my mom and Kiana this, and I couldn't either. They'd be even more suspicious.

Mom said, "*Because* is not a reason."

Go-boy is still working on that envelope the day after I get suspended from school. He has a card table set up. On top of the table is a miniature easel, and on the easel is his painted envelope.

He's standing in front of it, blurring parts of the chalk drawing with two of his fingers. Music is coming from his room down the hall. This is my first full day of suspension.

He says, "Leave your nets and I will make you a fisher of men."

He's wearing a white hooded pullover. It's a guy's version of a kuspak. I sit on the couch, behind the easel, facing Go.

He wipes red chalk on his jeans, says, "I need a copy of your essay about Wicho. Heaven starts today."

I haven't told Go-boy everything that's in the paper. He knows I ran with gangs back home and he knows Wicho is in prison for life, but I don't want to remind him, and I don't want him to know some of the more intense details. I'm sure that if Go knew the things I've done he'd think less of me, he'd think I'm a hypocrite. And I don't want Go to see the anger behind the paper. Something in me snapped. Something hit the inside of my forehead when I started working on the assignment about the U.S. presidents, and I got angry. I wrote that every president was a gangbanger. Every president had a clique. Every president sold drugs and busted through your door with a gun in hand and a blue rag over his face, raping your mother and daughter, jacking your car. Every new president rolled onto the scene and claimed territory for his clique—his banks—when that territory was already ours. Every president was a thug and I wished every president was in the car that day Wicho pulled a gun on those kids.

Now, with Go-boy and his eagerness, the paper is embarrassing. I say, "It's this teacher. What's the word for them, gussaqs?"

"Yeah," Go says, smiling.

"This gussaq," I tell him, reciting something I heard Kiana say, "from Ohio or someplace, on his postcollege adventure, roughing it with the Natives, teaching in the bush. He's only here so he can tell an interesting story at dinner parties when he moves home—so people will think he's generous."

"Gussaq is Eskimo for white person, but we don't always use it that way. Man, even Natives can act gussaq. It's more like an attitude than a race."

I find a small bag of chips wedged in with the magazines on an end table. The chips are crumbled but I eat them anyway. I say, "This guy is a gussaq. He told everyone Natives are no longer Natives, not unless they practice the old ways."

Go-boy smirks like smart people do when they hear something they disagree with. He has been doing that for the past few weeks— ever since coming back to town. He'll scratch the thin scruff on his chin—if he hasn't shaved—and his eyes will judge whatever he hears, like he knows something the rest of us don't.

Now I'm trying to get Go-boy on my side. I say, "That teacher said that about you guys. He said that Natives have lost their history. He said you guys just watch TV and never try to leave the village to better your lives."

"You're Native too," Go-boy says, wrapping duct tape around the flap-end of the envelope without sealing it shut.

"The teacher said that the missionaries were the best thing that happened to western Alaska."

Go-boy keeps tinkering with the envelope, taking a lighter and melting patches of the duct tape. He slaps at the envelope when it catches fire, says, "Everything we experience has meaning, if we let it. That's what grace means."

The reek of burning tape reminds me of Wicho's Ford Pinto when he tried duct-taping the exhaust so it wouldn't drag on the street. I've been trying to remember things like that. And remembering Wicho's Pinto makes me think of the scented green trees he hung from the rearview mirror.

Go looks up, says, "That's why I'm running for mayor."

I ignore him and pour more potato-chip crumbs into my mouth.

He says, "You're the first to know. I just heard it, just now— Mayor Go-boy." He waves his hand at the air above his head, as if he's revealing a banner, says, "Sounds real good, ah? And I've got to start heaven somewhere."

Go-boy walks over to the recliner and digs his Carhartt jacket out from under a pile. Then he parts the curtains. Kid handprints blur the bay window. He looks past them, outside, like he is expecting to see something. On the TV next to him are stacks of unfinished pizza on paper plates. Our house is a mess and Kiana has been stopping by, trying to clean, while spying on Go. Kiana and Mom have gotten each other suspicious of Go-boy's energy and optimism and his ignorance of everything that has happened. They've started sneaking around him, looking for clues. They're suspicious of why Go won't tell anyone where he went when he disappeared. A month is such a long time. I agree. I wonder about it too. Most everyone thought he was dead. But Go came back acting like he'd been home the whole time, and when anyone asked, he said he was *fasting in the desert*. So that prompted their skepticism. Kiana has been dropping by our place a couple times a week, trying to organize the muddy rubber boots and skate shoes in front of the door, asking him questions. When he isn't home, she'll walk into his room and shut that stereo off.

Go-boy turns from the window to put the Carhartt over his kuspak and says, "Man, you know what you need to do with this teacher?"

I fold up the empty chip bag and set it on the end table. It unfolds itself and falls to the floor.

"You need to give him a boat."

I stay silent because I'm not sure if Go is using religious slang for something. I'm still thinking about his idea to run for mayor. Down the hall, the music coming from Go's room is repeating something over and over, on top of electronic drums. It's a chorus I had stuck in my head a week earlier. Outside the window, a frayed piece of rope that is tied to a log fish rack tosses in the breeze. I wonder if Go-boy still uses the fish rack.

"Mayor?"

Go says, "My dad has an extra boat that's by the old dump at the far end of the marsh."

"I'm not giving that teacher anything. I feel like he owes me the apology."

"You need to give him a boat, man."

I assume this is one of Go's jokes. One of his ridiculous statements. Part of the string of ridiculous ideas he's been unraveling these last few days. And I'm learning that these are best ignored. So I turn on the TV, cranking the volume louder than his music.

He says, "This is your chance to be part of something big. A profound uprising. This is the New Forgiveness. The New Consciousness. You need to be a part of the New Forgiveness Conspiracy."

I say, "How about just buy me some drums instead. Then I won't need school."

"This," he says, holding up the envelope. "And you. And this teacher. And the mayoral election. Sometimes everything always comes together, just like now. There's no such thing as coincidence."

He shuts off his stereo and the TV. He tells me about how all the rich and powerful and famous people in the world are conspiring to make a heaven on earth. Senators, CEOs, rock stars, they're all in on it.

He says, "They'll first forgive the whole world's debt, which will erase poverty. Then they will devalue gold and create a new society. Literally, it will be heaven on earth. Salvation for everyone."

Go-boy tells me *we're* supposed to be a part of it. He quotes all sorts of books and musicians, even the Bible, and talks about a secret group called Christ Consciousness Collective. It's then I realize he hasn't spent any time with Valerie for a while. These ideas seem like the result of too much time alone. Valerie kept Go real, and centered, and I haven't seen them together since he's been back. I wonder if they're still dating.

I say, "I've never heard anything about a *good* conspiracy."

"It's happening now. We're reaching the peak of outward identity. Everything is crumbling. Everything is making the final switch to a feminine world."

Early in the summer the river is full of water. Snow is still melting up in the hills and trickling down over the tundra, through little streams, into the Bering Sea. Low tide doesn't expose enough shoreline to beach a boat, and high tide leaves everything afloat, reminding everyone how close we are to drowning. But the river shrinks in September, exposing sandbars and inflating beaches, and you can throw a stick from shore to shore without even trying. Anyone can.

Go-boy's idea was to rescue his dad's boat that was about three miles from the river. He told me long ago there was a high tide so high it flooded all around. It left the spit of land that is Unalakleet to tiptoe in the ocean like an impromptu island. When the tide went out it left piles of old boats and driftwood miles from any water. When he told me the story, I imagined the sight of a sea all around, swamping the road and the empty fields, with vacant boats like satellites orbiting town. Go claimed we could rope one of these little boats to a four-wheeler and drag it across tundra to the river. It was crazy. It was the kind of behavior his sister was worried about.

Kiana came over to our place later that night to clean and ask her brother all sorts of questions, trying to decide if he was mentally ill, trying to find out what he'd done when he disappeared.

"How's everything?" she asked.

Go-boy pulled all the yellow papers from his envelope and rewrote parts, scribbling out things with an ink pen and adding words in the margins. He also wrote on pieces of birch bark and toilet paper.

"Did you find work yet?" Kiana asked.

Go wasn't in the mood for interrogation, so he locked himself in his room with the envelope and his music.

Kiana looked around the house with a disgusted expression. She seemed to be getting more adult since living with my mom. Even more responsible. With her hair pulled back, the naked corners of her jaw seemed extra intense.

"This place is gross," she said.

We were always being reminded of Kiana's goals by the way she treated us—like we were children, like she was a celebrity pretending to care about regular folk. She couldn't wait to leave the village. She always talked about moving to a big city, out of Alaska. *When I leave the village . . . When I leave the village . . .* But now she was spending most of her time with my mom, teaching her all the Native stuff that Mom had forgotten, being *real village*, as Go put it. Kiana showed Mom how to cut and dry and smoke fish. Showed her how to boil crab, then spread it all out on the kitchen table and dig out the meat with scissors. Kiana took Mom on four-wheeler rides to the prime blueberry spots—to her secret spots—with a plastic tub roped to the front rack full of ice-cream buckets for the berries, bug dope, and a loaded pistol for bear protection. They came home tanned, laughing, their fingers stained purple and their attitudes full of accomplishment and purpose. I tried not to let their friendship get to me, but it was hard. The more Kiana ignored me, the more she buddied up to my mom. One time I went to their house and walked in on Kiana refreshing Mom on NYO—Native Youth Olympics. They were leg wrestling, but not taking it serious, just laughing and playing around, too caught up in the moment to say anything.

Kiana said, "Real gross."

She started cleaning the kitchen, scraping bacon grease from a skillet into an empty peach can so she could later give the fat to her uncle's dogs.

I told her Go was fine.

She asked if he had done anything strange like the day he'd walked into someone's house, stolen their TV while they were watching it, and taken it to the dumpster.

I said, "Man, they had asked Go-boy for help losing weight."

She was facing the wall and had a second garbage bag, filling it with the trash can's overflow and any other junk that was lying around. Something about the knobs of her elbows didn't look natural—a little too sharp, a little too much bone. Now she was silent. The only sounds were Go's muffled music down the hall and pop cans falling into the garbage bag.

Kiana hadn't been talking to me outside this place. And when she did it was only to get information about her brother. No *How you doing?* or *What's happening?* She was still mad at me. I knew she hoped to stay mad. She didn't care that most people thought I'd done the right thing. Since I was the one who'd seen what had happened, it was all my fault. Never mind that Go had seen it too and would've done the same thing had he been around. Never mind that if her dad had remembered what he'd done he would've turned himself in. And Kiana's anger shouldn't have been that big a deal, except I couldn't get that image of her out of my head—when she was drunk and I pedaled away from her, down the road to White Alice. I couldn't help think about how it was maybe that night that she slept with some random guy. And I couldn't stop thinking about sitting with her, watching the humpies jump, at the mouth of the river on a telephone pole, rubbing a gilly between my fingers, with the continuous splash of fish jumping by the shore and fish jumping farther down the river, in that cut-out moment when it seemed like Kiana felt something for me. I wanted to do it all over again. I wanted to claim that piece of land and that telephone pole and live there, and this time around I wouldn't care what she said, I'd ignore her so we could sit there a little bit longer.

Kiana filled a couple garbage bags and tossed them out the door onto the front step. She walked halfway down the hall, just outside Go's door, and stopped. She listened. This was how Kiana and Go-boy had been around each other. Kiana had been running back and forth between visiting her pop in jail and visiting her half-dead little brother in the Anchorage hospital, trying to keep her family together, and trying to forget why they were each in the places they were. Go wasn't paying much attention to any of his family. He just said his brother would be fine and his dad needed to follow his heart. Kiana didn't agree. And so the result was a cat-and-mouse thing—Go-boy dodging Kiana while she tried to record and analyze what he was doing and thinking.

Kiana turned, took a step back toward the living room, then hesitated outside her old bedroom. She looked inside. Left to right. Right to left. She seemed surprised about something. Surprised, maybe, that her room looked the same as it had when she'd lived in it. She looked at me for just a second before again diverting her eyes.

Back in the living room, she said, "Go doesn't even have a job. He should check-see if they need people at the new jail. Everyone's making money up there."

"We're working on some stuff."

She said, "You know what, I wouldn't have to bother you if you didn't live here."

I wanted to tell her that if she was so convinced I was the reason her family was in a wreck, then I wouldn't do anything to help her build it back up.

I learned drum basics like quarter notes and four/four beats. I learned you never hit a crash cymbal without kicking the bass at the same time.

The only drummer in Unk—Flo—was a quiet-looking Native lady who always wore a red bandana. She was maybe Mom's age but carried herself different. She didn't act like she was fighting with everyone for her share of life. She just acted content, like she didn't need or expect anything more than she already had. At school she was as tough and straight as a church pew, but when Flo sat down at the drums she was all emotion.

Flo said, "It's about rhythm. About synchronization."

I was learning on her set. *A classic*, she called it. The '63 Rogers had a pearl-gray finish. Each piece of chrome hardware shone and each curve and bend of the shells was a little rippled and scratched, but still glossy. The cursive *ROGERS* emblem on each drum was a cloudy chrome. The cymbals looked worn out like old pennies you find in the dirt and can't read, but they were crisp and clear-sounding. When she played, everything came together, all at once. A balancing act.

She said, "Drums are the voice of music's heartbeat."

A few days later I follow Go-boy to the post office. It's been almost a week since I was suspended and I still don't want to give that teacher anything. I follow Go-boy more out of curiosity than anything else. His plan is to mail the painted envelope, then borrow a four-wheeler from Uncle Stanley so we can tow his dad's boat to the river.

"Take this," he says, handing me the envelope.

"Where?"

Go says, "Put it in your backpack and bring it."

It's cold today and I pull my hood over my head and blow into my hands.

Go says, "Alappaa?" and laughs. I'm bundled in a hooded sweatshirt and hat. He's wearing just a gold t-shirt, no jacket, and he has on a pair of bunny boots.

A serious wind is blowing off the ocean. The clouds are low and silent and reflected in the puddles on the road. It hasn't dropped below freezing yet, and people in town have been talking about that.

It's not even October, but people say this is about the time winter starts—each week we lose almost an hour of sunlight. It's terrible. Makes me want to move back to LA.

People in town have also been talking about what Go-boy's dad did, and about me turning him in. Members of our family say I did the right thing. Friends of the family say the same. Yet I know there are people who think what I did was stupid. I can see it on their faces when I go to the store or the post office. They think imprisoning Go's dad does more damage to his family and the village than if he was free. They say he's no danger to society. They say it was a mistake. And yeah, it was a mistake—I get that, the police get that, everybody gets that—but where was I supposed to draw the line? At what point can I say, *Yeah, my brother killed two fifteen-year-old kids on a Wednesday, but he was the victim of his environment?* Because every day since Wicho has been locked up I've known he was innocent. Not in the *he didn't do it* sort of way, but in the *he's a good guy* sort of way. Wicho is a good person. I knew him, grew with him, depended on him. He was there for me in any and every way when Pop and Mom weren't. He's smart. He never forgot my birthday. He always asked about my day before he told me anything about his own. And after he went to prison my life got worse. He went to prison and I—the co-conspirator in a gang rape—I walked away free.

Stanley is sitting on the front lawn on the old passenger-van bench seat, next to his dog, fiddling with a broken-down snowmachine, and watching and waving at people who drive past on the road. The door to his house is wide open, and the smell of fish-stained plywood and fish-stained jackets and fish-stained burlap loft from the porch.

"What's up, Stan?"

"Up is down," Uncle Stanley says, and laughs.

I look next door to check if Mom and Kiana are home. Stanley's house is so close to Mom and Kiana's that if it were the same color it would look like an extension of their place. I need to tell Mom about getting suspended before the school does, before Kiana does. Mom will be angry anyway, but adding public embarrassment to the news will make it worse.

"We're gonna get my dad's boat that's by Old Dump," Go says.

Stanley makes a funny face, motions to the slough behind his house, and says, "I don't think so. His boat's right back here by mine."

"My dad's got a wooden boat that's high and dry off Old Road. Can we try-take your four-wheeler?"

Stanley laughs, waves his hand in the direction of the old dump, and says, "All them rotten boats over there below Amak Hill been there too many years all right. I think you're better off swimming!"

I hope this is changing Go's mind.

But he asks again, "Can we take your Honda?"

Stanley looks at me, smiles, and says, "I think Go-boy put too much punk in his peace pipe. You always run out of cig'rettes and smoke punk?"

Stanley is laughing and so is Go-boy, but Go is hopping on the four-wheeler anyway. He says, "All right, thanks, Uncle." And he starts the motor.

We're two miles out of town when Go turns us off the road and cruises over the mossy tundra. Sled dogs spin circles around their poles and jump on their houses and watch us approach. There are about thirty of the skinny mutts, lined in rows, and they all bark, thinking we are there to feed or run them.

We pull up next to this beaten sky-blue thing that is almost buried by weeds. Gigantic pieces of white driftwood tip the boat at an angle and pin it against more wood. Driftwood is everywhere—all gray and white. We walk to the boat and Go surveys the situation. He looks for his angle. He then tells me again about the highest high tide.

"The elders say it came and went so quick it left the roads covered with flopping fish."

I walk back to the four-wheeler. I want to tell him I don't think we can get the boat to the river. There isn't anyone in town who is using old wooden boats like this, and not a person, including this teacher, who would want to. Instead I say, "I'm not giving this thing to that gussaq teacher."

Go-boy runs the rope over the logs. He says, "The highest high tide was followed by the lowest low tide. The river went dry for a day and the Norton Sound receded so far that you could walk all the way to Nome."

I'm just standing there, watching him crawl over the driftwood, walking back and forth between the boat and the four-wheeler.

I say, "This isn't even my boat."

"But it's what we're supposed to do," he says, almost angry. And he keeps talking like this—*The New Forgiveness is the only real freedom . . . our generation has the tools to make it happen . . . we can only understand when we own the moment.*

He says, "Same-same reason I'm running for mayor. Unalakleet is ready to hear this."

When he first told me his idea to give my teacher the boat, I thought about ways I could sabotage it. Maybe let Go give him the boat and then tell the cops it was stolen. Maybe give it to the teacher, wait a week, and then drill a hole in the bottom and watch it sink. But now I don't care. Revenge feels stupid while I am with Go.

Go-boy turns the four-wheeler around and drives forward till the rope is tight. I walk up to the road to avoid whatever terrible thing I assume will happen. Two miles away I can see a truck fanning a yellow rag of dust as it drives in our direction, and behind that, flat clouds balance on the hills and shadow them like a navy curtain all around.

I want to ask Go-boy about Valerie, about where she's been. She hasn't stopped by Go's place in weeks. And when I saw her two days ago at Native Store, I said, "Hey," and I tried to make a joke about Go being home and being wound-up and hyper, but she just nodded and brushed out the door with her grocery bags and her hood over her head. It was strange. It made me think of the way Wicho's high school girlfriend acted around us after she got pregnant by another guy.

Go hits the throttle and the rope tenses and that bankrupt boat makes a strange creaking sound—wood on wood. It pinches against the logs but doesn't budge. The four-wheeler starts spinning in the mud, and nothing happens except engine noise.

Then everything lets loose and Go almost gets bucked off backward as the boat pops and slips free. It twists over the logs behind the four-wheeler. But only the front half makes it. The back of the boat is still with the driftwood. The rotten boat is split in half.

We look at the wreckage, not sure what to do. Where the front of the boat sat the ground is wet and smells moldy. Go-boy circles and then rubs his hand along the splintered bow.

Go hasn't noticed the truck out on the road, and when it comes to an intersection, it turns toward us, less than a mile away now.

I say, "It's a sign that I shouldn't be forgiving that guy."

Go-boy looks at me. He's more serious than I've ever seen him. He says, "When you hold a grudge, you live in the past. And the past is death."

That truck is right alongside us now and has slowed to see what we're doing. Go looks and waves, and the guy starts hollering.

"What?"

The old guy leans out the window and yells all sorts of outdated slang. His face is spackled with gray stubble.

Go says, "That's my dad's boat."

"Like hell," the guy says. He goes on yelling that the old boat is his and we wrecked it. Then he says he will get the VPO after us and peels out, kicking up rocks.

"We better leave, ah?"

When we're on the trail heading home I remember Go's painted envelope. It's still in my bag. But I don't say anything. I just want to get home. I'm relieved the old man saved Go from embarrassment. Instead I say, "Why didn't you try telling that guy about your New Forgiveness thing?"

Mom calls later that night. I think for sure I'll get yelled at for being suspended from school. Go-boy and me are eating pizza and she tells me that she just talked to Pop and he apologized for not visiting us.

Go is reading a newspaper and he folds it about six times so that the article he's reading is the only thing he sees. Mom hears the noise and says, "Did you hear me?"

I've only talked to Pop once since we moved here. It didn't seem like that big a deal at the time. Pop asked me what I'd been doing and all I could tell him about was my summer job counting fish. I remember the conversation because we ended it with an argument.

I told him high tide up here is at the exact same time as low tide in California. He claimed the ocean didn't work that way. But I told him it did. I said when we left home, low tide was at three o'clock, and when we got here, high tide was at the same time. He said I was wrong and that he had to go. I tried to tell him it could happen that way, that sometimes it did, but he'd already hung up.

Mom says, "Why don't you try-call him?"

Mom then asks me if I've heard the news. I haven't. She says one of the teachers died in a boating accident that morning. Valerie's dad.

I look at Go-boy, as if he could hear what Mom was saying. He looks at me and smiles.

Valerie's dad died before noon, and it was weird to think that all day, while we tried to unearth that wooden boat, Go maybe knew his girlfriend's dad had just died but didn't say anything about it. It makes me wonder again if they are still dating.

Go-boy drops the folded newspaper onto the floor and heads to his room. He thinks Kiana will try to talk to him after Mom is done, because she always does, and he's sick of justifying himself. He cranks his stereo. His dissonant indie rock seeps through the cracks of the door.

Mom says good-bye without mentioning school or wrecking a boat. And I'm alone.

I think about calling Pop. I'd tell him I wrote a paper about Wicho and he'd be glad. He'd tell me I did the right thing. Tell me my teacher was wrong and lame and was just trying to keep me down. Maybe Pop would ask for the teacher's phone number so he could call him. Maybe Pop would even buy me a one-way ticket home, or tell me he's talked to Wicho, or tell me he's rescheduled his flight to Unk. I think about all those possibilities and then go back to eating pizza—back to my life in Alaska, and Pop will have to stay at the other end of reported conversations from Mom.

Go-boy's music keeps echoing through the hall. The envelope he's painted and taped is still in my backpack. He's been so bent on making me a part of his New Forgiveness that he's forgotten to mail it.

To: Yoko Ono.

There is a circle of firelike orange around the address, like it's burning through the paper. Small stick-people line the bottom. Instead of a face, one stick-guy has the recycling logo as his head. A stick-girl has a heart and a brain drawn in, and arrows make a circle, connecting the two. It says, *SYNCHRONIZE*. On the back, by the burned patches of duct tape, it says, *TIME IS A REFERENCE TOOL*.

From the living room I hear Go sing along with his music, sometimes shouting along and sometimes hitting his legs or his desk—trying to follow the drummer. He's the most uninhibited guy I know, and these days, the happiest.

I peel back the duct tape, open the envelope, and pull out the stack of yellow papers. It's a letter, handwritten on legal paper—

dear Yoko Ono,

Meister Eckhart said earth has no escape from heaven.

I say today is heaven.

first: we know the Conspiracy is alive, because for the past few years, artists and businesses and politicians from everywhere have formed a community around the globe preparing the New Forgiveness—*SAVING THE WORLD!*

(2,000 years ago Jesus was a teenager)

second: how do I know the meaning of life? I know because you are now reading a letter from a full-fledged = completely ac-credited = card-carrying member = of the Christ Consciousness Collective.

so Yoko Ono,

I'm asking you for 7,000,000 dollars.

as a member of the Collective, I know I'm entitled to such ri-diculousness. honest? Yes. plausible? Everything! so let's go . . . my membership entitles me to Infinite possibilities and to need-ing nothing and already having everything, and it ensures that my past does not define me . . . and that it never will.

you're a member. your husband was a member. you know tHEse things. so I'm slightly embarrassed at how ordinary thIS request may seem to yoU.

yes Yoko Ono,

7,000,000 dollars.

I like big numbers and I love a girl named Valerie and I love a whole village called Unalakleet in western Alaska. everyone calls me Go-boy and I am charting my self-expression and the impact it has on those around me, and you should see what's happening! we're crEATing heaven by refusing to let fear and shame dictate our humanity.

but we're not all the way tHERE.

that is what this ordinary request is for—Valerie and my cousins and all of Unalakleet, and all of Alaska and America—for those who are asleep. this is for everyone on eARTh. the world looks around at all the mADness and says, No! yes we're exhausted but we believe in the otHER. we are waiting for a sign to know this is real. we are waiting for a miracle.

I Am the miracle and the sign.

yo Yoko,

imagine the billboards along Times Square: *HEAVEN IS HERE!* imagine the tv commercials flASHing in every corner of America. imagine the excitement at the gas station, in the factory break room, at the Sunday morning sermon in the state penitentiary. it's coming—our cities turned inside out, our people freed from under the tinfoil of material, a world of Self-Expression without judgment. Yes, it's coming.

Yoko,

meet me at Times Square on election day, this year. meet me where your *WAR IS OVER* billboard was. our war IS almost over. the spiritual—the feminine—is finALLy emerging victorious. let's celebrate. let's plan our next move. let's see the heaven in each other. I'll be there at noon.

Yoko Ono,

since I was a little kid I wanted two things more than anything—to know God and to have a woman in my life. I received both by simply writing a list entitled 101 Things I Love About Valerie.

#42: YOU VOLUNTEER FOR THE ELDERS' LUNCH PROGRAM.

#24: YOU NEVER ZIP YOUR BACKPACK ALL THE WAY SHUT.

#81: WHEN I ASKED YOU TO MARRY ME LAST NIGHT, YOU HAD A RED POPSICLE STAIN AROUND YOUR MOUTH.

I realized I am an individual, utterly and compLETely, and yet, I only became enlightened to IT through another BEautiful individual.

Y. O.,

Heaven lies not in perfection, but in the perfect perspective. and human beings were put on Earth to create heaven.

Valerie knows these things. she cradles them, secretly, within her heart, like a folded piece of paper in her pants pocket. and it will be her aWAKEning—to both our free-spirited romantic love and to this New Reality—that will be the defining story of our generation. a Love story to fulfill all stories before it.

all right Yoko Ono Lennon,

so give me 7,000,000 dollars . . . or don't.

I now feel I have the power to be ridiculous because I already have everything I need. I'm happier than I have ever been, and it has nothing to do with how people think of me.

Yoko,

Imagination is a tool of the heART—π.

Marley sang "The Redemption Song." all of us are singing the redemption song.

all of us are bursting with Infinite possibilities. it's starting right here in Unalakleet, Alaska, and I am the voice cALLing out with a megaphONE proclaiming to the world that we will all be in heaven, in this lifetime, on this PLANet, very soon.

see you at Times Square on election day (I'm so excited to finally meet you!)

—yes!
Go-boy

I get up early the next day and walk the long way to school, along the beach. The ocean is at low tide and mud stretches out shiny and wrinkled like worn-out leather. There is a barge docked up to the shore about three miles down, unloading Conex storage vans full of construction supplies for the new jail. It's the last barge shipment of the year.

Halfway there I see Kiana feeding her uncle's dogs. She's wearing bunny boots and is carrying a white bucket full of dry fish, giving each mutt two fillets connected by the tail. She once told me her uncle put the dogs on the beach during summer because the wind kept mosquitoes off them. She sees me coming. I raise my hand up and down when I'm close. She nods. And when she does, a piece of hair falls from behind her ear and brushes over her sharp cheek. But her nod isn't nice. It's just what people do—wave. Village routine. The dogs are barking for food and our eyes meet for a second but I don't stop walking, I can't stop walking.

Behind Kiana, the fireweed stretching over the tundra is shriveled and brown. A few of the flowers are still in bloom, but most of the purple-pink weeds have faded and are now indistinct from all the other greenish-browns.

Go-boy told me about fireweed when we were on one of our rides up the road this summer. He pointed to the tall flower, said, "The thing about fireweed is when it blooms all the way to the top, it means there's only six weeks left until winter."

In my backpack I have drumsticks and a letter I wrote to the teacher who suspended me. When I get to the school I stop in the principal's office. I hand the folded paper to Flo. She says that she'll give it to the teacher and will let him decide if the apology is acceptable. She says I can't return to school until he gives the okay.

But I don't care about rejoining the class or catching up on homework. I just want to play drums. I want another lesson. I ask her if I can. I tell her that's all I want—to play drums—to learn something new. She pauses, then says she'll compromise and show me one technique—a simple drum fill.

I follow her.

She says, "For any music to work, the drums have to be perfect. For the drums to be perfect, every fill has to start and end right on the beat."

On our way to the music room, Flo turns into the gym. There, under the farthest hoop, are her drums. Nothing else is set up anywhere. She turns the overhead lights on. The drums are on a small rectangle of carpet, and the room stretches around on all sides, big and empty. We walk to the set. All we hear is our footsteps.

Flo sits at the '63 Rogers. The hi-hats vibrate in the silence, echoing against the distant walls. She puts a stick in each hand. I memorize all of it—the seat squeak, the hum of the tom heads, the chains on the bottom of the snare drum rustling like a candy wrapper sliding down a sidewalk.

She says, "A drum fill, no matter how spectacular, is terrible if it's too early or too late."

There is anticipation to the volume she is about to create. A silent reverb throughout the empty gym.

And then she starts playing and the whole room comes alive, thundering and massive. Each of her legs and arms moves like this and that. The downbeat pounds with kick, anchoring everything. The two and four on the snare snap like guns firing off the high ceiling as she rolls and accents the ghost notes between each shot. Cymbals wash over the walls—the ride and hi-hats driving with sixteenth notes—the whole room encompassing what she does.

I stand there, watching, aware of my hands and feet and their need to produce feeling like that. And somewhere in the middle of it all—a simple drum fill.

She stops and holds out the sticks, inviting my turn. But for a minute I don't react. I don't know why. I don't know anything. I am brand new, trying to soak every last echo from the room. Every last ring. Each part of the kit is a noisy piece of old wood or metal that Flo has just merged with the rest and made into something real, something any person could make sense out of, even enjoy. And it all runs through the cymbal grooves and the wood grains of the '63 Rogers—the *classic*—and hits me at this place where the only thing I want to do is what she just did.

. . .

After the lesson I put my sticks in my backpack. Go's painted envelope is still in the bottom of the bag. So instead of going home, I walk to the post office, pay the postage, and in a way, I join Goboy's New Forgiveness Conspiracy.

BROKE

I needed money. I had been in Alaska long enough and it was time I moved back to LA because in LA I could pursue drumming—I could take lessons and make connections, and later on get some jobs—and that wasn't possible in Unalakleet.

One afternoon Kiana was at our house, looking for Go's checkbook, trying to see if he'd paid his bills.

She said, "What's this?" and held up some type of nasty car part that looked like a whistle or a pipe. She set it on a stack of newspapers. She wiped her fingers across the headline, leaving two faded smudges over an article about highway repairs in Anchorage.

Kiana and Mom were now certain Go-boy was crazy. They were just searching for proof. They were trying to convince me, and I was still staying out of the whole business. Kiana said Go-boy had probably *flushed away* his savings since he didn't have a job and had lost his college scholarships. Since birth he'd pooled all his Permanent Fund checks into a savings account. All his summers on the fish tower and summers crabbing with his uncles—saved. But Kiana couldn't find his checkbook and that meant something.

I said, "It means you can't find it."

Kiana again ignored me. This was the most she'd talked to me in weeks, so I was fine with her attitude, and besides, she'd just given me an idea—ask Go for money. I was broke, so what would it hurt? Because even if Mom hadn't spent all her money moving us up here, she wouldn't buy me a ticket back to California—for her California represented everything bad about Pop and Wicho and twenty un-successful years of her life, and she projected that onto me.

"How much money did he *flush*?" I asked.

Kiana held up a magazine that had a rectangle cut from one of the pages. She eyed the page a bit too long, then said, "He probably doesn't even know."

After that I figured maybe Go would give me the money because he was feeling good—he had all kinds of energy—and his tattoo had come back. He had drawn that Eskimo Jesus on his forearm almost every other day for a week and he showed me every time he changed something. He switched from black ink to blue ink. He added a whole background of angelic clouds and rain. The tattoo now stretched up to his shoulder. And since I had mailed his letter to Yoko Ono, he was treating me like I knew what he was talking about, like we were in this together, and for some reason I didn't mind.

So that night I asked Go for money. I told him I needed cash for a plane ticket so I could *follow my heart* and move back to LA and play drums. Maybe attend music school. I talked a little too much and a little too fast and Go-boy waited for me to finish. He told me he was worried I'd get back into my old life—that I'd be back run-ning with gangs. Then he paused and told me he'd think about it.

He said, "I'll lose the bet if you move back."

I smiled, said, "That's fine."

But before he gave me any money and before we could talk about it again, a forest just east of town caught fire.

The burning started one morning. We could see a thin trickle of smoke rising up out of the hills. The town's only fire truck filled its water tank and drove up the road, no siren, no lights. But by afternoon there was a gray wall from the ground to the sky, threatening to engulf the entire village. It had taken a few cabins already, including Flo's, and the Bible camp. It had gotten out of control. And then the planes and the helicopters arrived, dropping ocean water into the smoke, and the state newspaper ran a picture of Unk on its front page with the headline *BIBLE CAMP BURNS*.

GO AT SHAKTOOLIK

The smoke in the village was so thick that if you threw a rock you couldn't see it land. Even when the wind kicked up there was still a haze. The forest fires raged for a week, suffocating everything, putting some jobs on hold and even closing the school for a couple days. And since all the planes were grounded—nothing was coming or leaving—Go-boy told me another few days of this and AC Store would run out of food. But he laughed and said, "We got fifteen bags of French fries in our freezer." I checked, and we did.

At the smokiest times the world was reduced to twenty-foot sections, like islands of visibility—gliding into view of dim houses and telephone poles, then vanishing—the smell of burning in every sweatshirt hood and jacket collar. The streetlights blinked on at noon, or earlier, or maybe never shut off. The occasional Ford tried to shine through with high beams. Everyone in town stayed home and sealed their windows, and even the post office was closed. The entire village shut down.

This was when Go-boy told me about his idea of taking a boat from village to village, around the Norton Sound, letting people know about the *good news*.

I asked, "What good news?"

He reminded me there was a conspiracy in the works. A good conspiracy. One that would bring heaven on earth.

"I almost forgot," I said.

This conspiracy was why he would cruise up the coast to a place he called Shak Town—Shaktoolik—a village smaller than ours. He would let them know about the *good news*. And he claimed I needed to come with.

Go said, "The good news is that everyone is saved. Everyone is invited to heaven on earth."

He told me after Shaktoolik we'd hit Koyuk and Golovin and Elim and keep going right up the Sound to Nome. People were waiting for the *good news*. People were dying to hear the *good news*. People would feed us and give us places to sleep in exchange for the *good news*.

I said, "That's just begging."

And he told me he only listened to his heart. He said, "This is what I've always been meant to do. What we're now meant to do."

Kiana called on the smokiest day, asking for Go. She called every day to check on him, but this time was different. I'd slept past noon that morning because it was so dark outside, and when I woke up I couldn't even see our neighbor's house.

I answered the phone and Kiana didn't give me her usual attitude. She was desperate. Urgent. She asked for her brother and I told her I hadn't seen Go-boy all day, and then she made a noise like she would almost give up on something, a type of exhale. She said Uncle Stanley had passed out and needed to be at the clinic. All the smoke was getting to him. I knew Kiana didn't want to talk to me or ask for my help—she was still trying to ignore me, still trying to be mad—but I liked Stanley because he was always giving Go-boy shit in an uncle sort of way, so I said, "I'll come over."

I walked from Happy Valley to the other side of town, through the dark-gray shadow. Everything was empty. It was weird but kind of nice, like I was someplace else. When I got to Stanley's house he was hunched over the kitchen table and Kiana was forcing him to drink sips of water. It was no mystery why he was sick—the windows in his plywood shack just hung in the frames, with two-finger gaps in places. Other windows were covered with condensation, making the smoky view outside look watery.

"If he falls down I can't help him up," Kiana said, holding Stanley by the elbow.

Her index finger and thumb on both hands were stained a deep purple from picking and putting away blueberries. She had been out there on the tundra every day, despite the smoke.

We walked Stanley outside and Kiana put a ski mask on him. We helped him onto the back of the four-wheeler and I let her drive. I said I would ride my bike, but I didn't have a bike. So I just grabbed some neighbor kid's and pedaled off after the fading red taillights.

The nurse at the clinic said Stanley would be fine and put a breather on him and gave him air. There was nothing to be worried about, but Kiana was still acting nervous. A few more elders came in for oxygen. We sat in the lounge, waiting to hear if they needed to keep Stanley until the smoke cleared. Waiting to hear if we should wait.

Kiana said, "These places are starting to make me anxious."

She leaned forward and smoothed her stained fingertips through her hair, and I could hear her breathing. She'd been spending all her time either in the Anchorage hospital with Sean or at the city jail with her dad, and it was wearing her down. I could see that now. I turned and looked at a painting on the wall. It was a colorful village scene—a small house with a pill-shaped fuel tank and a Native in a red coat, happy and shoveling snow from the roof.

I said, "We can take off. Stan will be fine."

Everyone and everything around Kiana was breaking down. Everyone in the family depended on her, and Go was ignoring it all. And right then I felt bad. I wished I had agreed with her when she tried to convince me Go was crazy. I knew he was.

"We can leave now."

Kiana rocked her body back and forth, her black hair pooling onto her lap. She was wearing a thin, long-sleeved green shirt that hiked above her waist when she leaned forward. I didn't know if she had heard me, so I said, "Ready?" She was breathing hard now. I put my hand on the side of her shoulder and then lightly wrapped my fingers below her armpit, and pulled, and she didn't protest my hand on her arm, she just got up out of the chair. It was the first time I had touched her in months. It was nice.

We left the four-wheeler with Uncle Stanley and walked down Main Road. I couldn't look Kiana in the face but I knew she hadn't been crying. She was tough and wouldn't break down in front of me if she could help it. She was just stressed. It was getting close to supper and the smoke was still thick, but the sun had been dropping behind this grounded cloud. We walked in the empty gray tunnel like we were going nowhere.

Through the fog I could see a homemade banner of some sort—

it said, *#98: YOU DON'T TREAT DOGS LIKE PEOPLE*. Kiana didn't see it and I didn't say anything.

We didn't talk at all. It was the first time we had done anything together since I'd pissed her off and I hoped not to ruin that. The road couldn't disappear into the smoke long enough. I wanted to keep walking like this. I wanted this to last. But I didn't think she cared. And when we got back to Mom's place it was over, and all I could do was head back to Go-boy's.

She said, "Thanks."

She stood in the doorway and I stood on the bottom step, leaning back and holding on to the two-by-four railing. We could hear a truck coming down the road. The air was charcoal now. A lightbulb shined above us. Headlights popped through the smoke and passed the house in a blink. Then it was silent. Next door, at Stanley's house, we had left the front door wide open. I couldn't see his place through the haze, but I could hear a faucet running in his bathroom at the end of the hall. The high-pitched whistle of water washing into the sink seemed extra clear through the smoke. This was the faucet Stanley left running around the clock all winter to avoid frozen pipes. Even Stanley was expecting the first freeze any day now.

"What's that scar from?" Kiana asked and pointed at my cheek, drawing a boomerang shape in the air between us with her purple fingertip.

I touched the hair by my left ear and traced down to the corner of my jaw. "Accident," I said, lying.

"Car accident?"

I nodded.

She looked curious, like maybe she didn't believe me. I didn't want to tell her it was from a knife, from a fight. She knew a few things about my past and I didn't want to give her any more hints of who I had been in LA, or what I'd done, and I didn't want her to know I was trying to move back. Go might have told Kiana that my old friends would want me dead because I'd left the gang, but neither of them knew about the gang rape, and none of that seemed real while I stood there with her. Talking about LA with Kiana embarrassed me.

She didn't say anything and looked ready to walk into the house. I wanted to keep her there a little longer. She was holding the doorknob, and I could hear it start to spin and the door start to scratch open.

I said, "I think you're right about Go-boy."

She leaned away from the house, not breathing. She was looking right at me now, right on top of every word. I was waiting for another *thank you*, or some kind of sigh of relief. I was waiting for everything to slip into place. Ready for her to apologize, and mean it. But she didn't talk.

I told her, "I think he's crazy."

The smoke started to thin later in the week. Planes were still grounded and the town was still empty but from time to time an ocean breeze would push the smoke back and reveal a blue sky for a few minutes. This was when Go-boy left me a yellow note stuck to the on/off button of our TV—*MEET ME BY THE BOAT, TWO O'CLOCK. WE'RE SPREADING GOOD NEWS.*

He was talking about Shaktoolik.

The short walk to the slough seemed a little farther with the haze. I could see the sun behind this gray fog, a scar in the middle of the sky. Houses that were two blocks down the gravel road looked blurred. And the campfire smell, which had soaked into everything, no longer seemed like an issue.

I walked on Main Road, cut between a garage and a log fish rack, and walked down an embankment to the slough. Everything was dead and brown—the knee-high crabgrass, the weeds growing in the corners of buildings, the tundra that climbed the surrounding hills. Even the gravel roads had lost color. Before the smoke came it seemed things still had life, but now that the haze was lifting it looked like fall had already come and gone. This wasn't the typical forest-fire season and people were talking about that. People couldn't figure out why all those trees were burning so late in the year. And people couldn't figure out why, in spite of everything turning brown, the cold weather hadn't yet come.

Go-boy wasn't at the shore. In his boat was a rusty lawn chair next to the steering wheel. Next to that a backpack that had a rainbow flag sewn on with yellow fishing line, a box of Sailor Boy crackers, and a six-pack of pop.

I sat in the boat waiting for Go, floating a few feet from shore.

A cop in a pickup drove along the road that paralleled the slough, past a truck and two Honda four-wheelers parked along the edge. He drove slow through the haze, past the dumpsters and the garbage compactor to the edge of the bridge, then turned back around, rolled his window open, and yelled down to me, asking if I had seen Go-boy. I said no, which wasn't a total lie.

"We've got a restraining order to issue him," he said.

I shook my head and the VPO drove off.

I grabbed a soda and opened it. Soda was part of the reason the cops were looking for Go. He had been posting signs all over town. One big one said, *REASON #55: YOU LIKE PEPSI*, and it was stapled to an abandoned building across from the church. He'd started putting the signs up when the smoke was the thickest, and now, with the haze lifting, we could see them everywhere. Each poster was part of the list Go-boy had written for Valerie—*101 Things I Love About Valerie*. I'd read a few in his letter to Yoko Ono, but I didn't think he had written all one hundred and one reasons.

I opened the backpack to make sure it was Go-boy's stuff. I found wads of yellow sticky notes and legal pads and a couple books. I read some of the things he had written. Most of it was the kind of stuff people jot down to remember ideas. I dug around in some of the other pouches. He had a pocketknife. A foot-long chunk of black electrical wire. A cinnamon granola bar that had been in there so long it was now just a wrapper full of powder.

Then I found a small yellow package—an envelope—much like the manila envelope I had mailed for Go weeks before. It was addressed to Yoko Ono, again, and the address was framed in thin blue lines. Outside the lines, it read, IT'S JUST A BLUEPRINT. On the back, the flap side, there were a few philosophical quotes and prophetic drawings. Quick statements. Observations. The letter was also handwritten, but this time more like a formal letter and less like an outline. Some parts were crossed out but still readable. There were notes in the margins. I read the first paragraph—

> Dear Yoko Ono,
>
> Forget about the 7,000,000 dollars for a moment. I want to share a profound idea—a t-shirt design! I'm envisioning yellow-gold shirts with the phrase SAME-SAME across the chest in gold print. It is a village saying meaning two people are similar, like,

"Man, real same-same you two." On one person the t-shirt might not mean anything. But on two people it begins to mean something. So it's my plan to make thousands of these t-shirts, or maybe millions. Then it will begin to mean what we know it means.

I didn't read the rest.

When the cop was gone Go came running out from under the bridge, down the sandy shoreline. He had a can of Krylon spray paint, and he looked to the left and right.

"Ready?" he said, and walked past me and pulled in the back anchor.

I asked him where he was taking me.

Go fired up the motor, said, "See it?" and pointed at the Kuuk Bridge.

Right there, almost on top of us, in bright orange spray paint, crooked and covering about a quarter of the wall, it said, *#37: YOU WEAR T-SHIRTS INSIDE OUT.*

"And you're running for mayor?"

"Real upside-down world, ah?"

I gave him a confused look. He turned and picked up a red gas tank, shaking it, checking that it was full enough. He did the same to a second one.

He said, "It's like at this Indian's initiation one time. An elder told the boy, 'As you go the way of life, you will see a great chasm. Jump. It's not as wide as you think.'"

He backed the boat into the channel, its engine rumbling like a street-rod's, and I said, "Maybe it's not a chasm, maybe it's the deep end."

"Same-same, man."

"You know the cops are looking for you?"

He pushed the hammer down, and we took off toward the ocean.

The cop was after Go-boy because this list was scaring Valerie. She'd turned down his marriage proposal a few months back, but Go was still posting his love for her all over town.

The first sign I saw was while walking through the smoke with Kiana. After that I saw them everywhere. I read *#53: YOU SAY CROOK'D INSTEAD OF CROOKED* on Native Store's bulletin board pinned between a snowmachine sled classified and a Fish and Game flyer. I read reason number one at the post office and reason number seventy-six at the airport. I remember number sixty-one, tacked on the side of an abandoned Conex container. It said, *YOUR THUMB IS MORE WRINKLED THAN THE REST OF YOUR FINGERS.*

Go slowed the boat as we rounded a corner by the fish plant. He waved to an old woman who was backing a little flatboat into the water with her four-wheeler. The lady waved too. Around the turn, the mouth of the river opened up into the ocean. Buoys marked the channel.

Go-boy hollered at me above the engine noise and pointed at the seawall. Attached to the chain-link barrier, ten feet above shore, was a white bedsheet spread out like a banner. It said, *#71: YOU THINK THE APOSTLE PAUL WAS A REPRESSED HOMOSEXUAL.*

I looked at Go and he was smiling.

The boat thumped toward Shaktoolik and I had to talk myself out of getting seasick. I looked up at the patchy sky. I breathed deep. This was nothing like boating in the river. Even though the water was pretty calm, we were paralleling the coast and so the waves were hitting us at a side angle, jumping the boat in quick little S-shapes.

Just outside town we saw two guys sitting on the beach by a fire. They were drinking booze from Gatorade bottles and throwing rocks at an abandoned shoe that was set up as a target. Go-boy waved, and they waved back. He said it was Tom and Yobert.

"Yobert?"

"Yeah," he said. The guy's name was Robert but he always walked around town saying *Yo!* to everyone. All day every day, *Yo!* I hadn't met these guys. Go-boy said Uncle Stanley gave him the nickname after Yobert said *Yo!* to him.

Go said, "Until last week, those two hated each other." He said this like he had something to do with it, like it was because of him they were friends again, and this convinced me to find out if Go was crazy or not.

"How old are they?"

"Tom and Yobert?" Go said. "They're my age. We all graduated together."

"Do they work?"

Go paused, gave me a little smile that was supposed to mean something, and said, "Man, they're *working* right now."

When we were ten miles out of town we could see an island on the horizon. Go called it Besboro. It was shaped like the silhouette of an old Converse high-top. Besboro was how the airport knew if it was safe for planes to fly or land—if they could see the island from town, visibility was good enough.

"So what's your tattoo really mean?"

He held out his arm and looked it up and down. And then he told me he'd tried to kill himself after he'd asked Valerie to marry him, after she'd said no, when he'd disappeared for a month. He drank himself miserable till he was holding a gun against his head. He said if there were bullets, he'd be dead. But he passed out before he could find any. After that he changed everything—he discovered the meaning of life. At that moment, when Go decided he wasn't going to follow anybody anymore, he said he literally went to heaven.

"That's what your tattoo is about?"

He said, "I had been living for everyone else. I never trusted my own instincts, or my own thoughts or ideas. Only what others thought."

This was just days after I told Kiana I suspected he was crazy, and this was why I hadn't believed her in the first place when she said Go needed help—he always made sense. He always said the exact right thing at the exact right time.

"Look," he said, and shut the engine off. "Here's the truth. I've never liked myself. I've subconsciously believed there would always be heartbreak and trouble in my future. But when I finally realized that *I* was my own destiny, I realized that life or death was up to me. That's when I chose to follow my heart and live for myself. Victor Frankl said, 'Suffering, once articulated, ceases to be suffering.' I no longer suffer."

We were about halfway to Shak Town. The boat faced away from land. We were silent a few minutes and then Go-boy quoted a few more people—Socrates, Bob Dylan, Muhammad. He stood up and looked out over the ocean and exhaled, as if he was exhausted with his explanations too.

We floated. Then Go pointed about twenty yards ahead, said, "Right there!"

"What?"

"Beluga whales!"

I looked around but couldn't see anything.

"Right there," he said.

I was looking for big fish-colored bodies, but then saw white. It was two, maybe three white whales, like Chevy Suburbans floating at the surface.

"We eat those," he said.

"They're white."

Go said, "You've seen muktuk at potlucks. It's their skin and blubber."

I grabbed another soda from under the lawn chair. Now the boat was facing the waves and the up-and-down motion wasn't as sickening. The whales blew out of the water a few times and disappeared.

I still didn't know if Go was crazy. I didn't have proof either way. I said, "You love this girl because she drinks Pepsi?"

Go-boy laughed a little but didn't say anything.

Sometime after I opened that pop we both sat on the floor of the boat, facing each other. With our knees bent in front of us, we leaned back against the welded blue walls. The silence of wind and water was audible with the engine off. We just floated. The boat rolled front to back over a constant line of waves and slurping, but we couldn't see the ocean over the sides. Just sky. Saltwater shot onto the floor and washed toward the rear drain, sliding past our legs like spit on windshields. And the air above us hollowed out, not near as smoky as in town.

"I originally was going to make the list ten thousand reasons."

I laughed. But Go was serious. I said, "Where would you have put them all?"

"I wanted to show myself that I could simply appreciate another person."

"But there's not even ten thousand places in town," I said.

"I wanted to prove that I could appreciate a girl without always wanting something back."

Go pulled out a bag of coaster-sized crackers and offered me one.

I asked, "And now the cops are after you?"

He told me that the notes all over town might not be the real reason the cops were looking for him. It might have been something he'd done on the smokiest day. It was the same day I had gone to the clinic with Kiana. Go-boy had been trying to talk to Valerie, but nobody would tell him where she was. All her relatives were protecting her. They thought Go was being too forward, too aggressive. Her dad had just died. She needed space. But Go-boy called it *honesty.* Called it *destiny.* He even used the word *free.* Valerie didn't see it that way—she was freaked out.

Go-boy said he wrapped himself in red Christmas lights from head to toe and wired them up with nine-volt batteries. He walked to Valerie's house like this, carrying a boom box. He said in the smoke it must've looked cool. The daytime, dark, choked inside a cloud of dishwater gray. The town empty. The airplanes grounded. The whole village on pause until east winds would be trumped by stronger winds from the west. And Go was in the middle of it all, walking alone, walking down a gravel road, glowing red, a boom box on his shoulder.

I laughed.

He told me it was just like Valerie's favorite movie. I didn't know which one he was talking about, but I guessed how Go's story ended—he stood outside the girl's bedroom window, afraid but shameless, her favorite song booming from a stereo; Go-boy, in love, laying it all out there, letting nothing get in his way of pursuing this girl. And that was what he did. But the stereo died before he got to Valerie's, so he sang a Ben Harper song called "Forever" with no music.

I said, "I'm not surprised she called the cops."

"Pretty good, ah?"

"That kind of stupid's got to be illegal somewhere."

Go said, "Give me a lever and a place to stand and I will move the world."

He pulled a small baggie from his coat and tossed it to me. It was weed. My weed—the weed I'd left in Uncle Stanley's cabin on one of my bike rides up the road. Most of it was gone.

Go smiled, said, "When we see ourselves without judgment, then we'll begin to see and accept others without judgment. We'll turn the volume down on the external world, and we'll see we're all connected, we're all same-same."

He passed more crackers. It seemed the waves had stopped.

I thought about the fact that Go's actions never seemed crazy when he was explaining them to me, or when I was witnessing them. It was only later, after a day or two, when all his stories blurred to-gether and I knew something wasn't right. But maybe I just wanted to believe he was nuts because of what I had told Kiana. I wasn't sure. Go was acting crazy and doing dumb shit, but he still didn't seem like he needed help. He knew who he was and what he was do-ing and what he wanted. For once, Go seemed content.

At some point we both stood up and saw that the boat was beached, stuck hard in black muck. The motor buried in mud. We had floated too long and the waves had pushed us at an angle till we'd hit shore. We checked up and down the coast. Nothing was anywhere except this enormous mound of rock, towering above us. A cliff, hundreds of feet high. The face was cut with diagonal lines as if hacked by a butter knife. I remembered asking a girl in town what had caused those crooked grooves. She was an MIT grad and told me rocks weren't her field, but it was probably from glaciers. We were stuck right below this. And there was something comforting about it.

"Tide's going out."

"Shit," I said, not worried.

He started laughing, and we each sat on an edge of the boat.

"Is this part of your plan?"

He laughed again.

I grabbed the Sailor Boys and we ate more crackers and drank more pop, and for about an hour we watched the ocean pull away while the sun beat down on top of us. Down the coast we could see the clouds of smoke from the forest fires, still burning, still fogging Unk. We didn't talk about anything, or if we did, I don't remember what we said. It was the perfect moment to forget. It was the first time in months that there was no tension pushing and pulling between us. We were just living. Wanting and needing nothing. Planning nothing. We were ourselves and in agreement with everything else around us. Long after this day passed, I would look back on this moment—the moment I couldn't remember—and feel as if it were my first religious experience.

After an hour or so, Go said, "How much you need for a plane ticket?"

"To LA?"

"Yeah," he said.

I hadn't even checked to see what it would cost. I didn't expect to get an offer. At least, I didn't expect it to be so easy. Since our bet—when I'd first arrived in town—Go had been convinced that I would stay in Unk forever.

"Maybe a thousand?"

I said, "Maybe."

"Okay," he said, and pulled a wallet from his backpack and counted out a thousand dollars in twenties.

"What?"

"Yeah," he said. "Take it."

I waited. I wanted to tell him about the gang rape, the girl, and everything that had led up to it. He had just given me his life story and now he was trying to give me this money, and I felt like he didn't really know who I was. I felt like he maybe thought we wanted similar things and believed similar things and had experienced similar things. But we hadn't. And I was afraid to tell him about the gang rape because I was afraid he'd realize we weren't the same.

He said, "I think we need a member of the conspiracy in California."

Then he smiled, and I took the cash.

We both fell asleep in the sunshine and when I woke up the sun had started to set behind the water. Go was gone, and I wasn't surprised. Go was always walking off without telling anyone. Even when we were doing things together he'd manage to vanish.

I took my shoes off, rolled my jeans, and hopped out of the boat into the mud, sinking to my ankles. Go had tossed an anchor onto shore so the boat wouldn't float away when the tide went back up. I hit the shore and cleaned my feet with my socks, then left the socks on the stones and slipped barefoot into my shoes.

I walked for what seemed like hours. I got a blister on each heel and I didn't even mind. I knew if I followed the beach long enough

I'd get home. Even in the trailing smoke that was getting thicker the closer I got to town, if I walked too far I'd run into the river and the seawall.

I thought about stopping by Kiana's place. I now had a reason to talk to her and wanted to see her again. I'd tell her the cops were looking for her brother. That Go had planned to make the list ten thousand reasons long. That he'd given me a thousand dollars cash. All proof he was crazy and needed help. All proof that Kiana should be okay with me again. That I was on her side. But was I convinced?

After Kiana and me took Stanley to the clinic and I first told her I thought Go-boy was nuts, she didn't say anything for a long time. I stood on the bottom step and she was in the doorway. I continued to listen to the running water from Stanley's house. After a while Kiana shook her head, said, "I don't know anymore." She said, "I don't think so."

"But you've been saying this for weeks."

And she said she knew that, but now she thought it was more simple. She thought Go was in love. "You really think he's crazy?"

"He disappears for a month, then comes back acting like nothing is weird, then he decides to run for mayor. You've been right this whole time. Something's off."

She said, "But that's just Go. He's always been impulsive. I think he's just lovesick."

Afterward, before I turned to walk home in the smoke, Kiana ran her stained fingertips through her hair, and when she did that, the sleeve of her shirt fell to her elbow, and I saw she was wearing a wristwatch. My wristwatch. I had left it on my dresser along with all the other things I'd left behind in my room, along with all my stuff that Kiana had boxed up and moved to storage. The wristwatch was simple—leather band, black face, silver trim and hands—but there was nothing simple about her wearing it. The watch looked good on her bony wrist. It was good to see she wanted to wear—and have—something of mine.

Kiana then said good-bye, smiled, and said thanks, like maybe me and her had a chance. And then I didn't care about anything else.

I knew I was close to town when I walked past those two guys sitting by a fire. Through the lingering gray fog I saw a small flame. They were burning a big chunk of driftwood, the smoke rising up from shore and then blurring into the rest of the cloud. One guy was passed out. The other looked at me like he didn't know what was happening. I nodded, stepping over the branch of driftwood that wasn't on fire. He acted like he couldn't see me. I said, "Yo!" as I passed. He kept looking and squinting. I just walked.

Piles of dull driftwood ran parallel to the beach, pushed up by storms. I turned away from the shoreline, climbed the logs, and walked along the chain-link fence that bordered the airport runway. There were signs attached to the posts every thirty feet or so, saying *AIRPORT, KEEP OUT.* I knew I was close to the road.

Then I saw a homemade sign tacked below one of the airport's. It was a coffee can, no label, cut vertical and flattened. In white paint, I read *#101: WHEN WE HELD HANDS FOR THE FIRST TIME, WALKING ACROSS THE BRIDGE, AND IT WAS PERFECTLY SILENT, I COULD HEAR YOU SMILE.*

As I walked farther down the beach I smoothed the stack of twenties between my fingers in my jacket pocket. I had a thousand bucks. I had possibilities. I had known people to get shot over this kind of cash. And it was right there in my pocket, and I could use it. I had wanted to leave the village all summer and now could do whatever I wanted. Anything. But for some reason, it was unsettling.

So I kept walking and smoothing the cash, the thick stack in my hand. I kept walking even when I got back into town, right down Airport Road, right past our house. The smoke was the thickest it had been. I stepped around puddles and watched the hazy gravel road unravel ten feet in front of me. There was a loose dog in the ditch next to a rusted dump truck. The mutt scratched at something in the dirt. And I kept walking with that money, all over town, like maybe if I stopped walking, it would disappear.

SOMETIMES WE ALWAYS

The three of us were eating pizza for dinner every night this week. It was Tuesday. I'd taken the first slice and sat in front of the TV while Kiana and Mom were folding back the covers on three boxes—pepperoni, black olive and green pepper, and supreme. I'd been trying to get some alone time with Kiana for days now, but she wasn't picking up on my hints.

"This pizza's got too much sauce," I said after one bite.

Kiana was talking about alcoholism in the village. Mom had just landed a job—her first in years—working at the clinic with a new community alcohol treatment program. It was just an internship, but she was excited all the same. And she was superexcited to talk to Kiana about it. Those two were now inseparable, their conversations never-ending—rocketing from a laugh fest to a therapy session to these types of social problems. It was like they needed to impress each other. For Kiana, Mom was a Native who had lived outside Alaska. For Mom, Kiana hadn't yet forgotten how to be Native.

With my mouth full, I said, "The cheese slides right off."

Kiana told Mom that she thought Unk should be switched from a *damp* village to a *dry* village like some of the other small towns in rural Alaska. She said, "Booze always makes everything worse."

Mom agreed. "But it's not different anywhere else in the world."

We were guinea pigs each night this week for the new pizza joint that was having its grand opening on Friday. It was going to be a community Halloween party, with free pizza and pop and a whole Disney theme for the kids. And everyone in town was excited for a village event that wasn't the result of something sad.

This new restaurant was right next door to Mom's and the smell of melted cheese had been blowing through her house. We were supposed to call the owner with our comments. But after Monday night I knew how the rest of the week would pan out—Mom and Kiana would eat and talk for hours about anything but the pizza, and then when it was time to report, Mom would say she wanted something with mushrooms, and Kiana would say the sauce was too pasty.

It was Tuesday and it was already shaping up to be that way.

Kiana showed Mom how to make akutaq—Eskimo ice cream— and she kept talking about booze. Kiana had quit drinking just two weeks earlier and she was now some kind of expert on the whole thing. She said, "I want to be part of a solution around here." She was starting to sound like Go-boy. And since my relationship with Kiana was based on one drunken night, I knew what she was saying.

I said, "The pepperoni tastes like plastic."

Kiana ran a pizza cutter across each pie. "Real crooked."

Mom wrote each of our comments with marker on a chunk of pizza box that she'd torn off. This was as organized as we would get the whole week. And it was pretty damn good pizza to begin with, but given the opportunity, anyone becomes a critic. So this first list of comments on the chunk of cardboard was the end of our advice, and it would land in the trash.

Mom had just called off her engagement to the dog musher, so the pizza was the last thing she cared about. Mom explained to Kiana why she felt so good about breaking up with her fiancé.

"I realized I was addicted to men. I've never *not* had a guy around, and I was depending on that kind of relationship. My heart told me it was time to be single."

Mom was starting to sound like Go-boy too. And I knew she was talking about why she'd let Pop walk all over her for twenty years, but I didn't care about Pop anymore. If she would've said this stuff a month ago I would've gotten mad. But now, nothing. Mom had a new job and a new idea about how to live her life, so I was happy for her. I was glad she had become so contented and motivated. But as Mom talked about her past problems with men, I could see she was putting ideas into Kiana's head, giving her lots of reasons not to let me and her happen.

"And anyway," Mom said, wincing, "this guy always had real dirty fingernails."

"At least he didn't drink."

Mom said, "Lot of people don't drink."

"Like Go-boy," I said.

Kiana breathed like she was going to say something about her brother, but didn't.

"Has Go-boy ever?" Mom asked.

Kiana shook her head, no, and she and Mom shared some kind of suspicious look, like maybe they thought a person who had never made big mistakes didn't have the same credibility as someone who had. I'd heard that line a hundred times back in LA. But it seemed like those people who always had to be reminding everyone about their credibility didn't believe they had it.

"Where is Go?" Kiana asked me.

I shrugged, lying. Go-boy had left for Seattle that morning.

Go-boy was how we'd gotten hooked up with the free pizzas. According to the owner, Go was the inspiration for his restaurant. Go-boy had encouraged the guy to *run straight at fear* and *take enormous risks*. Go told him, "Whatever you can imagine happening, will." The guy bought it all. He decided to open the only eatery in the village—a pizza place that would serve Unk and all the other villages around the Norton Sound. He called it To-Go Pizza. People from any little town could call in an order and he'd make the pizzas, and then he'd throw them on the next Bering Air flight, or any other passenger plane, for delivery. Go-boy told me it was revolutionary for western Alaska. And I said, "Know what else would be? Roads." Go laughed.

"I like the crust," Kiana said, stuffing the last bite into her mouth. My watch hung from her thin wrist. She was still wearing it, and still hadn't said anything about it.

Mom said, "You know what? Natives have the highest rate of alcohol abstinence of any race in the United States. Like fifty percent. They taught me that today."

I said, "What about Muslims?"

"Muslims?"

"Yeah."

Kiana said, "Muslim's not a race."

"But I bet they don't drink."

"I could never be Muslim," Mom said. "Gotta always wear that big scarf on your head." She traced an invisible head covering, and both girls laughed.

"The Eskimo men always try-scold you when you take off your malaghai?" Kiana said, joking, and both girls laughed more.

When we were done eating I wanted to ask Kiana if she would like to take a walk, but before I could Mom dug out the photo albums and the two girls started in with the kid pictures and the family stories. This was how it had been these days.

Then the phone rang. I answered. It was Wicho.

"Hello . . . hello?" he said like he couldn't hear me.

I said, "Yeah. There's a delay."

"Hey, little bro, how you doing?"

I couldn't remember the last time I'd talked to Wicho. I only remembered playing out conversations in my head, scenario after scenario, ever since he'd been locked up—going back to when I was convinced I would get him out of jail by merits of a college degree, to times I was frustrated at him for being gone, to times I was sorry for moving to Alaska. Even though we'd talked on the phone the first few years he'd been locked up, I imagined talking to him more than I did.

"Listen, kid, I don't have much time."

His voice was almost unrecognizable. It was thin, and too cool. And I wondered why this was the first we'd spoken in almost a year. He maybe had phone privileges every day or week and could call whoever he wanted. Through the phone I could hear booming voices in the background. They stopped. Wicho said, "I'm sending you my journals from the first couple years I was in here. Okay? You there? Hello?"

"Yeah," I said.

"Read them, okay? I want you to know this about me. About your older brother. Okay?"

After he hung up I wondered who he usually called. If he had phone privileges, that meant every day or every week he was calling somebody besides us. Did he still have a girlfriend? Did he have a kid somewhere? There was so much we didn't know about him, so much that had been lost.

"Who was it?" Mom asked.

"Nobody."

I left that night without saying anything to Kiana. On my walk back to Go-boy's house, the most bizarre thing happened. I was bundled in a canvas jacket with the hood cinched around my head and my hands in my pockets. It had been getting colder every day, with the sun setting earlier and the temp dropping with it, so I walked quick. Down the road, the frozen puddles were smashed out and now were just skeletons of ice bordering muddy water. Every night these big puddles on the roads would freeze over, and every morning the kids would stomp them out on their way to school.

The bizarre thing happened when I was halfway home—all the dogs in town, like they were in a choir or something, reared back and started howling, all at the same time. I was walking down Main Road, and a few dog lots along the slough started in, and then dogs by the bridge answered, and then more from the ocean side of town echoed until every mutt was singing. Even dogs past the airport and on the other side of the river were howling along. I walked for an extra ten minutes just to hear if it was all of them, and it was, maybe a couple hundred or more, yipping and barking together. And then, just like that, in unison, they stopped. This was at eight o'clock.

. . .

The next night I snooped around Kiana's bedroom—looking through her drawers, her closet, and the boxes under her bed. Inside a plastic crate that served as a nightstand, I found a white ring made of ivory. It was the same ring she'd worn on her thumb the night we sat together and watched the humpies jump and splash in the water. The band was smooth, sort of thin, and at one point it got wider. At its widest spot it had a single hole—the size of a pen tip—with two blacks dots on either side. I slipped the ring onto my pinkie finger, and it fit. On my way to Mom's for pizza, I removed the band a couple times. Nervous. Not sure about wearing it. But ready to try.

I stopped at Uncle Stanley's on the way. He was digging ankle-deep holes at the corners of a shed next to his house. This bare-wood building was rotten and graying and looked ready to tip. And it appeared to be without doors.

"Damn mice," he said, burying a white bucket so the rim was flush with the ground. He filled each one half full with water from a hose—mousetraps.

"Just burn it down."

"Wouldn't take much," he said in his soft voice.

People had been trying to buy this property off Stanley for years, but he'd refused to even listen to offers. Go-boy told me Stanley had always been way too stubborn about the building, saying he used it, saying he had stuff to store in it. But the thing didn't have any doors and must have been supported by the wall-to-wall junk inside.

"Mice always eat in their plants," Stanley said, swatting his hand at the neighbor's vegetable garden—a small rectangle the size of a pickup and fenced in by chicken wire.

I said, "I'll push it over with Go-boy's car."

"Okay."

"We can bury them together."

"Wouldn't matter," Stanley said, waving to the building and the land around. "I'm selling it next week."

This was when I knew something funny was going on around town. Like the flu, but instead of sick, everyone was trying to do good. Go-boy had predicted something like this would happen ever since he'd decided to run for mayor, ever since I'd moved in with him a few months ago, or even since I'd moved up here five months back. He'd always talk about the potential and endless possibilities of everyone. And when he predicted that the village would *catch fire*, Go made it sound like *he* would be the spark. Now he wasn't even in town to see it start.

A week before this Go had been hired to help finish the new jail. They had the roof on the building and electricians and plumbers were crowding inside, racing to get everything working before the first freeze. But yesterday Go-boy had quit and snuck onto the Northern Air Cargo plane heading for Anchorage—he climbed inside an empty dishwasher box that was stacked on a pallet of construction supplies. He'd told me he'd bring some snacks and a blanket inside the box and just wait to be unloaded. In Anchorage he was going to visit his little brother at the Native hospital. From there he was flying to Seattle to see a band called Built to Spill, and then from there he was going to New York City for what he called business. He had no place to stay and didn't even have a ticket to the concert, but he told me it would all work out. He said he'd be back sometime after election day.

My life had become routine now that I was back in school—classes, drums, eat at Go's, then head back to the school for open-gym. I'd see Kiana throughout the day, here and there, but she was in all the advanced groups and was even taking university classes over the phone and computer, so it was always in passing. After school I would spend an hour or more at the drum set. I would start with a simple beat—something to get me going. And then, depending on my mood, I would either try new techniques, new fills, or new rhythms, sometimes stopping and starting again, or else I would play a continuous beat, letting it progress, closing my eyes and letting the room disappear while my muscle memory carried the rhythm.

I stopped at the gym after Stanley's. It was ladies' night but some guys were hanging around, shooting at the side hoops. The high school girls were running five-on-five. Bum One was dribbling two balls beside the bleachers, listening to music through the earphones he always wore. It felt like years ago when I'd first met him, when he took me to a gravel pit and shared his beer and tried to scare me about the winter, when he let me fire his handgun.

He said, "Did you hear?"

Bum One always had the rumors, whether they were true or not.

"Did you hear what girl is pregnant?"

I hadn't. I said, "Who?"

"I don't know, man. I just heard someone is pregnant."

Bum One looked at the girls running the floor—all ages of high schoolers. The girls shuffled their feet. They moved without the ball. They shouted each other's name, called *shot, switch*.

Bum One pulled out one of his earphones, elbowed me, and again said, "I don't know. I don't know who. I just heard someone got knocked up."

I was late getting to Mom's place, and when I got there she and Kiana were already done eating, but there was still a whole pizza left. They were watching a movie. I sat down with a couple slices and asked how the food was this time, but they were talking about other stuff and ignored me.

Mom said, "He's real fat, ah? Should probably pedal an exercise bike while he watches."

They laughed.

"I'll never have TV around my kids," Kiana said, shaking her hand in small circles so my oversized watch rotated in loops around her bony wrist.

Mom shook her head, agreeing but skeptical. She said, "We never had it growing up. I was in California before TV ever came here."

"I remember when we just had that one channel—RAT-Net."

Mom said, "They should never have let TV into the village."

"We never watched any, not like kids now," Kiana said. "We just played bat all the time."

They both laughed, still staring at the screen; then they quick-shifted to silence, sharing a memory that was similar but experienced a full generation apart.

Even though neither of them looked at me, I kept my left hand—and Kiana's ring—hidden in the pocket of my zip-up sweatshirt. I could feel the ivory. I could feel the weight of something so delicate hanging on my pinky finger. And I kept that hand hidden in my pocket.

Kiana asked Mom, "If you could be any age again, how old would you be?"

"Twenty," Mom said without hesitation.

I left before I was done eating and carried a box of cold pizza with me. I passed the old BIA school, which still had one of Go-boy's posters stuck to the side of it. It was a cardboard cutout. *#41: YOU STAND UP WHILE DRIVING A BOAT.* A lot of his reasons were still hanging all over town. Valerie had already moved to Anchorage for college, but these signs that were intended for her still hung proud—the only billboards in the village. And although most would be removed, it seemed people in town didn't mind the idea of Go's romantic gestures in their public spaces. On the water tower, it said, *#79: YOU LAUGH WHEN YOU SEE PEOPLE FALL DOWN.*

When I was halfway home, just like the night before, all the dogs in the village started howling. It was gradual like the first time, with a few starting and a few more answering, until the whole town was nothing but a dog siren. At that moment, when you could hear the layers of dogs nearby and dogs in the distance, it was as if nothing else was happening. It seemed everyone in town had exited the stage for these chained-up pups to get in their one collective word for the day.

Something about how I felt reminded me of when Go-boy had disappeared for a month. I now had the same directionless feeling I'd had while riding that BMX up the road every day, looking for Go. I had the same mix of edgy boredom.

And it was then I wondered if Kiana was the girl who was pregnant.

Thursday afternoon I went to the airport and made a reservation to Anchorage and then a reservation from Anchorage to LA. One-way tickets. A month from now. Unplanned. Unannounced.

The agent said she could only take a credit card. I still had the thousand in cash from Go—it was in my pocket—but I told the agent I would have to come back with my mom's card. The agent said she would hold the reservation.

When I got to Mom's that night I explained to them about how all the dogs in town had been howling at the exact same time, in unison, every night. "At eight o'clock. Every dog in the village."

Mom said, "So what? They always bark."

Kiana wasn't listening and looked worried about something. There were three white boxes on the kitchen counter in front of her labeled *SAUSAGE/PINEAPPLE, CHEESE, THE GO-BOY SUPREME.*

I said, "Not like this, though. They're howling at the exact same time." I told them when I walked home from eating pizza every night, I heard them. Dogs by the slough and dogs along Main Road and even dogs by the airport.

Mom told me they just get antsy when the weather starts to get cold. "Have you seen Go-boy?"

Kiana was sliding my wristwatch up and down her forearm and looked up when Mom said that, her eyes rephrasing the question.

I said, "I don't know."

"He's missing again," Kiana said, turning, already surrendered to the idea.

"He's not missing."

"Where is he, then? Nobody's seen him for days."

I shrugged. "He's probably around. He's not missing, though."

Kiana wasn't listening to me anymore. She and Mom were already plotting out what to do next. Go-boy hadn't given me a specific day that he'd be back from Seattle, but I knew he was fine. What bothered me was Kiana and her games and how every time things got cool between us she'd start to act like she wasn't interested. Right now I felt like I could announce that Sean had come out of the coma, but she wouldn't hear it unless Mom told her. She seemed to be acting too coarse around me, too distracted, and at first I thought she was trying to hide her attraction for me—the same attraction I had for her—the attraction I thought we'd both felt walking home together through the smoke after taking Stanley to the clinic; but now I hoped her distance was just that—distance. I hoped she wasn't hiding anything.

With another slice of pizza in hand, I said, "You know what, I haven't seen Go for a few days."

"That's it," Kiana said. "I'm calling around."

Mom asked, "Who? Just wait a minute."

"Whoever. The police."

Mom said, "We should calm down a minute. We don't want to start overreacting."

I took a bite of my slice, and said, "Call the pizza place. Tell them this sauce is the best yet."

Mom gave me a look but I shrugged and noticed that neither of them was eating. Kiana grabbed the phone and tapped the wall, dialing, then waiting for an answer. She said, "Nobody."

"We should talk to Stanley first."

I said, "Stanley's been drowning mice."

"Are you sure you haven't seen Go-boy?"

I nodded with confidence, pulled my left hand from my pocket—the hand with Kiana's ring on my finger—and rested it on the table.

Kiana said, "I'll call the clinic."

Mom might not have remembered the best berry-picking spots or how to squeeze the oil from whitefish to make Eskimo ice cream, but she knew how to deal with missing boys. She said, "We need to check all our bases before we make any calls."

Kiana stayed on the phone anyway, bouncing her heel on the carpet. She looked across the kitchen table at my pizza, then next to it, at my left hand. She recognized her ring. She saw it, focused harder, looked me in the eyes for a second, then looked away and began talking to someone on the other end of the line. When she did that, when she looked at me, it took all the energy I had not to pull my hand off the table.

Stanley showed up along with one of the other uncles. Kiana ran down a list of possible places to search, people to contact, clues to watch for, as Mom tried to stay in charge. This was exciting. I heard Kiana tell them I hadn't seen Go-boy for days.

"Cesar said Go hasn't been at home either."

It was the first she'd said my name all week.

Mom again warned everyone not to make too big a deal out of it, saying there might be a reasonable explanation, and for Go-boy's sake, they shouldn't get too many people involved. She offered everyone pizza. She said, "Slow down." But Kiana argued that Go had almost died the last time he'd disappeared. I wanted to interrupt, but a full-on argument had started between the two women. According to Kiana, Mom wasn't alarmed enough, and she said Go was her brother—the only immediate family she had around right then—and she had every right to freak out.

"Hey, Stanley, you heard all the dogs howling last night, right?"

"Huh?"

I said, "At eight o'clock, every night this week, all the dogs in town have been howling, all at the same time."

Stanley laughed like I had said something stupid, or like I'd made a joke.

I raised my hand to my mouth, feeling the ivory on my chin. I said, "They really are."

Mom and Kiana weren't saying anything to each other. It was that silence that hovers after the argument has already started but hasn't yet exploded.

Kiana sat in the chair next to me. She looked like she was thinking about what she would argue next. It was getting close to eight o'clock, so I turned to her and said, "Want to go listen to the dogs?"

News hit town on Friday that a grant for rural Alaskan transportation had been received. Within two years all the roads in town would be paved, including the airport runway. It also included subsidies for fuel and plane-ticket prices for everyone, which was huge. It had been costing people about eight dollars a gallon to fill their truck or snowmachine, about fifteen hundred a month to heat their house in winter, and about five hundred dollars to fly round-trip to Anchorage to see the dentist, or doctor, or buy new clothes. Now the village cost of living would be a little more on a par with the rest of the country.

Kiana came to Go's house Halloween morning—the day of the restaurant's grand opening. I had rolled out of bed an hour earlier and was eating cold pizza and reading through a Bentley service manual that Go-boy had received in the mail for his AMC Eagle. His car was now dying after it warmed up. So every time we drove, we ended up pushing it back home. The trick was to run it in short enough stints that it didn't heat up until we got back to the house. Sometimes it died as we coasted into the driveway.

"Where's your costume?"

Kiana ignored the question and said, "Was Go here last night?"

"No."

She went straight to his bedroom. I hadn't been in there in months, so I followed her, and the first thing I noticed was that the walls were plastered with pieces of yellow legal paper, each containing a random thought or drawing. On the wall opposite his bed he had a fish net, stretched and nailed, with newspaper and magazine articles pinned behind. Red buoys hung at the corners. The curtains were pulled shut and the room was messy, and it smelled like he hadn't cleaned the fish net before he'd hung it.

Kiana was digging in Go's drawers. I noticed she was no longer wearing my watch. I eyed her body, looking for pregnancy weight, but there was none, and she almost caught me looking.

I said, "That party's tonight, huh?"

She turned on a desk lamp and leaned over piles of papers and books. The documents Go-boy needed to fill out to run for mayor were on top, completed and signed but now overdue—he wouldn't be included on the ballot. Kiana unzipped a money bag and pulled out a wad of phone numbers and business cards, set them all on the desk, and started fingering through. She asked, "Have you looked at Stanley's cabin?"

"I thought it got burned in the fires."

"No," she said.

The stereo was on and something soft was playing, stuck on repeat, with the volume at zero. I turned it up a few notches.

Kiana sat on the bed and looked around the room for clues, even though she appeared ready to quit. Shadows were cast on her eyes and neck from the desk lamp, emphasizing her unforgettable attractiveness. She looked at the corner of the room like she was listening to a conversation. It was a mystery to me how certain faces, like hers, with just one glance, could be so memorable among millions of carbon copies. She was beautiful and for a minute I liked the idea of having a baby with her.

Kiana said, "He might be at the cabin."

I knew Go wasn't coming back for another week—after election day—whenever he could sneak onto another cargo plane back to the village.

"I'll run upriver and check it out if you want."

Kiana then smiled a little.

I told her I'd go there later that day. I was lying. I said Go-boy might be up there, maybe doing some bird-hunting or soul-searching. I told her things had been normal around the house and that Go hadn't given me any reason to think he would disappear like he had a few months ago. I was still lying.

"His bunny boots are here," she said. "He would've taken them."

"I think he has others."

I sat next to her on his bed and showed her a Polaroid I'd picked up off the dresser. It was me and Go pushing his station wagon back into town. We were both laughing. This was the first time his car died on us. We were up in the hills because Go wanted me to take pictures of him overlooking the ocean and the village for his mayoral campaign flyers, which I thought—and hoped—was just a joke. On the way back to town the car died on us and we pushed it about two miles, Go leaning into the driver's door and steering through the open window, me shoving against the rear hatch. When a construction worker saw us he stopped his truck and asked if we needed help, Go said, "Yeah, man, could you take a picture?" and handed him the camera.

"When was that?" she asked.

I was holding the photo in my left hand. Kiana's ivory ring was still on my pinkie finger, visible just at the bottom edge of the photo. I'd forgotten about it. Right away I became embarrassed and set the picture on the bed between us.

"Maybe a month ago," I said.

She picked up the photo, examining it, and laughed. But after a minute, while still staring, I could tell she was no longer seeing the picture.

She said, "Quyaana. Thank you."

"For what?"

"For helping."

I said, "It wasn't much."

"For everything this year," she said. "A lot has happened."

Then she turned and leaned into me. She wrapped one arm around behind me, and with her other she grabbed my hand and wrapped her fingers around my pinkie, holding her ivory ring. It was weird that she was embracing me on her brother's bed, but I thought of the night we'd had sex, the way she'd leaned in and kissed me first, the way she'd shifted herself above me and taken her t-shirt off before she'd taken off mine. She moved with such confidence, such coordination. I didn't remember much. But I remembered the way everything was controlled by her, and how quick it progressed, and how I couldn't stop thinking about it months later.

She said, "Tell me Go will be fine."

Maybe she hadn't been ignoring me this week. Maybe I'd imagined the whole thing. With her one embrace I wanted to admit I was lying about Go, and I wanted to admit all the things I hadn't told her, from both this summer and back home in LA.

"He's okay," I said, wrapping an arm behind her.

Kiana relaxed. With her fingers still holding that ring, she slid it off my hand and slipped it onto her thumb. Her chin then leaned heavy onto my shoulder. She inched us back, lowering us to the bed, with our legs still hanging off at our knees. She kept embracing me for a minute or two without moving. And then Kiana slid her face along my cheek. She shifted her torso so I was on my back and she was on her side, next to me but still above me. She ran her hand along my jawline. Everything moved gradual. I let her orchestrate it all. She guided our noses beside each other. She slid her fingers back behind my shoulder, pulling my other arm around behind her. Our breaths mixed. I could smell her skin—a warm, wheat-bread smell, with no perfume. Still above me, she brushed her mouth across mine, inching left to right, just barely touching our dry lips together, and I knew right then we wouldn't kiss or do anything more than that. She traced her face over mine—I felt her eyelashes on my cheeks, her exhales past my ear, and her hair pouring over my jaw and down my neck. And we kept doing that on Go-boy's bed, longer than it seemed two people could do something like that, and it was more like sex than any sex I'd ever had.

I went to Mom's house before the pizza joint's grand opening. I passed a group of trick-or-treaters. One kid wore a white bedsheet over a snowsuit. Another wore a parka over his Darth Vader costume. And another was a pear, or maybe a green M&M.

Kiana and Mom were in the kitchen and they weren't talking to each other. The TV was off and there were no free pizzas. There was a card from the owner saying, THANKS FOR THE ADVICE next to a bowl full of candy.

"Did you check the cabin?" Kiana asked.

I nodded but didn't say anything. I sat in the living room, facing the kitchen, and that was when it hit me that a few more days of this might do some damage.

Stanley and three other uncles came over, standing in the back doorway just inside the kitchen. They said they'd checked with the ticket agents at the airport, driven the entire road to where it ended looking for an abandoned car or four-wheeler, and checked the slough where Go kept his boat. He hadn't bought a plane ticket out of Unk; there was nothing on the road; and Go's boat was still anchored along the shoreline. They were clueless.

Trick-or-treaters came to the door and everyone smiled at the kids as Mom handed out candy.

I could see the pizza joint through the open door. The owner had hung orange balloons and streamers inside. There was a sign on the front, made from a pizza box, that said, *GRAND OPENING TONIGHT*.

"I knew this would happen," Kiana said.

"We still don't know that anything's actually happened," Mom said.

"Yeah. Go's gone. He'd be here if nothing was wrong."

"It'll be all right," Mom said.

"How were we convinced that he didn't need help?" Kiana said, talking straight at my mom.

"It's not *my* fault."

There was another knock at the kitchen door. It was the owner of the pizza joint, and he slid in behind Stanley and the other uncles. He asked, "Still gone?" and the men nodded. He said he was going to cancel the grand opening. Go-boy had played such a big part in encouraging him that with Go missing, he and the rest of the town wouldn't have fun.

Right then I got up and walked to the doorway between the kitchen and the living room. Mom looked surprised to see me charging into the conversation, taking an interest, but this was getting stupid. I wasn't sure what to say and I wasn't sure how Kiana would react, but I started with, "There's nothing to worry about."

Then the phone rang. Everyone looked at Kiana and she leaned past me and answered it, then turned back around and faced the kitchen, with her shoulder almost touching mine. I wondered if it was Wicho again, checking our box number. I wondered what was in his journals that he thought I needed to read. Was there something for me to learn? Or did he just want to be known by his family? Either way it was always like this, every time I'd just about forgotten him something would pop up, remind me of my brother in prison, in California, the brother we had abandoned. But now I had a ticket home. I would see him again—in person—for the first time since the guards had hauled him out of the courtroom over five years ago.

Go-boy was on the phone.

"Where are you?" Kiana asked.

Everyone was silent.

"Anchorage? We've been worried."

I could hear Go's excited voice.

She said, "We've been looking for you for days. Why didn't you tell anyone you were leaving?"

And here it came. I could've sworn I heard Go say my Eskimo name in the little phone speaker—Atausiq. It sounded like he might have said it twice. Kiana turned, facing me, her mouth open a little, and said, "You knew?"

"What?"

Kiana leaned back into the phone, said, "You told Cesar you were leaving?"

For the first time that whole week it was silent in the house, and maybe silent in the whole village. Kiana tilted her head into the phone as if listening in private. The long cord hung to the ground and she was standing on the curled wire with a firm foot. Everyone in the kitchen was tense.

Two kids dressed like clowns knocked on our door. They could see us through the window, but nobody opened the door for a moment. It was strange. Everyone hesitated. Then Uncle Stanley let them in and gave them candy bars.

And that was when Go-boy did something amazing—just like all the dogs howling at eight o'clock every night, and like Stanley selling that shed, and like Mom and Kiana taking charge of their lives, and like the whole village on the cusp of a renaissance—Go told his sister that he'd made a mistake, that he hadn't clued me in on his travel plans, that he'd forgotten.

"You can't just leave without telling anyone," Kiana said.

The uncles shifted, exhaling, then sat at the kitchen table and started talking about the news of paved roads and cheaper gas. The pizza joint's owner turned to leave, maybe to fire up his ovens and start cooking food for the grand opening. Kiana walked with the phone down the hall. More kids came to the door for candy. And in the middle of this kitchen, as the volume turned back up, I caught Mom looking at me. Staring even. She wasn't peering into my soul or holding an expression of wisdom like she had known I was lying all along, or she knew I was going to admit it; she just looked at me like only a mother can, like she was watching a nostalgic movie, like she knew something about me that I didn't. She looked like she missed me. She didn't even know Wicho had called and that was why this was strange. It was the first time I'd ever noticed my mom watching me.

I went back into the living room. Kiana hung up the phone and sat down on the arm of my chair. She rocked us back and forth, her big toe digging into the carpet. She was still wearing the ivory ring on her thumb.

"He's okay?" I asked.

She chuckled a little, looking forward at the blank TV screen. Mom was in the kitchen getting something ready for the party, maybe the Eskimo ice cream.

She said, "Go is at the hospital visiting Sean."

Go had told her that even though their little brother was still in a coma (pushing four months now), he believed Sean would be healed and would return to normal health. *Tomorrow*, he told her, *Sean will wake up*. Kiana asked if the doctors had said that, and Go said no, they still thought it looked bad. They had been preparing the family to make a major decision about Sean, the major decision. The survival rate after a few weeks in a coma was low, worse yet after four months. But Go kept telling her—*within a day*. He said, *It's going to be so remarkable, an Eskimo miracle*. He said after Sean woke up he was going to Seattle and then to New York City. He told Kiana she should fly to Anchorage right away so she could be there when Sean woke up. Kiana ended the conversation saying she needed to think about it.

"I'm so glad he called," Kiana said. She let her hand fall on my thigh and left it there.

We could hear the uncles talking about a pregnant high school girl.

"Really!" Mom said.

I asked Kiana, "Who's pregnant?"

She rocked our chair faster, hesitated way too long, then said, "Four girls. All juniors."

Mom overheard Kiana and came to the doorway of the living room. She said, "Four!"

"That I know of."

"Don't they teach these kids what happens when you put tunggu in utchuk?" Stanley said, and all the uncles laughed.

Mom asked, "How many girls are in the junior class, like six?"

"I went to war when I was their age!" Stanley said, getting louder.

"Seven junior girls," and Kiana listed the four who were pregnant, with which guys, and how far along each was.

Uncle Stanley said, "They just gotta try-round up all them boys and fix 'em like reindeer. Rubber-band their balls and slap 'em on the ass and send 'em out on the tundra."

The uncles laughed again.

Mom laughed too, turned back into the kitchen, and said, "Araa you Stanley."

"So Go-boy thinks Sean will come out of this coma?" I asked, almost in a whisper. "Tomorrow?"

Kiana nodded, hesitant, like she wished he'd never mentioned that. I could feel she was close to crying. She said, "At least he called."

Kiana kept rocking our chair. The grand opening for the new joint was starting in the building next door and we could smell the pizza. Kids wearing masks and face paint were already there, lining up for games, for candy, for pizza. The next flight to Anchorage wouldn't be until the following afternoon. I asked Kiana if she was going to see Sean and Go-boy, and she shrugged. She didn't know. She asked, "How can he predict when Sean will come out of the coma?" I said, "With Go-boy, anything's possible." I was joking, but Kiana nodded like it might be true. And yeah, I thought, maybe it was true. So I told her I could give her some money if she wanted to buy a plane ticket. I had a thousand bucks and she could use as much as she needed. I told her that Go-boy might be right, there was a chance. She was still looking straight ahead at the blank TV screen and smiled like she had earlier in the day when I'd offered to help look for her brother, but this time what I offered wasn't a lie.

We sat a little longer, rocking, and when it was almost eight o'clock, I said, "Want to go listen to all the dogs howl?"

FOUR

SO THE UNKNOWN WOMAN COULD SLEEP

The first person in the village to go to work was the person who found her. Before the sun popped above the horizon, before the wind stirred things, when the only sound was an occasional dog chain dragging in the dirt, someone saw a woman sitting on the road. That person might've been a construction worker in a dump truck or a man on his way to open the little airport or even someone heading out of town, hunting. It could've been me or Go-boy if she'd been there a few months before, when we'd worked mornings on the fish tower. But whoever it was, they found her—the unknown woman—sitting on Main Road in the middle of everything, crying and confused, her fingers clutching handfuls of gravel. Later that day someone would theorize that she had fallen from the sky, but the first person to see her early in the morning didn't care where she was from—he just went for help.

Go-boy and I heard about the unknown woman sometime before noon. She was still incoherent—crying and lashing out at the air all around. The police had taken her first, trying to learn who she was and where she was from and how she'd managed to get to Unk. She had no bag or purse or wallet. No plane ticket. Go-boy said a person could walk to town, but the nearest village was fifty miles. And he said fifty miles over the bare tundra was like a hundred on solid ground.

"Probably take a week," he said.

By the time the ladies at the clinic heard about the unknown woman and demanded she get medical attention, around eleven, the police were ready to give up anyway, frustrated that she wouldn't speak. Mom called us when the unknown woman arrived at the clinic, asking Go-boy if we could help. She asked him if we could search around town, find out if anyone was missing a visitor or expecting a visitor. And Kiana also got ahold of us, asking for help with distributing unknown-person flyers. When she called, Go answered and handed me the phone. He said, "It's for you." He was pretending he didn't know his sister. I talked to Kiana and she was genuine and concerned, not gossiping but motivated to join this unknown-woman thing. She was soft and assured. Her voice had energy and it brought me into the cause, making me want to participate—partly for the woman, partly for Kiana.

"We should help," I told Go.

He was busy and distracted, flipping through his new auto-repair manual. His nails were framed with rusty grease and he left dirty fingerprint smudges on the corner of each page. And because of the way he ignored me right then—flipping pages and not answering for a moment—I became suspicious.

"Kiana wants you to copy flyers."

He turned page after page, not reading. After a while he said okay and closed the book—maybe out of the loyalty he carried for his sister—and we left the house. But in that brief time when he waited to respond, I knew something was up.

"Let me first try the Eagle," Go said, sliding behind the wheel of his AMC wagon—the car he'd been reading about, the car that had just stopped working altogether.

With the driver's door open and his left leg hanging out, Go-boy turned the key and let the engine roll over and over for a minute or more until it slowed, then only clicked.

He said, "I'll jump it."

I was standing at the end of the little driveway, almost in the road. "It won't fire," I said.

"I'll try-pour gas down the carb. Maybe it's out of gas. Or maybe it's flooded."

I told him there was no spark, but for some reason he wouldn't hear me. He wasn't listening to what I said about the car, or what I said about anything.

Go-boy had just flown back from Anchorage a few days earlier, and since then he'd been strange. He no longer made eye contact, acting distant and nervous like a person being videotaped. He no longer asked me questions—didn't ask me to do anything, didn't ask me what I thought about anything. He wasn't interested, I guess. And when I asked if he had gone to Seattle and then to New York City, he waved off the question, walked away.

This morning he'd been fixated on getting his car to run. He camped out at the dining room table reading the repair manual. He hovered over the engine of the AMC with a handful of tools. He ran warm water in the kitchen sink, thawing his cold, oil-stained fingers. But that was just today.

Yesterday morning he'd decided to make paper, shitting up the whole kitchen with a washtub, a screen frame cut from a brownie pan, and a blender full of something he called slurry—a pasty soup of paper mixed with crabgrass and dried fireweed. But he didn't finish that project. He quit before lunch. In the afternoon he set out to record his family history. He interviewed Uncle Stanley, filled up two pages of notes, and photographed the wooden crosses of dead family members; then he dropped the idea and tried to start a recycling program before dinnertime. When he didn't get immediate support from the city, he quit. Sure, Go always had projects, but he always finished them. I'd never known Go to be such a mess. Or so disconnected. He seemed out of control.

I said, "Man, that engine isn't getting spark." I told him when the engine doesn't fire it means bad points or wires or distributor, or maybe messed-up timing. But he didn't listen. And regardless if the car could run or not, the whole town was only a mile from end to end, and the clinic was just two blocks away, so I said, "We can walk."

Go-boy continued to hook up a battery charger and turn the engine over till it twitched. He poured gas from an empty pop can down the air intake, then he tried to start it again, and a few flames shot back through the carb.

"There's some spark!" he said.

"It's in the wiring. There's a bad connection somewhere and the juice isn't getting to the cylinders."

"Not necessarily, because one time I had a bad fuel pump act just like this."

I went in the house to warm up, and like I'd been doing for days, I waited for him. When the car still wouldn't run after almost an hour of his troubleshooting, Go-boy came into the living room and said, "I need a different battery charger."

He dug in a closet. He threw a parka into the hall. Then skis. A tackle box. Bunny boots.

I said, "Are we going?"

"Yeah, in a minute."

"Do you know if the mail came today?" I asked.

He didn't know. Or just didn't answer.

Yesterday and the day before, planes had been flying in and out of town like normal—clear skies, no wind—but for whatever reason the mail never came. I asked around town but nobody thought it was that big a deal. It was just something that happened.

I was waiting for those journals from Wicho. He'd said to look for a package this week. I still wasn't sure why he was sending them to me. I didn't know his angle or if he even had one. Wicho and me would always be brothers, through this—his life sentence and me living in Alaska—and through anything, and yet, since he'd been locked up, brothers or not, we'd had no relation to each other at all. Not until this idea of the journals. But even now it was more of the same. More waiting. Guessing. And then more waiting.

Mom met us in the lobby of the clinic. They'd been giving the unknown woman fluids, thinking she might be on drugs because she had dark circles under dilated eyes and looked like she hadn't slept in weeks. The nurses were successful at calming the woman and had convinced her to lie down. And even though she wouldn't close her eyes and rest, she seemed to be a bit more relaxed in the company of health workers, who had brushed her long hair free of tangles, cleaned the gravel from under her fingernails, and pooled together some clean clothes for her to wear.

We wanted to see what this unknown woman looked like.

In a hushed voice, Mom said, "I checked with the airport; in the past couple weeks there's only been a few strangers fly in, and they're all accounted for. She didn't fly to Unalakleet."

I asked how else the unknown woman could've gotten here, and Mom said maybe by the ocean. The police were checking for mysterious boats along the shore, which was easy this time of year because most people had pulled everything they owned from the water, fearing that first overnight freeze. But Mom was less interested in how she'd come to town and more concerned with her condition.

While she talked about the woman's health issues, Go-boy wandered down the hall and snooped around in a supply closet. He pulled out tongue depressors and stuffed his pockets full.

Mom said, "You guys need to go door-to-door. There's seven hundred people living here and with enough help we should be able to talk to everyone."

The day Go-boy returned from Anchorage he was in good spirits and handed me a gift as soon as he got back to our house. While in the city he'd had two t-shirts made, one for me and one for him, that said, SAME-SAME. It was a yellow-gold shirt with gold print, and I wasn't surprised because I'd read about his t-shirt idea in the second letter to Yoko Ono, but I didn't want him to know I'd read either of the letters, so I faked like I was surprised, held the shirt by its shoulders and forgot to say *thank you*.

"Sometimes we're always real same-same," Go said, and laughed.

I wondered if this shirt had been meant for Yoko Ono. I wondered if he had even made it to New York City.

I forced a smile, looking at how the second SAME was flipped, mirroring the first.

Go said, "It's just village, man. You just sometimes always never understand." Then he pulled his over his head. "Same-same is like your Eskimo name—Atausiq."

"How?"

"Atausiq means one."

This first day he was back Go acted like the normal Go-boy— energetic but relaxed, funny but intent. It was maybe the following day that he started unraveling, acting like he'd disappeared behind a curtain, but instead of him vanishing, it was as if everyone and every-thing around became invisible to him.

I left that t-shirt in the living room for a few days, sitting on an end table the way he'd handed it to me—shoulders and waist folded behind, the words SAME-SAME framed on the front. When Go saw I'd left it there, he said, "If you don't want the damn shirt, give it to Ki-ana. She'll wear it."

And right then I knew—he'd finally heard about me and his sister.

The unknown woman was still a mystery when the clinic closed at eight o'clock. She still wasn't speaking and was frightened by any people or noises. Go-boy and me had helped the search mission, running door-to-door with a poor-looking pencil sketch of the woman that Kiana was distributing, but nobody recognized her—she wasn't from Unalakleet or anywhere around the Norton Sound.

After fifteen minutes of walking Go ditched me, leaving me alone with that picture. I didn't find him for three hours. And when I did find him, he was behind the fish plant, pulling carburetor jets off a four-wheeler engine that was propped on a fifty-five-gallon barrel.

"What the fuck, man?"

He said, "These might work."

Mom agreed to take the unknown woman in for the night, or even longer if necessary. With the help of Kiana, they would try to give the woman a comfortable bed and a room with enough security so she could sleep. They started by bathing her. Then they wrapped her in a bathrobe and added blankets. She lay on the couch in the living room afterward, motionless. Mom said, "It's to get her acquainted with me and Kiana." They found she relaxed when listening to Buffy Sainte-Marie and drinking lukewarm hot chocolate, and soon realized she liked anything sweet. Mom reported all this over the phone. After a while the woman wasn't scared, and in the company of the ladies, she began behaving normal. She pulled her own hair into a ponytail. She sucked on a piece of hard candy and left the wrapper on an end table. By ten o'clock she was finding the bathroom, flipping the lights on or off, and flushing.

We got sent on an errand to a pie social at the church. Mom wasn't letting us see the unknown woman yet, theorizing that she was uncomfortable with men, thinking she might have been abused by a boyfriend or a husband in the past. Mom wanted us to stop at the church and buy two whole pies because she thought sweets were helping the woman. She said, "Her blood-sugar level is probably real low."

In the basement of the church, about forty people sat beside long card tables, laughing and eating dessert. The popular conversation topic was the unknown woman. We wove between tables and heard all the different theories. The city mechanic thought she might have come through town on a connecting flight to some other little village along the coast. He said, "The airport wouldn't have any record of her then." As we stood in line, waiting to buy pies, we heard another guy theorizing that scientifically it was possible she'd just appeared, saying, "Basically, it's like she fell from the sky." He claimed that it happened more than people knew—living and non-living objects entirely disappeared and relocated to some other place in the world, or some other year. He said, "Half the time, when we think we've lost an ink-pen or a gas cap, it's actually vaporized to some other location." And Uncle Stanley, sitting next to that guy, said, "Talk about science, maybe she's the new teacher." Everyone laughed.

"What do you think?" I asked Go-boy. "You think she's maybe White Alice, reincarnated?"

Go puffed a quick laugh. He hadn't been as interested in the un-known woman as the rest of us. Go acted like she didn't exist. At first I thought he might have had something to do with her, but the one thing Go couldn't do was lie, at all. So I knew he just didn't care. He'd never been into gossip or rumors. And yet he was always into helping people, especially those who were powerless, and especially when it related to the community. It was as if Go had now become self-centered overnight.

"I think she's whacked out on some kind of acid trip." I told him maybe she could've lived in town with us all summer without anyone knowing who she was. It was possible. A village of seven hundred is big enough to disappear in. She might have had an apart-ment somewhere or even been sleeping in some garage. Maybe the one person she knew in this whole town was on vacation. It was possible.

Go said, "No way, man. I've lived here forever and I know every person I see."

"She could've stayed home."

"What would she eat?" he said, picking up a crumb of pie crust from the counter and tossing it into his mouth. His hands and wrists were cut up with fresh gouges and scrapes—puffy and reddish-pink spots on his sensitive skin—from working on the AMC. The cuts looked like they would start bleeding at any moment. "The minute she'd go to AC Store to buy some bread, half the town would see her."

"But you don't know any of the fishing-lodge tourists."

We paused to check out the pies. The whole room went quiet for a moment, with just a few murmurs here and there, like every conversation lulled at the same time. That was when Go spun around like he'd heard someone shouting his name from the stairs. It was abrupt and his face got pale and limp for a quick second. He dropped his napkin. It was startling. But nobody said anything. As he stared across the room it was like the air between us had pushed me onto my heels. And it was then I knew Go needed my help.

Go-boy turned back to the pies, said, "Man, that's because we know they're fishing-lodge tourists from the moment we see them."

"What if she looks like them? You haven't seen her."

"Believe me, man, she doesn't look like one of them."

Go-boy then ordered two pies for my mom without consulting me. We handed a young girl some money and her friend grabbed tin foil and napkins. Behind us we heard a man telling people he thought the unknown woman was a prostitute. He said they sneak onto cargo planes out of Nome. After they do a few jobs and have enough money, they buy a one-way ticket back. "It happens," he kept saying. He guessed she came to Unk and didn't get paid, and that was why she couldn't leave and why nobody *admitted* to recognizing her face. I couldn't tell if he was joking or not.

The postmaster was eating a slice of pie with a couple young kids and I flagged him down to ask about the mail.

"It came today," he said. "Lots."

"All of it?"

"Well, I assume so."

Go and I walked back to Mom's house, each carrying a pie—Go-boy had blueberry and I had rhubarb. The huge sky above us was black with the smoky texture of clouds, looking ready to dump sleet, or hail, or even snow. The air collected our breaths in short bursts of fog.

We walked on the road that curved past the point where the river met the ocean. It was the long way to Mom's, and it seemed appropriate not to take any shortcuts. The road straightened out and the Bering Sea was spread out on our left side. The only thing between us and the ocean was piles of pale driftwood illuminated by a streetlight, stacked in rows all the way down to the water. There was a tangled fishnet knotted around one of the branches.

Go-boy handed me the pie he was carrying. He said, "I've got to leave."

"Where?"

"Home," he said. "I know what's wrong with the Eagle. It's the intake gasket."

"You can't work in the dark."

"I've got to find some Form-A-Gasket," he said. "Try-patch it."

"The problem's not a gasket. The engine isn't getting spark."

Go-boy turned and walked straight down the road.

"Don't you want to see the woman?" I asked.

"No."

"Before she's asleep? Before they take her away?"

Go then turned and ran straight at me. His hair blew back and his eyes were intense with anger and I wondered if he was going to throw a punch. He stopped in front of me, right in my face, and yelled, "I can't help her! I can't."

His breath was all stale coffee and I stared back at him for a second, not sure what to say, not sure if there was anything to say.

He turned and walked away, quicker than before.

I said, "I'm sorry."

But Go was already half a block away, and I would've needed to yell for him to hear me.

I got to Mom's just as the rain started. All of the lights were shut off and there were small candles placed throughout the house. She and Kiana were in the kitchen, drinking ayuu tea—tundra tea—and whispering. Steam blurred the windows and caught the glow of orange candlelight. Mom put her finger to her lips, urging me to be quiet. She mouthed, *sleeping.* I set the pies between them and the sound of tin foil sliding on the table seemed too abrasive for the moment. Kiana looked relieved I had arrived. It was peaceful, giving me the idea that maybe we had something real growing between us. I hadn't seen her all day and now I wanted to sit her down and tell her everything that had happened since we'd last been together. I'd tell her about Go. How I was worried. How he'd almost hit me. Tell her what people were saying about the unknown woman. Tell her about the mail and how the journals from my brother hadn't come, and that I'd been thinking about her. I had been thinking about her. I wanted to tell her everything. And again she looked up at me with the same expression, and held it.

"Can I?" I said, hoping to see the unknown woman.

Kiana stood up. I grabbed her arm just below her bony elbow and held it for a second. We moved to the edge of the kitchen, where the linoleum met the carpet in a small doorless frame, where the living room began. We stood shoulder to shoulder, looking. And right there, three steps away, on the same couch I had sprawled on many times to watch TV, the unknown woman slept.

She was younger than I'd imagined. Her face was wide and square and she had black hair that disappeared into the cushions behind. The candlelight gave her a dark orange hue. On her cheeks there was soft, transparent fuzz where men grow sideburns, denser than it was on most women, but not quite facial hair. One of her hands had spilled out from under the blanket and was dangling from the edge of the couch. It was thin like a piece of bread, darker than her face, and each finger was perfect and straight. Her hand and her whole body were this way—slight, fragile. She looked weightless, like she could walk up old stairs without making a sound, like she could fetch a snack from the kitchen without the three of us noticing. . . . And she even looked so light that when she burst out of the house later that night—while Mom and Kiana and I slept in the living room chairs—and ran down the road with only a bathrobe around her, running straight off the fifteen-foot seawall at the mouth of the shallow river (and surviving), I was surprised that she didn't fly up and blow away to some other unsuspecting small village down the coast.

I stood in the doorway with Kiana, watching the unknown woman sleep for maybe ten minutes or more. Kiana leaned into me and we were hypnotized by the feathery breath that lifted and dropped the woman's small chest. In her breath we couldn't see that the doctors in Anchorage would call tomorrow and say that Sean had miraculously woken up; we couldn't see how ill Go-boy really was and how his situation was even worse than we knew; we couldn't even see that I would cancel my tickets to LA; but we could feel, all in this moment, that something was about to happen.

We kept watching the unknown woman sleep. She was covered in quilts, but as we stood there I wanted to blanket her head to toe with something very thin. I wanted to take a picture so I could show Go-boy what it was like to watch the unknown woman—to show him what I now saw. This house and town were nowhere to her. She was alone and unfamiliar and didn't know where her real life had gone. She was isolated, and her helplessness held us captive. And as I stood there, I wished Go were there with us, standing in the doorframe of the candlelit room, the silence all around. I wished Go-boy were there so he could watch a person who wasn't known by anyone, sleep.

T-SHIRTS

There were eight hundred t-shirts under Go-boy's house. I had slept at Mom's—the second night straight since the unknown-woman incident—and when I got back to Go's place, there they were, these t-shirts, in boxes, under his house. It was exciting because Sean had just come out of his coma—just as Go had predicted, only a little later—and Kiana and Mom were all bubbly with happiness. These t-shirts seemed to be a part of that excitement.

Go's house was set on steel posts about four feet off the ground. Most of the time that space below was filled with bikes and baseball gloves belonging to whichever kids Go had let play video games, or kids Go was giving rides around town, or kids getting drinks of water, trying to recruit Go-boy for a pickup game of softball in the field next door. But today Go filled the space below the house with all these t-shirts that had arrived on the cargo plane. An empty pallet stood on end, leaning against the stairs.

I crawled under the house and peeked inside a box. There were wads of gold t-shirts.

Go-boy came down the steps. I watched his feet. He bent over to see me crawling around in the dirt. He was wearing one of the tees—*SAME-SAME*. It was the exact shirt he had given me a week earlier.

He said, "I thought you were someone else."

"Are you coming to Anchorage with us to pick up Sean?"

I hadn't seen much of Go since our fight, but I assumed he was happy about Sean's health and didn't need more serious talk. I told him he should come over to Mom's for dinner. It had been a constant party over there. Everyone—all the uncles and cousins—had been in and out of the house, looking for updates on Sean's recovery, sharing hugs, dropping off presents for him. I told Go that Kiana and I were flying to pick him up in two days. I told him he should come with.

"Maybe."

"What are these shirts for?"

Go-boy turned back into the house, distracted, and said, "One for everybody in town."

I knew Go wanted to deliver each shirt himself to all the residents of Unalakleet, along with an inspirational message, and from there he would watch something amazing transpire. But something amazing already had transpired—Sean was alive, and we were all celebrating that.

Later that day I saw Go-boy's t-shirts at Native Store. They were parked at an end cap next to cases of outdated, half-priced pop. The original boxes were opened. The shirts were in a mound, spilling out onto the floor and hanging on the nearby shelves. Next to the mess was a small sign—a sheet of yellow legal paper—*FREE SHIRTS*.

BURN THE HOUSE DOWN

Go-boy hung himself.

It was the same day city workers were preparing to demolish the old jail. They tied ropes to the support beams so they could pull down the place with front-end loaders—dropping the ceiling into a miniature implosion.

Go-boy tried to hang himself from a rafter in our house, but it didn't work. Go tied the rope wrong. And instead of cinching around his neck, it knotted on itself, then slipped and burned over Go-boy's chin, breaking his jaw. I found him right after—his face swollen and bruised—as he attempted to retie the rope.

The old jail had been scheduled to be torn down since the beginning of summer, but with each problem during the new building's construction, demolition of the old one was delayed. People weren't talking much about this. People in town never really complained or showed emotion about anything anyway. They just said the new jail was up on Air Force Hill, and that it was bigger, and that we'd be able to see it from town. And people were right. If you stood in a certain place, like next to the old jail, and looked between a couple houses, you could see a corrugated steel roof where there used to be nothing but trees, four miles out on the only road. This was next to the city dump—the place where the old jail would be thrown. And of the seven hundred people who lived here, if you asked any one of them about the old jail I bet none would say they were sad to see it torn down. It was a busted, unpainted wood house that the police had been using for many years. It sat next to the post office right on Main Road, right in the middle of town, rotting. You couldn't do anything around here without passing the place two or three times a day. And the only thing that would make people happier than seeing it destroyed would be not needing a jail at all.

The day before he tried suicide, Go-boy asked me to ride around in his station wagon. His AMC was running again and he asked me to drive.

"I have school," I said.

But I could see this was serious. I could see Go was too preoccupied by something to drive himself.

"Where to?" I asked, adjusting the rearview mirror, the engine idling up and down in short throbs of rhythm, the rusty muffler vibrating under our feet, the oily steering wheel all smooth except for a small crack at two o'clock. I felt good sitting behind the wheel.

"Just ride."

We looped around town a few times. I waved to people walking, people driving four-wheelers and trucks. Go-boy wasn't ready to talk. It was then I should have seen something coming—he never let me drive.

"You want to stop at Native Store?" I asked.

Go-boy hadn't been saying anything, so I decided to drive back through town and head out toward the hills. We drove past the old jail on Main Road. It had police tape marking the perimeter, cornered with orange cones and fifty-five-gallon barrels, and city workers were bouncing in and out, preparing its demolition. I waved to a group of kids wearing their SAME-SAME shirts, but Go didn't notice. When we crossed the bridge at the edge of town, Go started talking.

"I need to get lost for a while."

He'd done that plenty of times without telling anyone.

I asked, "Where? Upriver?"

"Out of here."

"Nome?"

"No, farther," he said. "Maybe out of Alaska."

We were a mile out on the gravel and I didn't need to ask him why because Go was already into the story. It had something to do with his ex-girlfriend, how he'd freaked her out bad and betrayed her trust—he said it was all worse than I thought. Something about being expelled from Bible college back in the spring. Something about putting his family through loads of stress. And a lot more about his ex-girlfriend and his past struggles. He told me he had terrible secrets.

I said, "Nobody feels betrayed."

But Go felt guilty and wouldn't believe me. He thought he'd let all his friends and family down. He kept saying he always did this— let everyone down—every time he tried to be happy. He said he was ashamed.

"Don't be," I told him.

Go scratched at a glob of dried paint on the dashboard. His nail clicked, back and forth, back and forth. He said, "When I ran away I ended up in Nome for a week. I was drunk and gave away money to strangers and decided to end my life. I slept with a prostitute as a way to tell God to fuck off. He destined me for a shitty life and I wanted to burn myself in hell because of it."

I thought about telling Go-boy that those things were in the past, stuff to forget about. Instead I said, "Where were you the other three weeks of that month?"

He leaned back in the chair and looked out his window. The distant hills were covered with a light dusting of snow. He said, "Everyone thinks I'm nuts."

"No way," I said. "Everyone looks up to you."

"Everyone's been talking behind my back. They still are, man. I know they are. There's this cloud over me and there's nothing I can do about it."

I said, "I've done some stuff you can't even imagine."

Go wasn't listening. He couldn't get out of his own head and I couldn't persuade him otherwise. We were on Air Force Hill and came to a T in the road under a stop sign that had been mangled by gunshots. To our right was the dump, and up farther, the new jail. I turned the car around, put it in neutral, and shut off the motor. And with the town and ocean mapped out below us, we rode out of the hills in silence, coasting down along acres of brown tundra.

We rolled to the edge of the village and I parked in the middle of the single-lane bridge, just like we had done when I'd first moved here.

Go said, "You always been dealing with my shit this whole time."

Right then I decided that all he needed to do was get everything out, to say what was dragging on him, and in the process would be his cure. At least, that's what I hoped. That's what made me decide I had to tell Kiana about my past, because that's what was dragging on me. She and I were now dating, but there was something standing between us. I had tried to convince myself that it was a problem with her—the stress about her little brother, the stress of her dad in jail—but I knew the problem was me. Kiana only knew parts of my past and the things she didn't know had put us on different levels. She didn't know about the gang rape. Nobody did. And up till now I hadn't thought Kiana would ever need to know. I didn't think she could handle it. I felt that if she knew this, she would never forgive me, and she would never see me the same. I wasn't sure I could deal with that. And if she asked me questions, what would I say? I wasn't sure how I felt about the girl who'd been raped. I hated being there when it happened, but I also hated the girl and I hated how everything led to that moment. I was sorry I had known that type of life, and sorry that because of me, Kiana and Go-boy would know that type of life too. Maybe this was why I had to tell her. Her not knowing about my life was worse than her hating me for it.

I told Go-boy, "And you've been dealing with me this whole time too."

"It's not the same."

"You're right. It's same-same."

He didn't laugh or smile or anything.

This was how I understood Go's guilt—I didn't think he was sorry for his mistakes but sorry for how they related to the people he cared about. It seemed to me the only difference between a kid and a grown-up was that a grown-up couldn't help remembering all the shitty stuff. It seemed like this was where Go-boy was. Remembering too much. And he needed to tell someone and release each memory. So I let him talk some more. He said, "Valerie will never forgive me," but then he stopped—hesitating to tell me why, and I didn't press him or ask any more questions. I backed off. I became nervous.

I said, "It's been a good year. Don't you think?"

From there I started the engine and drove us home. Go didn't seem finished, but he seemed to feel a little better.

A few hours later Kiana and me were on a plane to Anchorage to pick up Sean.

Doctors had been calling her little brother *the memory kid*. They said, "Five months in a coma and he comes out and beats all of us at the memory game." They were exaggerating, but nobody cared about what the doctors were saying now that the scare was over. Now we were about to escort him home to a family who was relieved that he still remembered their names and where they came from. A family who was relieved he was even alive.

We spent the night with Kiana's aunt, and the next day—just before Sean was released from the hospital—we went shopping. We filled boxes with groceries. We made a trip to a hardware store to buy wood clamps for Uncle Stanley. And we ended the morning walking along Fifth Avenue, engulfed in the downtown buildings and one-way streets, looking for a birthday present for Sean.

"Should we call Go-boy and see if he needs us to pick up anything?"

Kiana said, "He was just here."

It was my first time shopping in months. Downtown Anchorage had the tourist boutiques with racks of Alaska wares. Art shops. Fake bears and fake moose. Jewelry. Fur. It was the tourist scene you see on a travel channel. But every other part of the city was stacked with megastores, parking lots, strip malls, cul-de-sacs. And all of it was part of the state that I'd never seen before—this tourism and commerce—and it was a whole other world from Unalakleet. After six months in the village, Anchorage seemed like any other part of the country, like a frozen Los Angeles. It wasn't the Alaska I'd come to know—Go-boy's Alaska. But I was glad to smell cheeseburgers again.

Kiana breezed past everything without interest. It was cold and she was wearing those big bunny boots. This village girl seemed even more confident of who she was in the city, moving past flyered lampposts, panhandlers, and our reflection in windows, unaffected, unimpressed.

We passed a small courtyard with benches and concrete sculptures and then found a street-level toy store. Once inside we split up, looking for the perfect out-of-hospital/birthday present for Sean. I browsed the action figures and Legos and kid tool sets. When I found Kiana she was picking through stuffed animals.

"Isn't he four years old?" I asked.

"He just had his fifth birthday."

I looked at the animals she was holding—a monkey in a sleeveless red shirt and matching hat, and a polar bear with a pink tongue—presents for a baby.

"Five?"

She said, "This isn't necessarily for him, for right now. It will mean something to him later, when he's older."

Kiana bought the monkey and we walked back down Fifth. Now that she wasn't scanning for toy stores I noticed she was looking at people, at each face, like she was trying to remember who everyone was. This was also when I noticed her eye was getting red.

"What's wrong with your eye?" I said.

She looked at her reflection in a Thai restaurant's window. A few of the early lunch customers glanced back through the glass as she pulled on her lower lid.

"It doesn't feel hurt," Kiana said, blinking one lid at a time, checking her vision.

At the hospital that afternoon the doctors would shine a light in her eye, flirt with her, and tell her a blood vessel had burst, and it was harmless, and that she only needed to see a doctor again if she went blind. They laughed. But now, walking along the sidewalk, I couldn't stop looking at it. The white of her eye was all red. Even her lid looked irritated, and sagged.

We walked past a fire station. It had kids running in and out and I figured they were on a field trip, but they seemed too old to be at a fire station. Ninth graders, maybe. Inside the garage doors, to the left of a bright yellow and chrome truck, a firefighter wearing a yellow coat was standing at the bottom of the pole, catching kids who slid from the second floor. One after another they spun down the pole and walked away with a smile. Maybe they were eighth graders. The sound of their giggling and goofing was swallowed up in the brick building, sunken and hidden from the rest of the street.

"They still do that?"

Kiana raised her eyebrows.

I pointed, said, "The fire pole."

"What's that?"

We stopped walking. "The pole. When there's a fire they slide down quick and change clothes and hop in the trucks."

"I never knew they did that."

She was holding the monkey under its armpits, the same way the firewoman caught each kid, and she was impressed, and not the least bit embarrassed that she hadn't heard of it before.

I said, "I didn't know they still did that."

We boarded the airplane that afternoon with Sean. At about the same time we ducked our heads and crawled down the thin aisle to our seats, Go-boy was at home and had decided to end his life. I'm not sure how he did all of it, but I saw the aftermath, and from that I could guess.

He started with a chainsaw. He cut a hole in the ceiling, exposing a rafter to attach the rope. After that he cut a hole in the floor, sawing through the joists and exposing the dirt ground four feet below the house. It seemed to parallel Go's worldview, his catchphrase, part of the tattoo he was still planning to get on his forearm—*You've been the clouds, you've been the ocean, you are now the rain.* But that phrase was meant to be hopeful.

His cutting the ceiling and the floor must have taken about twenty minutes, and by then Kiana and her brother and me were in the air. Clouds were thick at all elevations and they suspended us in a blank glow. The plane was about half full, maybe six people on board, plus the three of us at the very back on a bench seat. Kiana was between her brother and me. Her legs were stretched out in front. Her bunny boots filled the aisle. The engine noise hollered all around us. We all wore earplugs until I pulled out one of Kiana's.

I said, "I need to tell you something."

She smiled. Her bloodshot eye made her look like she'd been crying.

"I need to tell you about LA."

I was holding her yellow-and-orange earplug, palm up on my thigh, rolling the plug back and forth between my thumb and index finger. I never thought I would be in this spot—this needing to share my past. She shifted and then waited, and at that moment I wanted to disappear in her wide, smooth face. I wanted to hide behind her stable expression.

I told her I had stabbed a kid. It wasn't a total lie, but it wasn't what I needed to say either. I needed to tell her about the rape, but I couldn't, so I told her this.

"A knife fight."

"When?" she said.

"Maybe a year ago."

I told her I'd been running hard with a gang and that she had to remember how different things were now, and how when you're in the game, everything is something else. She asked what happened and why, all at the same time, and I told her a couple of us tried jumping some kid for his gold chain and the kid pulled a knife and I pulled a knife and it all just went to shit after that. I told her I now felt terrible.

Kiana didn't say anything. She looked around the plane, left to right, with an expression that was different from what I expected. Even with that bloody eye there was confidence in her face, like she knew something I didn't. She almost looked content. Kiana then turned to see Sean, who was asleep, and she straightened his oversized t-shirt.

"Where?" she asked.

"LA," I said. "Santa Ana."

"No, where did you stab him?"

I glanced down the aisle. Most everyone slept except for this one guy near the front—maybe a state construction worker—who had his legs crossed in a triangle, reading a newspaper.

"Armpit."

Kiana's mouth dropped open a little and it looked like her blood-shot eye started to water. She mouthed, *armpit?* I could have said shoulder or chest because I didn't know for sure—from what I remembered, it was a gash at the most, similar to the wound that had left a scar along my jaw—but for whatever reason I said armpit.

Kiana asked, "Did he die?"

I shook my head no and said, "Doubt it. He ran off."

By now we were less than an hour from home. Maybe Go-boy had already sawed the floor and ceiling open with that chainsaw. Maybe he was starting in with the duct tape, draping strands from ceiling to carpet throughout the living room—mystical and indus-trial—prolonging the suicide process. Afterward this was what gave me hope that he didn't want to die, even though a noose was the most effective method. He spent so much time preparing that it seemed he was leaving room to turn back. Or be discovered. Or something.

Kiana stayed silent. The plane bounced as it started its descent. Kiana turned in her seat and looked at me like she was about to speak. But she stayed quiet. She could spend silence better than any-one I knew. She said, "Do you know—" and didn't say any more, just cut the sentence off and held her steady focus. The red in her eye was brilliant. Kiana then grabbed her earplug and stuffed it back under her black hair. I didn't know what would come next, but I knew I had to tell her about the gang rape, and didn't, and because of it nothing felt different. I felt worse. And I thought about me and Go-boy in his wagon the day before, on the bridge. I knew he hadn't told me everything he needed to. I knew there were more secrets, but I cut him off and didn't let him say everything. Now I was worried. And I didn't want to get off this plane without telling Kiana about the rape.

At home, on the tall strands of duct tape that crowded the small room, Go was writing his suicide note in blue marker. He wrote out the same things he'd explained to me the day before. He felt extreme guilt for what he'd put everyone through over the summer—if his family and friends couldn't trust him, he no longer had the right to live. He claimed he'd failed his community and was responsible for all the sadness and hardships the town had experienced over the past summer. If people had heard Go say these things, they would have shaken their heads. They would have said, "No way." They would have said that if everybody lived like Go-boy, the town would've been almost perfect. But Go held on to a guilt that few could comprehend.

Outside Go-boy's place, a snowstorm had come and gone, but a wind was still swirling, blowing snow under the house and up into the living room through the hole he'd cut.

Down the road about a half mile, at the old jail, city workers had made precision cuts to the support beams and load-bearing walls. They had run ropes through doorways and windows and attached them to the loaders that would later block Main Road and, in unison, shift into reverse and pull the jail down.

When Go-boy finished the note, he went back to his bedroom and collected all his yellow legal pads and papers that contained his ideas and theories. He dumped all these into the hole in the floor. Some of the papers blew back into the house, sticking to strips of tape or blowing into the kitchen, but most of them landed on the ground and were swept away.

People in town had been hearing his crazy ideas so much that none of them seemed shocking or weird anymore. Go was always talking to people about their *true self* while waiting in the checkout line at AC Store or sitting with kids on the steps at Igloo, eating sour candy and telling them they'd experience paradise in their lifetimes, or even dropping prophetic flyers into everyone's mailboxes. And although he had now become frustrated that this good news hadn't affected people in radical ways—in ways he could measure—I think he had made a difference. Go-boy believed in everyone.

After he dropped the notes through the hole, Go hung the thick rope from a rafter, and while referencing a secondhand Boy Scout book, he tied the noose, and he tied it wrong.

At about this same time, when Go stood over the hole in the floor with the rope around his neck, about to drop, our plane flew past the village, making a big circle out over the ocean, lining up to hit the runway. I'm sure he could hear us pass.

When the small plane descended out of the clouds, we saw how everything at home was different—the trees and the hills and the gravel road running into town were all covered by the season's first snowstorm.

"Finally," Kiana said. "Real late this year."

It had snowed a few times this month, but nothing had accumulated. I figured Kiana was so happy about her little brother that everything was good news. Even this. And it was the first thing she'd said in almost twenty minutes, so it must have meant something. She looked out the window as the town passed below us. Her brother, next to her, was still asleep.

"You're ready for this?"

She nodded. Even smiled.

I said, "I don't know how anyone could be ready for this."

The plane aimed at the snow-packed runway. It was hard to believe that I had been in Alaska for six months, and that it was winter
already.

From the sky it looked like a thin dusting over the tundra, maybe
an inch or so, but when we landed we saw it had dumped almost a
foot, and the snow was windblown—drifts swollen to the size of
dump trucks, piling between homes and ramping over roads.

"You'll get used to it," Kiana said.

By the way she looked at me, I thought she was talking about
her eye.

That was when Kiana leaned into me. The plane taxied to the
small airport building and she dropped her head against my shoulder and chest. She slid her arm around behind me. I was tight with
nerves, unsettled, and even more unsure of everything. Kiana then
put her face in front of mine, with our noses almost touching, and I
stared into the shattering of red veins in her left eye.

The last thing Go-boy did, as he stood with his legs straddling
that hole, was color his right forearm with a marker—solid black,
elbow to wrist, over the ghost image of his ink-pen Eskimo Jesus.
Then he dropped.

A big group was at the airport when we landed. Kiana's little brother
had ladies squatting to hug him and dads messing his hair. Everyone was now calling him *Memory*. "Little Mr. Memory!" they said.
Kiana loved this. She loved the nickname. She loved having him
back home with everyone around. It was good to see her so happy.

We left the airport and I told Kiana I wanted to walk home, alone.

"In the snow?" she said.

She and Sean were getting into a truck, and I told her, "Yeah." So we made plans to meet up in a few hours to watch the old jail come down. It was something a lot of people in town were waiting to see. I hadn't yet thought about it.

I walked to Go's house from the airport. The road was drifted over in a few spots, the wind still moving. Somewhere behind me was the distant sound of ocean, somewhere on the other side of town, with that constant shouting of waves, like a crowded stadium.

When I got to Happy Valley I saw garbage tumbling over the road, over the fresh white fields of drifts and white rooftops and white hills along the sky. It was yellow papers gusting sideways. It was Go's notes and theories blowing through the village. It wasn't right. I dropped my bag and chased down as much of the paper as I could. And although I wasn't dressed for it, I chased pages over drifts and between homes. I chased pages under cars and into ditches and under fuel tanks. My shoes and socks were frozen and my hands were numb and I continued to fall over bushes and dive onto snowbanks and sink into hidden holes, all the way back to Go's house.

I opened the front door. A strange draft hit me from inside. Everything was dark. I held on to the crumpled notes and walked through the entryway. Snow dusted over the carpet. A breeze swayed the yellow curtains side to side in the living area, bending the light like the place was floating. It was cold, and the wind made a whistling noise beneath the house, and the furnace was running. Everything in the place rushed back at me.

Go's jaw was broken. His face was swollen and his eyes were irritated as he looked at me from the middle of the room. I said, "Your papers," and held out a handful of his yellow notes. He ignored me, acting like he wouldn't stop trying to retie the rope or stop trying to kill himself just because I'd arrived. But he did. That broken jaw and rope-burned neck and face was the best possible situation I could've run into. Later I would think about that, about how walking into that small house to find Go-boy hanging dead in the middle of the room—hanging through a hole in the floor with his hands and arms dangling just above the carpet and not willing to save himself, before his time, before our time—how that would've been something I couldn't have dealt with. No matter what had happened before that, walking into the house to find Go dead would've defined everything for the year and for years to come. I would have replayed everything leading up to it. I knew he was in trouble long before this. I had a summer of evidence. We all did. We all had suspicions and fears, and yet, in some way, we all pretended that we didn't, that none of it existed, but it was all right there with us the whole time. If I had walked into that house to find Go-boy hanging, there would have been no release from what I'd known. His death would have sealed something shut. Even finding him as busted as I did—envisioning his first attempt at falling through the hole, with the rope ripping over his chin and face, snapping his head back, and Go dropping to the dirt ground outside—even that was enough to change everything.

I rushed at Go and grabbed him by the shoulders. Strips of duct tape stuck to my coat. He wouldn't look me in the eyes, but he let me walk him out of the house and over to the clinic. He wasn't wearing a jacket, but it was only a block and I didn't want to stop for anything. From the clinic I called Kiana. Go was with the health aids. When she answered the phone I said, "I don't know what to do."

. . .

The last thing city workers would do that day was pull out the support beams of the old jail and watch the ceiling drop. After that they'd clock out and head home and wouldn't start cleaning up the mess until early the next morning.

A group stood around, waiting for the jail to fall. There were maybe fifty people and none of them were Kiana. The temp had now jumped above freezing and the wind had stopped and the street was getting muddy, decorated with puddles and slushy piles of brown snow. People were kicking at the melt and talking about the crazy weather. It was like spring was already here. I had a weird feeling in me. It was both relief and regret.

"Makes you glad all the roads are getting paved," the postmaster said, looking at his feet and laughing.

A few people asked about Go-boy while I waited. It had only been a couple hours since we'd gotten him medevaced to Nome. Kiana and me were waiting for a Bering Air flight that would make a special stop here so we could be with Go in the hospital. Our plan was to watch for the plane as the jail was flattened.

Word had spread through town fast that afternoon about Go-boy, and it wasn't gossip, it was like a hero had fallen. Like in a similar way all those *SAME-SAME* shirts meant something substantial to Go-boy, his suicide attempt meant something substantial to the village.

Kiana joined the crowd and stood next to a parked truck. A woman with long, streaky hair leaned from the driver's seat, talking through the open window. The woman reached to Kiana's chin and turned her head, checking out her bloodshot eye. She was the village-based counselor and Kiana was maybe asking and answering questions about Go-boy. Kiana had been strong that afternoon, stronger than I'd ever seen her, marching head-on into this mess with Go while I stood by and watched. All I did was call her.

Kiana joined me. We stood shoulder to shoulder, looking opposite directions, silent. She was checking out the action down Main Road and I was still watching the old jail. Kiana's hip leaned into me. After a minute she turned around, and I looked into her blood-shot eye.

"We should get to the airport," she said.

"Just another minute. We can maybe see this."

She looked past me at the old jail. The red in her eye had spread and the color had begun fading.

She said, "Nothing's happening."

But I told her I wanted to see this go down.

Many people had gotten impatient and left, leaving about twenty of us, with the occasional kid on a bike stopping by to see what everyone was doing. To the kids this had always been a jail. But to the others, to the older folks, this house had been many things. Some knew it had first been a dorm for orphans, then a pastor's home, then offices for the BIA school, then a single-family house, then empty. They recalled the time they'd spent living alongside whatever was happening in this building; first with its promise and hope, then through the years of its decline and vacancy, and now, the most recent years—its rotten years—the years it had been used as the town's jail.

I looked up the road at the town, at the scattered maroon and light-blue homes stacked along the street under a rapid sky. Everything seemed to point to the jail. There were only two city workers on the job, with two loaders facing the building, idling sulfur, with ropes secured to their buckets. And it would only take these two to pull the whole house down.

A small beige plane flew overhead. We knew it was time to leave.

"We can't wait," Kiana said.

I held out a full five minutes, and when nothing happened, we hopped in someone's car and hitched a ride to the airport.

We heard about it later, from more than one person. The city workers removed the ropes from the loaders at four o'clock that afternoon, without destroying the old jail. They planned to return the next day and do the job, start to finish. People who were there laughed, saying it was typical of them to procrastinate.

The real story happened a little bit later. Sometime before supper, a few teenage kids showed up at the old jail with hammers and baseball bats. They tore the yellow police ribbon away and started swinging and shattering windows and busting through rotten wood. They were no doubt some of the sons and brothers of men who'd been locked up there.

Then the younger kids passing on bikes joined in, throwing rocks and kicking at walls. This started as just a few teenagers raising hell, waiting till their parents or the cops came by in trucks, chuckling and telling them to knock it off before they got hurt. But instead some of their older brothers and cousins showed up. They brought sledgehammers and crowbars. And when I heard about this, I wished I'd been there, more than anything. I felt I should've been a part of it, and in a way, as if I needed it to happen. I did need it to happen. I needed to help destroy the old jail.

Depending on who told the story, they'd say either some of the kids were wearing SAME-SAME shirts or everybody was. But everyone agreed it was superwarm that night—in the forties—which felt like sixty at this time of year and melted all the snow. And everyone agreed that lots of people were wearing Go-boy's gold t-shirts, and they agreed it was intentional.

When city buildings were taken down in the village, locals were invited to salvage anything they wanted—steel posts or windows or boards—before it was all hauled away. So that was what most of the kids thought was happening when the adults came by in trucks. The sun was starting to set and the sound of chainsaws and Sawzalls started to fire. But instead of salvaging, grown men and women grabbed the ropes that were still attached to the support beams, and the kids joined them, and everyone reared back and pulled that place into a dusty heap of trash. The old jail fell.

The mood wasn't festive or comical. Nobody was excited. Every person was focused on destroying this building. Elders sat on four-wheelers and lawn chairs, forming a perimeter around the place, watching, as if this were a task that needed to be overseen through completion.

The old jail was nothing but a yard of trash. Flattened. An hour had passed since kids had first started beating the house. That was when city workers arrived with their wives and kids, driving personal vehicles. It had gotten dark and the guy who owned a construction company had hauled those tall job-site lights, the kind on wheels with a built-on generator, and illuminated the mess in a stage-lit glow. From there the men and women began sawing pieces of plywood and bending chunks of steel roofing into smaller sections to be hauled away. Nobody was salvaging anything. Every piece of that building was trash. Every person in town with a truck was running loads a few miles up the hill to the city dump. And when the entire jail was gone, when every nail and shard of broken glass was thrown into a pile in the middle of the landfill, they flooded it with kerosene and set it all on fire.

Everyone saw the blaze that night. A rocket of flames stretched thirty feet into the sky above the shadowed hills. People back at the site of the old jail stood around and watched the fire for a few minutes, talking more casual with the job completed, even laughing. I understood the feeling they all had. It was what I hoped for. They all felt something was finished. They all felt relieved.

Afterward everyone made their way to their family's home, friend's, aunt's or uncle's place, or gram's or sister's, and they stayed up later than usual, not speaking about the old jail or what had just taken place, not even mentioning Go-boy or what he'd done, but now free for a moment to talk about anything else.

IN REVERSE

I told Go-boy about the old jail—about how all the kids started destroying it, how the older folks pulled on that rope, and how the whole town hauled it away and piled it in a corner of the dump. Set it on fire. I was rambling, avoiding the awkwardness of a silent hospital room. I said, "They were all wearing your *SAME-SAME* shirts."

He sat at the end of the bed, his feet flat on the floor, his posture rigid, his eyes staring at the space between Kiana and me—at his own reflection in the bathroom doorknob. He forced a nod.

"Joe," Kiana said. She was sitting on a chair next to him. She lifted her hand from her thigh and almost touched his forearm, almost caressed him, but pulled back. She said, "Sean's perfect. Or, he's . . . it's like nothing happened. He's so funny."

I could see she was unsure how to tell Go-boy about their little brother's healthy recovery. She too was uncomfortable with the silence, a first for her.

"Sean keeps telling everyone that he wants to catch some humpies. When I tried convincing him he had to go to school, he was so
confused, and he said, 'What happened to summer this year?'" She
paused. "Everyone calls him Memory now."

Go-boy was wearing the same clothes he had on the day he tried
to hang himself. This was our second visit and Kiana had remembered to bring a small duffel bag full of t-shirts and socks. I wondered why they didn't make him wear a gown. They must have made
a special exception for the behavioral health patients.

Kiana pulled a ratty stuffed animal from the duffel bag. It was a
brown otter and it must have meant something to the two of them.
She set it on the end table. Go-boy didn't look at it, but he could see
it in the doorknob's reflection.

"Joe," Kiana said.

Go-boy blinked. His jaw was still swollen. It had turned out it
wasn't broken, just dislocated. Fluid had filled his cheeks, dilating
his face, making his eyes look sunken and small. His expression
made me wonder if we were doing any good by being here. He'd
only been in the hospital for five days and had, by law, another nine
before he could leave. Go stared at the doorknob. In it I imagined he
saw the whole room in reverse.

"Joseph," Kiana said.

He looked at her for a quick second, then turned and looked out
the window behind me.

"Joe." She was trying to talk to him now for real, trying to start
one of the hundred sentences she'd planned out ahead of time. Encouragement, no doubt. Support. She had been carrying it all for
her family, all year, and now she was carrying it for Go-boy too. And
even though Go knew everything she needed to say, she still needed

to say it. But it was impossible—with his new medications and the hangover of emotion, he seemed both angry and inebriated.

I said, "I got some drums. From the school. Flo got a new set and so I put her old one in my room."

"Joseph," Kiana said again. Her bloodshot eye had almost faded to normal, but now, here, in the hospital, trying to get her older brother's attention, both of her eyes were getting red.

"The drums are good enough for me. They're old, but they sound good. The kick pedal is crap, though. Flo said I can use them until I get my own."

I looked at Go, then followed his line of sight and saw the doorknob. The silence he was giving was predictable, and still impossible. I kept talking about nothing.

"Joe, everything—" Kiana started, then hesitated and trailed back into thought.

I didn't try to talk anymore. I just waited. I leaned back against the window. I wanted to let Kiana and her brother have their silent struggle without trying to break it up with distractions. I didn't want to change anything. Kiana's desperation and pain had always been private, until now. I wanted to see all her stress—and all the year— all catch up to her, right here, in the hospital. I wanted to see this, not out of spite but because it was making me feel something too.

FIVE

GO & VALERIE

Go-boy told me the whole story when he was in the hospital for a second time, five months after he tried to hang himself. It was the middle of April. Spring wasn't here yet, not even close—still snowing, still freezing. Go hadn't attempted suicide this time but he said he almost had, and that was why he had checked himself in. I visited him in the Anchorage psych ward and he told me everything that had happened over the past year.

The story of Go and Valerie had started just before I'd moved to Unalakleet, and it unfolded all around me, all summer and fall, but I knew hardly any of it. Go said he needed to tell someone, to release his guilt, but I think the story transported him away from the hospital and the therapists, away from the heartbreaks he couldn't seem to separate himself from, and back to Unk and Valerie. The story went like this—

. . .

It was the worst time for Go and Valerie to fall in love. It had started exactly a year earlier, in April, more than a month before I would move to Alaska, during an early, atypical west coast Alaskan spring that only stuck around for about a week. It started when Go-boy entered a contest. He placed his bet at the Unalakleet Native Corporation, and there she was—Valerie—a girl who smiled like she'd been waiting for him.

The town had a contest every spring. People would bet on the exact day and hour and minute that the ice in the river would break up and float out to sea. They'd set a tripod on the frozen water near the mouth of the river, with a long cable running from the top to a digital timer set on shore, recording when everything finally started to inch its way out to the ocean. I'd never seen anything like it. But people said sometimes the breakup could be phenomenal—the deep cracking of ice that had been frozen for seven months, thundering through town, resisting the push of the water underneath and the warmer air above. Many times the enormous plates backed up on themselves, like a rush-hour jam, and could pile over the banks and rip out trees and buildings that lined the shores. Other times it would break up quietly and flow to the ocean without much of a stir, sometimes while everyone slept.

Go-boy and Valerie had both grown up in villages around the Norton Sound, mostly Unalakleet through their teenaged years. Go-boy graduated from high school when Valerie was only a sophomore. He was off to a Bible college in Anchorage, studying and doing whatever else he spent his time doing, before he could even pay attention to Valerie. It wasn't until April—when Go turned twenty-two and placed his bet—that he really noticed her.

He bought only one ticket and guessed the ice would go out on April eighteenth at seven forty-two in the evening, earlier than usual. Valerie entered his info and took his twenty dollars. She was wearing an old t-shirt inside out, the print underneath giving the shirt texture, like a scar.

He said, "Hi, Val."

"Only one ticket? Go-boy's feeling lucky this year, ah?" Valerie laughed.

He smiled nervously.

Go had always been confident around girls, but according to him, that had changed after he'd moved to Anchorage and gone to college. Something switched during those years. Maybe the conservative school instilled guilt in him. Maybe he already had guilt and it didn't wake up until he left home. Maybe it was the intimidation of the big city. Either way, standing there with Valerie, he knew he'd stumbled onto something great.

He said, "I've never won before. Not yet anyway."

Nobody knew Go-boy had just been kicked out of Bible college. According to his adviser, he had too many incomplete grades, but Go told me they kicked him out because he was a threat to the sterilized Christian bubble they had created for themselves. Go-boy had unordinary theories and beliefs. He constantly questioned his professors' doctrines and ideologies. That year he had incited a renaissance on campus. Some scholars called his angle Universalism theology, but Go simply called it *real spirituality*. He claimed that everyone was saved—every person on earth—and that the concept of eternal damnation was hyperbole, along with the idea of hell. His evidence was biblical. Students around him began catching on to these ideas. When Go-boy accumulated enough incompletes, the school kicked him out, even though there were plenty of students with as many incompletes or more. Go told his adviser that Jesus was treated the same way by the Pharisees.

Go asked, "So what you been up to these days?"

Valerie told him about her job.

"I'm working upriver at the fish tower this summer," he said. "Whenever kings start running."

Valerie told him she would be going to the University of Alaska Anchorage in the fall on a scholarship. She was a year out of high school and would be starting college as a freshman after having spent the previous year taking care of her gram.

He said, "Real champ, Val."

She smiled.

Go told her he was taking a break from college.

It wasn't necessarily Valerie's appearance that had Go hooked that afternoon. When I first saw her, I thought she looked a little too rounded and her short hair was too mannish. But she had the type of beauty that grew on you, and regardless, it was something else that Go-boy latched on to, something else that would intrigue him and keep him awake late almost every night that week, and many nights the rest of the year. He just explained it by saying they were same-same.

Go said, "We should try-take a ride."

"Okay."

"A boat ride to Blueberry. I got potential gas money right here," he said, waving his ticket.

Valerie was excited because she was feeling the same as Go. The temp wasn't even forty. The river was still frozen. The slough was still frozen. And the ocean still had ice that stretched out a couple hundred feet. But Go said he would tow his boat with a snowmachine to the edge of the open water. Uncle Stanley and others had already gone out to the ocean this way, seal hunting, so Valerie didn't even think twice when they made plans to meet in two days. Although two days didn't feel soon enough for either of them.

Go said, "See you then," and left the building, already contemplating the possibility of going back to school in Anchorage that fall to be near her.

They met two days later at Go-boy's boat just below the Kuuk Bridge in the slough.

Go had spent the morning getting everything ready. He'd charged the battery. Shot lithium grease in all the right places. Turned the engine over to check if it would fire. Topped off the red jerry cans. Shoveled out the slush behind the steering wheel console and drained the standing water. Go busied himself. He was nervous.

When Valerie got there, the first thing she said was, "I made you this," and handed Go a sealskin wallet. She'd been impatient to give it to him.

Go said, "Man." And that was it. He loved her.

Valerie had lunch in her backpack. She was unsure what Go liked, so she brought some Eskimo food—black meat, Yukon king strips, and herring eggs on kelp—along with simple stuff—peanut-butter-and-jelly sandwiches and Doritos. She was packing the traditional food that day to impress Go-boy. She could sense that he was attracted to modern women who were grounded in old-fashioned ways. How? She didn't know. But she was right.

Go only brought a six-pack of pop.

Valerie sat in the boat as Go dragged it behind his snowmachine. She was wearing her parka, sunglasses, and a smile. Go had brought a rifle just in case they saw an ugruk. It was warm in the sunshine and there were large drifts still unthawed on the other side of the slough, lining the snow fences.

When they got to the open ocean water, Valerie stayed in the boat as Go pushed it off the ice. She was always nervous in the sea—ice or no ice. She said, "Iisragii, Go-boy. Be careful." He laughed and fired the engine.

"Can I drive?" Valerie asked.

Go said okay. He liked a girl who went straight at her fears.

They motored out past a few large ice floes, looking for seals. They each were wearing bunny boots, parka, fur malaghai, and sunglasses. The cold wind cut at their exposed faces. As Valerie handled the boat north, parallel to the distant coast, driving like she did this every day, overcoming her fear of the ocean in front of Go, they didn't talk but just shared glances back and forth, smiling.

This was Go-boy's ideal date. Something simple. Outdoors. Without the distraction of a movie or a crowded restaurant. There weren't even theaters or cafés in Unk to take her to, and that was good because Go was a guy who liked to jump right into the heavy conversations. It was almost a requirement for him in order to move to a deeper level with a girl. And that was what he wanted—riding along the coast, watching Valerie weaving around random icebergs and shielding her exposed face—was the deepest of possible connections.

Can you hear this?" Valerie said, holding out her hand and moving her thumb after the boat had stopped just west of Blueberry Hill. Her joint clicked like a loud clock. "Fishing accident."

Go laughed, said, "Real Native, man. You always been get seal finger too?"

They both laughed.

Go was definitely in love. Valerie knew she soon would be.

The ocean was calm so they didn't anchor up to any ice but stayed floating that afternoon, drinking pop and eating most of the food from Valerie's backpack. Go-boy had been talking about school and his decision to leave, and about his most recent beliefs regarding heaven and salvation and everything surrounding those theologies. He felt the modern Christian church was misrepresenting Jesus.

"I'm not sure if I believe in heaven," Valerie said, tearing the skin from an oily salmon strip. "Or God."

They had been talking so freely that afternoon, agreeing about everything, even finishing some of each other's thoughts, that Go-boy just assumed she believed as he did.

"I know you have your faith," she said, "but I haven't figured it out yet. For myself." She explained her skepticism of a god who would let suffering and pain happen so regularly and freely. She doubted why a god would want so much worship and attention, as if he were an insecure teenager.

"*She,*" Go-boy said, speaking of God, "is the sum of us all, and of everything." But that was the most he said about it. He didn't explain to her that the problem about pain and suffering wasn't all that difficult. To Go-boy it was simple—in order for humans to experience any real life, with real choices and real celebrations, God had to limit her own power. If God protected any ounce of the natural world from pain, or limited creation in a way that removed suffering, then no person could ever know the sweetness of true salvation and true awareness, true enlightenment. And no person could ever be free. Go-boy didn't say these things to Valerie that afternoon in the boat, and didn't say anything else about spirituality, but their difference in worldview deflated him. He doubted he could date a girl who didn't believe as he did. But sitting there, talking and laughing past suppertime and into the night, Go-boy knew he was already in love anyway.

Valerie and Go kept dating after the ice in the river went out. Go-boy didn't win the contest—he was only six minutes off, but the winner was within three. They watched the ice flow out to the ocean. This year was one of those loud, destructive years, where the seawall was left mangled and wooden fish racks were broken into piles of kindling. To Go-boy, seeing it with Valerie was worth more than any cash prize.

They fished trout and went goose-hunting together in May. In June they fished king salmon in North River. Valerie filleted and stripped each fish with an ulu that Go-boy's dad had made. They delivered food to the seniors in town as part of an Elders' Lunch Program. Valerie even agreed to sometimes attend the church with him, although her beliefs hadn't changed, and because of it Go-boy still doubted the relationship's future. But Valerie was now in love with Go. She hadn't said that—neither of them had—but they were both very much in love. And even though there was plenty of sexual attraction, they hadn't had sex, or even kissed. They did everything together and their relationship darted to levels deeper than many married couples ever experience, but neither of them minded that the sex part was slow—it was what they both needed.

This was when I moved to town, in the middle of June. Go-boy and me started working together at the fish tower, counting fish, but I didn't know that he and Valerie were so close already, not while all of this was happening. They were shy about their relationship. The only way Go publicly showed Valerie affection was by calling in to the radio program *Open Line* and wishing all of his love to Ripper—Valerie's obscure nickname. I suppose that's the way to do things in such a small town, where everybody always knows everything. But I didn't find out about most of their relationship until it was over, until Go was in the Anchorage hospital, telling me everything that had happened, and more.

For the town's Fourth of July celebration, Go and Valerie entered the raft race on North River. Contestants started at the bridge and floated a few miles to Main River, using only homemade rafts. Go and Valerie weren't interested in winning, so they found an abandoned Volkswagen, stripped everything, leaving only the body and floor pan, attached a few long pieces of driftwood to the bottom, and entered the race. They set lawn chairs where the driver and passenger seats had been. They brought a cooler full of pop and snacks. The water was ice-cold, always was. They mounted their raft and floated alongside about fifteen other contestants.

North River was about as wide as a downtown city street. It had a swift current and turned itself over and back many times. Evergreens hung over the eroding banks, showing signs of the river's own reshaping, and the water ran clear like thick glass.

From the start of the race it was obvious Go and Valerie would lose. The old Volkswagen's body, although feather-light for a car, was too heavy. At the starting line, people laughed and cheered them on. But a few bends into the race, with all the other teams far ahead, it was apparent that the VW was sinking. Not only was it too heavy to keep pace with the others, it was too heavy for the driftwood it floated on. They surrendered after a mile and banked the raft onto a sandbar somewhere between the North River Bridge and the river's mouth.

And the Volkswagen stayed there all year. At first people were surprised to see it along the river, but by the end of summer it had become a part of North River's scenery. High school kids camped out and had bonfires on the same sandbar, some tagged it with graffiti. Families beached their boats and picnicked beside the VW, some even stretching ratty chunks of burlap across the hood and using it as a table for cutting fish. And the VW would stay there all winter, until the following spring, when the ice would break up and scrape out everything along the river, cleansing itself, and people would see a VW bug floating past town in a frozen flow.

Valerie and Go laughed when they beached onto shore that Fourth of July, pleased with themselves. To them, this signified their love—their willingness to lose the race, or more so, lose themselves, for each other.

Three months of their relationship had passed when Valerie left a note on Go's pillow. She had written a list—*TEN THINGS I LIKE ABOUT GO-BOY*—on a page torn from the Bible. Go received the letter on the same day we went to the funeral potluck at the bowling alley for his friend Trilogy. He showed it to me then. The note was funny and cute, with simple reasons. I didn't read the whole thing. I didn't read what Valerie had written at the bottom of the letter—*I want to kiss you tonight.* She wrote that she had wanted to kiss him on their first date, right when they had passed through the mouth of the frozen river. She wanted them to ride out to that spot that night, and float, and kiss for the first time.

They met at Go's boat around eleven, both a little nervous—Valerie because she wanted everything to be perfect, Go because he didn't think the relationship could last. Go brought two cans of soda and a box of Otter Pop popsicles.

As Go drove the boat from the slough into the river, a sudden hesitation passed over him. It was a moment when he lost all confidence, and every uncertainty and fear made Go-boy's eyes lose focus. He felt like he was watching himself crash—leading this girl on. He felt like every teacher and pastor and parent was watching this accident. This was something he'd always struggled with—this self-doubt—and at that moment, he hated everything about himself.

As they neared the mouth of the river where it opened to the ocean, Go turned the key off so the boat died and floated to a stop, its wake pushing up from behind and disappearing. They were short of their planned destination.

"What's wrong? We gas-siaq?"

Go thought for a moment. The sun still hung above the horizon, out over the ocean, and wouldn't drop till after midnight. And later that night, millions of humpies would crowd the river in search of their spawning grounds.

"I think the fuel pump is bad."

Valerie walked to the back of the boat. She traced fuel lines from a red gas tank into a coffee-can-sized filter. Go was facing the ocean, unable to do anything, wondering what he should say, feeling stupid, feeling lost. That was when Valerie pulled a screwdriver and pliers from Go-boy's tackle box and drained water from the fuel filter. As she worked, she said, "I think I've always believed in God. Not the church's God, but some type of unity in all of us." She said, "There's something there, I think."

Go-boy turned and watched how Valerie's young fingers moved through the pieces of the fuel lines and filter with confidence. She had the engine cover off and was checking each of the three carburetors for water contamination. Go then knew this was no longer an accident—this was meant to be. He watched her bite her lip as she scraped gunk with her fingernails and removed and reattached pieces of his boat that Go knew nothing about.

Go later said this was the moment he realized he could no longer live his life by social codes, by what others expected of him. He said it was then he saw the importance of individual strength and the ability to not care about what others thought but to follow his own heart. He said that Valerie, by being herself and fixing his fuel pump because she wanted to kiss him, gave Go-boy the confidence and inspiration to truly be enlightened, to truly be himself and live from his heart. Even if it was ridiculous.

That was when Go knelt down on one knee and said, "Valerie, will you marry me?"

She turned from reinstalling the filter, her fingernails framed with gunk and smelling like gas, a red Popsicle stain on her upper lip. She laughed. She didn't think he was serious.

"What?" she said, smiling. "Yeah, okay, maybe someday."

Go-boy said he was serious, now. He said he wanted to marry her as soon as they could. "I love you."

"Let's try-turn the motor," Valerie said, her smile relaxing as she moved past him and spun the key of the boat, firing the engine.

He said, "I know we'll get married someday. Why wait?"

Valerie's expression slipped into concern. Her shoulders dropped. It was like Go-boy had just slapped her. She couldn't believe this, not then or even later. "Araa! I'm only nineteen," she said.

"I'm only twenty-two."

"Let's not ruin this," she said. "Everything's perfect. Don't ruin this."

But by the look on Go-boy's face, Valerie could see he'd already ruined it. He was serious. His face sparked with excitement and he couldn't hear her disagreements or her concerns. She hoped this would pass, so she slid behind the steering wheel and turned them back to the slough. She beached the boat and jumped out before Go could say anything else, before they could have their first kiss.

That night Go-boy started his list—*101 THINGS I LOVE ABOUT VALERIE*. But he didn't finish it then. This was when he and I saw his dad put Sean in a coma, that next morning. It was the same morning all the humpies swam into the river. Valerie's rejection and his dad's outburst pooled together, creating some type of guilt and self-hatred for Go-boy, and he vanished for a month.

While he was in the hospital, this was where his story would start for counseling sessions. This was the start of his summer-long mania, according to his therapist. Although he had experienced many ups and downs before this, they had never seemed like anything but puberty and identity-searching. But this summer was noticeably different. His therapist would tell him it was a common beginning of a mania—drastic emotions, the desire to change everything by tomorrow, the feeling that life had suddenly become lucid.

. . .

Nobody knew where Go went that month. There were plenty of rumors. Plenty of search-and-rescue missions. Some stories in the Alaska papers and even on the six o'clock news. But after a week the media lost interest, and the State of Alaska called it quits on the search. His family kept looking, though, for the whole month, hoping for the best and bracing for the worst. Every weekend Uncle Stanley and a few others would load up their boats with extra gas and drive up the river for hours and hours until they couldn't get any farther. Bush-pilot friends altered their flight patterns and flew lower, looking for anything suspicious. And I was looking too. And just like everyone else, I grew pessimistic when the days without clues piled on top of one another. There was so much empty land—the nearest villages to the north and south were forty miles, and to the east about eighty miles, and in between there was nothing. And when Go told me this whole story about his relationship with Valerie, he still left out most of the details about what he did while he was gone. Earlier he'd told me about his drunken week in Nome, but when I asked about the other three weeks, he said he didn't want to talk about it. He said at the time it felt like something phenomenal, but now his therapist was telling him it was all just a mania, nothing real, so he had to forget about it.

Valerie had been hired to work on the fish tower to fill in for Go and me after we were fired. During this month that Go-boy was gone, Valerie and I got to know each other. She'd call me, checking to see if Go had resurfaced. She was nervous, almost hysterical, feeling like she was the reason he'd disappeared. She'd cry over the phone, and in person. It was awkward for me at first, but anytime people cry in front of each other they either become friends or ignore each other. We became friends. She would stop by my mom's house and show me the things Go had made for her. One time she showed me the ulu with the glass handle. "It doesn't work very well," Valerie said. "The glass is too slippery to hold." The handle was made of gillies melted together. It was lumpy, but all the layers of different-colored glass added a vibrant depth, like individual worlds inside and around and connected to each other. "It's beautiful," Valerie said, on the verge of tears, again. She was a mess. She had stopped combing her hair and always wore the same red sweatshirt and paint-stained jeans.

"Here," I said, and handed her a black ball cap.

She laughed. "I look that bad, ah?"

"You can keep it."

Then Go-boy returned with no explanation of where he'd been, and even more hopped up than when he'd proposed. Valerie was elated when he reappeared—relieved he was alive and that she wasn't responsible for something terrible—relieved that there was a chance to do everything over again—relieved that Go might be back to normal. But her excitement wore off in a day or two. Go was acting, it seemed to Valerie, as if the marriage proposal had never happened, or even sometimes like she'd said yes. He avoided talking about it. He only wanted to act like they were in love, like they were married, and like their futures were the same.

"I can't do this," she told him. "It's still too fast."

Go reacted as if this were a challenge he not only could rise to but had already conquered. He never left her alone. He called several times a day. He drove by her house. He left notes. He called *Open Line* and on live radio revealed embarrassing facts about his love for Valerie—*I want to touch your soul more than your body. . . . I want to kiss your lips because of what you say and how you say it.* It was annoying, yet still flattering to Valerie.

She tried to explain to him that a lot had been changing in her life. Go had prompted some of these changes—she was thinking about spirituality and God like never before, especially when he'd disappeared, but probably not in the ways he'd hoped. She was merely accepting the possibility. She was open to someday, if nothing else, teaching her kids to believe in God.

Go told her, "*Our* kids will know God in ways we can't even comprehend."

But Valerie knew she would never believe the way Go-boy did and wondered if anyone actually could. He was always bothering her, talking about their perfect love and his theories for how they would change the world together. It was making Valerie lose interest.

And then, just after I'd moved in with Go-boy, Valerie's dad died. It was the middle of summer and I had started playing the drums. Valerie's dad was checking his nets in the ocean, and on his way home he had a heart attack. He was alone and he passed out behind the wheel of the boat, driving right by town at forty mph and ending up a half mile down the coast before the whole thing ramped onto shore, throwing him from the boat and mangling his face and neck. Afterward people hoped he'd been dead before the boat hit the shore. But nobody found out for sure.

Funerals in the village were an all-day event, open to everyone. The church service was around two hours long, with the first half led by the pastor reading through scripture and giving a sermon; the second half was like a wake, with silence and open-mic time for people to share their stories and memories of the person who died. Afterward the coffin was loaded into a family member's truck and driven down Main Road a mile to the cemetery, which in rural Alaska was usually set right next to the airport runway. The coffin was always made by friends or family. The hole in the ground was dug ahead of time by a backhoe. The coffin lowered by ropes. The ground shoveled in by all the men. Many times songs and prayers broke out at the burial, sometimes in Iñupiaq. The younger the deceased, the longer everything took. At night there was a potluck in the community center or gymnasium. Tables were lined up, thirty feet long, stacked with every kind of Eskimo food and modern dish you could think of. People sat around on folding chairs, talking, sometimes watching a video, looking at pictures, sometimes laughing, sometimes crying. Kids were always running around. And usually this lasted hours.

The church was packed for the funeral. I wasn't there, but Mom and Kiana were. Valerie looked around the sanctuary, hoping Goboy wouldn't show. But he was already in the building somewhere. He was waiting for his moment. He knew the town was in need of a prophet and that the timing was perfect for him to emerge. He knew this would both shine light into the town's pockets of darkness and win Valerie's heart.

The funeral lasted just over an hour. Valerie's dad had been in the church choir, so there was an emotional time where all the members stood around his coffin and sang a hymn translated into Iñupiaq.

After the sermon the pastor opened the microphone to anyone who wanted to share memories of Valerie's dad. Her uncle spoke—a best friend of her dad's, followed by a woman who was a member of the choir and coworker, followed by Valerie's mom, who could hardly get out halves of sentences at first. Her mom told a story of when they were just married and living in Koyuk, and it had been a bad year for fishing and hunting and she was pregnant with Valerie. She was offered a job at the University of Alaska Fairbanks, but she decided she didn't want to take it; she wanted to stay home that year with her firstborn, stay in Koyuk. So Valerie's dad, struggling to feed himself and his wife and struggling to pay rent, began carving miniature fish and ulus and whales from small pieces of petrified wood, and made them into earrings with fishing-lure leads, and started selling them to tourist shops in Anchorage. She said, "Real Native art, I guess," joking, and the people in church laughed. But the earrings helped get them through that year, and became a popular tourist purchase, and ended up getting them through a few more years after. As she told the story, she brushed her fingers past her ears—she was wearing the first pair he'd ever made—little seals. Valerie had on a pair too.

There was a long pause after Valerie's mom spoke. A collected breath of air. Cheeks were starting to relax after being sore from the exhausted laughing, and the tears that had followed the story were starting to dry.

This was when Go-boy came to the podium from a side room.

He said, "As some of you may know, I asked Valerie to marry me over a month ago. I was serious, and I would do it again. I *am* doing it again, right now."

At this point there was some uneasy shifting in the church. One person laughed.

"She's an amazing woman, and it's a testament to her parents. To her mom, who shows such strength and compassion, who shows us that God must be a woman, and to her dad—a man who no doubt had problems, who hurt, who struggled, who even stole some gas from Garage one time. We remember that. Man, we've all stolen gas from Garage. And we've all given gas, or fish, or kuupiaq to someone who needed it too. And we've seen today, in this dead man, how a person can turn from stealing gas to near perfection—before death, before the afterlife, right here on this planet.

"So today we honor a man who was prepared to make heaven a reality. Let us learn from him. Let us release the things that keep us in the past, the things that keep us silent, the things that hold us back from becoming what our hearts want us to be. Today we shall all become exactly who we want to be. I want to be Unalakleet's youngest mayor. This day, right now, it's official—vote for Go-boy—Go-boy for mayor."

There was a silent shock throughout the room, followed by anxious mumbling.

"When I'm mayor we will all find heaven, here and now. It will be new and beautiful! In this new day the whole village will live without judgment, and we will be free to express ourselves. We will never forget that the moment is all there is, and we will see that we are true. Time is our tool to watch perfection unfold—and Unalakleet will become perfect. I'll act as the most transparent leader and I will bring the New Consciousness to politics. There will be no more poverty or crime, and we will turn the new jail into a rural Alaska college for the perpetual study of awe and wonderment. The town will operate as a cooperative, and everything—from milk to airfare to postage—will be based on a sliding-scale fee. I will appoint a poet laureate to inspire our senses, and students will be paid to attend school, and every seven years we will redistribute all the wealth throughout the co-op—"

The pastor finally walked to the podium and cut Go-boy off,

leading him out to the side room. A couple people laughed, but none were from Valerie's family. And Valerie was devastated. She was angry. Go had turned her father's funeral into a showcase for his beliefs. Most importantly, he'd turned the attention on himself. She knew she would never again believe the things Go-boy wanted her to believe—much less love him again. At that moment she was sure of it.

Valerie moved to Anchorage two weeks after her dad's funeral. It wasn't to attend the university but to get away from Go-boy. He'd been relentless and she couldn't hide from him in the small village.

Her last week in Unk was when forest fires blanketed the whole town with that yellowish-gray haze of smoke. She was scheduled to fly out at the start of the week, but each day the flights were canceled, and Go kept up his relentless pursuit—posting his reasons for love all over town and knocking on every relative's and friend's door looking for her. So Valerie's mom called the police and Go was issued a restraining order. And although Go had never gotten forceful, or even disrespectful, and everyone who knew about the situation mostly just thought it was cute, Valerie was scared.

Go-boy made one last attempt to *save* Valerie. At least, that was how he saw it. He was convinced she wasn't listening to her heart. That by some kind of trauma, some kind of deep wound, she wasn't setting herself free. So after she moved, Go found out where Valerie was living. This was when he snuck onto a cargo plane, intending to eventually fly to New York City to meet Yoko Ono. In Anchorage Go-boy broke into Valerie's uncle's house. Go found Valerie's room and left a note that was attached to a gill-net buoy. It said, *I KNOW*

YOUR DAD MOLESTED YOU. He was convinced not only that she had been hiding this shameful secret but that this *miracle* of him knowing would be the key to her healing and the key to reinstating their awesome love for one another.

He was absolutely wrong in all these assumptions. Valerie was crushed.

Valerie wanted to forget about Go-boy, so she convinced herself to fall for someone else. After a month in Anchorage she began dating an engineer from Montana, a short guy who was eight years older than her. He made decent money working for an oil and gas company and spent his weekends playing hacky sack on sidewalks along Fourth Avenue and his nights drinking in the bars on that same street. He loved to pick fights when he was drunk and would often come back to his apartment sweaty and bruised and out of breath. Valerie started drinking as well. This new boyfriend supplied her with a fake ID.

Soon after, Valerie's uncle told her if she didn't stop getting *wasted* she'd have to move out. So Valerie did, and moved in with Montana. At first the arrangement was temporary because she had no desire to live with him, or any guy, so soon, while she was so young. But another month passed, and plans were forgotten.

I think I'll go to school," Valerie told Montana. At this point the deadline for spring semester was nearing and she was still unemployed. She knew he would tell her to forget about it. She knew he'd say what he always said, that she didn't have to worry about a career because he made enough money for both of them. He would say this, thinking it was nice, thinking he was a better man for offering. But Valerie was dating him as a fling. That was all. She and Montana had already been together two months—two-thirds as long as she and Go-boy—but Valerie felt more like a roommate to Montana than a lover, like they'd been arbitrarily paired up for a set amount of time. After the intense start and then sharp fall with Go-boy, this was all she needed—something mindless—something simple— a fling.

But this time, instead of talking about the money he made, Montana only said, "Why do you always wear t-shirts inside out? You look like you're poor." He was making a joke, but Valerie didn't find it funny.

She thought about Go-boy, remembering the list he wrote for her, the reason spray-painted on the Kuuk Bridge—*YOU WEAR T-SHIRTS INSIDE OUT*.

Valerie went into the bedroom and put on a different t-shirt, a solid navy shirt, right side out.

The Unalakleet River had finally frozen. Just as spring had been unusually early, fall had been unusually late—a long summer altogether. It would still be a month before the ice was thick enough for snowmachines. This was just after the unknown woman came to town; at least, she was unknown for a few days until she was flown to a Nome hospital. There she was identified, and according to the rumors, she was healed in a week and was back to her normal, domestic life. But I still didn't know how she had gotten to Unk. Nobody did. And it seemed nobody ever would—it was a mystery that only this small town would ever ponder.

Go had been detached that week, emotionless, all the while tormented by his own compulsions. Yet, a few times, when I was close to confronting him about his uncharacteristic sadness and detachment, Go would have brief moments of normalcy. During those times he would show a fleeting interest in his family, in me, and in the unknown woman. It was enough to keep me confused and unsure. At times he was fun. During one of these breaks Go tried to theorize about how the unknown woman had landed in town.

"She could've floated on an ice floe from Point Hope," Go said. "It started the size of a parking lot but melted real slow, and when it reached our beach it was the size of a pillow, and gone by morning."

"She was frozen in permafrost a hundred years ago," I said. "And when the forest fires came, she thawed and came to life."

"Permafrost!" Go said. "Nice. But how would a family claim her?"

"They were lying."

"Maybe they were thawed by the forest fires too!"

Not more than a week after this I found Go trying to tie a rope around his neck.

Valerie heard about Go-boy's attempted suicide three days after it happened. He was still in Nome at the hospital, so she tried to do what she'd been thinking about doing anyway—call him. But Go-boy wasn't taking calls, not from Valerie or anyone. He was only talking to me and Kiana, and that was because we were there at the hospital. Even then I couldn't get many words out of him. He fake-listened every time I tried to ask questions or give him encouragement. I tried to tell him about how everyone in Unk had torn down the old jail. How the kids had started smashing the ruined building. How it sounded phenomenal. And Kiana told him about Sean, how he beat the doctors at the memory game and how that was his new nickname—Memory. But Go didn't react. His brain was busy, ruminating over something. He led the doctors on, letting them hear the right types of responses in the right order. And by the time they let him leave, Go hadn't changed much. He was drugged now, but Kiana and I could tell he was still denying his condition.

For weeks after, Go was unstable. He was accepting of his disease but unhopeful about his situation and future. And he and I would have variations of the same conversation over and over—

"You can hold on to all of the good things from the summer," I'd say. "Take the accomplishments and forget about the rest."

"I hurt so many people," he'd say, meaning Valerie.

"People bounce back. We can take it."

"Man, I can't even trust myself."

"You know more about yourself now, though. You can learn."

"It was the best year of my life, and it was all a lie."

Go-boy's therapist had told him he couldn't live like he had been. That it wasn't normal. He'd been manic all year, and his brain chemicals were out of whack. The therapist told him all the things he'd believed were actually distortions created by his overactive, and very ill, brain. To Go this meant most people would in fact be sent to hell, and there would never be a heaven on earth, and his love for Valerie was a sickness. The therapist told him he was manic-depressive, and would always be, and that he would always need to be medicated. This frustrated me. I mean, I was no doctor, but the all-or-nothing approach just seemed stupid, especially for Go. He thrived on positivity.

I said, "What if you really were living on a higher level of consciousness? What if you really were enlightened?"

"Then I wouldn't have tried to hang myself."

I said, "That was just the crash, man, the rest of us bringing you back down. Don't you think Jesus seemed a little fuckin' manic too?"

But in his current medicated state, saying things like this was unreasonable. It wasn't even funny to him. It couldn't be. Go was now consumed with doing everything he could to stay focused on the simple, the immediate, the concrete. He arranged potato chips in order of size, then ate them largest to smallest. He organized his music collection from A to Z, then by year, then by genre. He separated change. He counted clouds. He took hours to do everything. When he wasn't engaged in those chores, he slept.

One time, just before Christmas, we hopped in his AMC to go to the post office. We had to let the car warm up, so we sat in the driveway waiting, with Go behind the wheel, me sitting shotgun. Go blew into his bare hands, warming them. I adjusted the radio. After a while the car sounded ready to drive, but Go still waited. He waited ten minutes. Then fifteen. Then twenty. We were warm by that point but still not going anywhere. Go, behind the wheel, looked arrested by a thought that paralyzed him. It was disturbing.

"Hey, Go," I said.

He didn't respond.

"The post office is only open another two hours. We better hurry."

He laughed a little, but it was more for show than anything. Then he said something I never thought I'd hear him say. He said, "What if this is it? What if this is the best we can do?" He motioned to the whole village, but I knew he was talking about the two of us. "What if God is just a sadist?"

I wasn't sure what he meant, but I could feel his despair, and I wanted to be quick and smart so I could reinstate his hope in life. I wanted to prove him wrong for his own sake. Right then I wanted to know impossibly more than I ever would. Yet I couldn't respond. I'd start with, "But—" or "Think about—" and wouldn't finish. I'd spend the holidays trying to remember what Go said, and then I'd try to answer his doubts and fears. And in a way that only Go could, he had me thinking about the purpose of life. He had me thinking about the role of perspective in our lives. He had me unlocking questions I never knew I had.

During Go-boy's funk people were always stopping by our house, bringing cookies and sweetbread and smoked salmon strips. Most people were strangers to me, but they knew who I was, and it felt nice. It was even busier during Christmas. People were worried, and they wanted to visit with Go, but he wouldn't allow it. So our kitchen counter became clogged with plastic bags full of food. Breads and salads and cookies and fish, and most of it would get moldy or stale.

With Sean home, Kiana and Mom had a new project—raising a kid. Mom put all her energy into Sean. She seemed rejuvenated by the responsibility of raising a boy in Unalakleet. And it suited her. Although she and Kiana were there for Go-boy when he needed them, they weren't as aware of Go's health as they had been before the suicide attempt.

For New Year's Eve, over half the people in the village went to the bridge at the edge of town to watch a fireworks show. The sled-dog club hosted the celebration. It was a pitch-black night. Head-lights from trucks cast long shadows over the snowy bridge and tundra all around. Bodies stumbled into each other, blinded and disoriented, waiting patiently. When the clocks finally hit midnight we could hear gunshots echoing throughout town—people firing off round after round from their .22 rifles and pistols. Then the pyrotechnics started and the sky lit up and you could finally see people—wrapped in fur parkas and fur hats—their faces lit up red and blue and orange below a low cloud of truck exhaust and frozen breath. I wove between trucks and four-wheelers and through the people, wondering where Go-boy was. I wondered how long his funk would last. I wondered if he needed to have his medications adjusted or if maybe this was the real Go-boy, the Go who'd existed before I'd moved to town, the Go who would struggle to raise a smile the rest of his prescription-filled days. He was not only depressed like he had been right before and right after his suicide attempt, but he was now frustrated with all the medical stuff—the diagnosis, the drugs, the therapy. He blamed the medication for many things. He said it made him foggy all day. He said he could no longer read books—not being able to focus his eyes. He said some of his favorite foods and drinks, like pop, tasted horrible. Through all of this, Go kept himself locked up inside our house. He kept the curtains shut and the lights dim. There was never music in his room anymore. Kids stopped by from time to time, but Go wasn't visiting with anyone.

The church was openly praying for Go-boy during worship services. They operated a prayer chain—members phoning each other, passing along a prayer request for Go over the phone. The pastor stopped by our house weekly. There were times when Go-boy refused the pastor—didn't even let her in the house—and other times when they sat together, drinking coffee and watching daytime TV. But Go had stopped going to church, stopped talking about God. He even told me he no longer believed in Christianity.

A couple months passed, and in my weakest moments, when I would see Go still depressed and imprisoned to his own distorted emotions, I wondered if it would have been better if I'd never caught him trying to kill himself, if he might have been better off. Like Valerie, I was undecided about what came after death, but living with Go while he hated every ounce of himself and his life—hidden behind the curtains and walls of our house, avoiding people at all costs—made me feel like there had to be something better waiting for us, all of us, if not in this life, then after. Maybe death really would've been okay for Go-boy, to avoid this spot he was stuck in.

But we still had a lot of living ahead of us. And maybe that was the reason Go never tried suicide again—despite the worst of it. Maybe he was open to the idea that hope could someday come back to him.

Around March Go-boy started to rejoin the community. He worked part-time shifts at the airport. He played in the Iditarod basketball tournament, helping his team get third place, receiving his own All-Tourney trophy and sweatpants. Go-boy had been learning to read his moods—he called them phases—and kept a journal dedicated to tracking his patterns and changes. He watched what he ate, reducing his sugar and caffeine intake. He still didn't trust the mental health industry, but he stayed on his medications, adjusting the dosage to his own liking—low enough so he still had energy and could read books, yet high enough to regulate the extreme ups and downs. It was a struggle. It took lots of work. In late March he felt a rapid change again—like the year before—and talked to his doctor, getting the okay for a higher dosage for a couple weeks, for safety. It seemed, Go-boy was learning, that he had a straightforward annual manic episode—one long mania for most of the year, and one long, dark depression starting sometime in late winter.

By April Go-boy was ready to call Valerie. It was around the time people were guessing when the ice would break up. Some were thinking the end of May, others even theorized as late as June. It seemed spring would never come. Always cloudy. Always cold. I'd been in Unk for almost a year at this point, and half of it had been during this winter, during the never-ending blizzards and nonstop wind, through day after day of layering winter clothes for school and trips to the grocery store, with the occasional basketball or wrestling tournament in the school gym. Kiana and I spent all our time together. We'd make out and watch movies in Go-boy's living room, ignoring the poorly patched hole in the floor and trying to get Go to play board games with us.

Go-boy talked to me about calling Valerie. He asked if I thought it was a good idea. Then he ran through his monologue a few times, and it sounded good—safe—so with me sitting in the room, he called and left a message.

"Hey, Valerie. It's Go. I . . . wanted to call and say hello. I guess a lot has happened this past year that I haven't apologized for. . . . I know you know. . . . So I won't even try-say anything. I just wanted to maybe be friends again. Either way, I understand. At least, I'm starting to. Okay, see you."

By the time he hung up the phone he was already worrying.

I told him she probably wouldn't call for a while. A month, to be fair. She was a smart girl and would need time to think things over. She had loved him and had gotten hurt, and that wasn't something to just bounce back from.

But after hearing the message, Valerie knew she would call Go.

Everybody did. She wanted to forgive him. Hearing his voice was what she needed. She had been missing Unk more than anything, and the sound of Go's voice reminded her of boat rides upriver, and family picnics on sandbars, and aunties sitting around for hours with coffee and little kids, laughing and talking about nothing. But she also wanted to wait before calling Go back, maybe a week or so, to not get him too excited. She wanted to show patience.

The next Go-boy heard about Valerie was from a stranger the following week. He was at the post office, checking his mail, when one of his former teachers told him.

She said, "How are you? Are you okay?"

"I'm okay," Go said, assuming the teacher was talking about his depression. He fingered through the *Bushmailer* newspaper—bulk-mail coupons for rural Alaska.

"She was too young."

Go looked at the teacher, confused.

"Haven't you heard?" she said.

Valerie had died in a car accident on the Seward Highway, heading south out of Anchorage with her boyfriend.

Some would theorize that Valerie had been trying to break up with Montana. Most of Valerie's friends guessed that she was going to use their road trip that day to give him the news. She was that type of person. Thoughtful, but not always with the best timing. Those who held to this theory thought she had maybe already told him, before the accident. They thought maybe he deliberately crossed lanes and drove head-on into the logging truck. Afterward police found alcohol in Montana's blood. He wasn't drunk, and there weren't any bottles in the car, but any alcohol in his blood was enough for Valerie's friends and family to blame him. They had already been blaming him for Valerie's drinking.

Of course Go-boy blamed himself. He left the post office, and by the time he got to the other side of town, to his house, that *cloud*—as he described it—had resettled over his life. He couldn't take any more tragedies. His immediate thought was suicide. End everything. That was it. End it all. He was the reason Valerie had died, and he couldn't live with that. He didn't deserve to live.

Go blamed himself because of what he believed. He believed people planned out their lives before they were born, like reincarnation, in order to live a number of different times to experience everything, yet individuals and circumstances derailed those plans every day with free will. Go-boy believed in avoidable tragedy. And Go-boy believed he was the cause of Valerie's tragedy.

By the time I heard the news, Go-boy was long gone. He disappeared like he had a habit of doing.

I searched through Go's room, looking for clues to where he might have gone. I dug in his dresser drawers and pants pockets and backpacks. Among a stack of notebooks I found a journal. It was titled GO & VALERIE. On their first date, they had started this journal together, writing their feelings and emotions out, separately, in this little black book. They addressed each entry to one another—DEAR GO; DEAR VALERIE. I'm sure they passed it back and forth. There were many entries early on, sometimes two a day from each of them. Both Go and Valerie wrote about their love with an energy that now seemed ridiculous. About a quarter of the way through the journal, Valerie's entries stopped, from the time Go had asked her to marry him. And about halfway through the book, there was nothing but blank pages. I guessed that to be around the time of Go's attempted suicide. But as I flipped through, I found a recent entry, near the end of the journal, dated the same day Go had heard about her death. I read it start to finish, thinking it might reveal his whereabouts—

Dear Valerie,

I remember so much, almost more than could have possibly happened. I remember the way you drove a boat up North River and how you stood up while steering. You said that it was in order to view the channel and any snags in the water, and I trusted you because you were a good driver. But I remember something else: sitting next to you, seeing you, and sensing how you savored the feeling of water rushing beneath your feet, how if you could've had the choice, there would've been no need for a boat at all. With the strong current against you at those times, you would've steered us upriver, around each bend and sandbar, through the deep spots, under the hanging trees, and I would've never doubted where we were traveling. I could've put my hand on your leg and held on, but it wouldn't have mattered, and you wouldn't have noticed, because at that moment we were already together.

Sometimes always a bend or two behind,
—Go-boy

I tracked Go down in Anchorage, at the psych ward of the Native Hospital. He'd checked himself in, feeling so unstable he couldn't trust himself. I spent most of my remaining five hundred dollars—from the thousand Go had given me—on a plane ticket to see him. But since he'd checked himself in, he could refuse visitors, and he didn't want to see anyone, not even Kiana. Not even me. He felt too guilty. So I explained the whole story to his nurses, and on my behalf they tried convincing him to let me visit, but it didn't work. I was turned away to the sidewalks of Anchorage.

Standing there in front of the hospital, I looked up at the third floor, at the black windows reflecting sky. I wondered if Go was up there behind the tinted glass, looking down and seeing me on the sidewalk with no place to be. And I wondered—if he was watching, what did he see? Was I just another cousin who scoffed at his fanatical ideas? Was I just another jaded skeptic who didn't pay attention to spirituality, who didn't appreciate the hard questions about life? Was I just a phase for him, a passing memory, a time to look back and laugh about—the year his cousin from LA lived with him? How funny it was when this cousin couldn't fit into the village scene. How this cousin talked a lot of shit about moving home and playing drums. How this cousin had a fling with his sister. How it would be nice to see this cousin again for old time's sake, all the while knowing this cousin would never return to Unk, not even to visit.

This was what finally pushed me to change my name to Atausiq. I started the legal name-change process because of this—the idea of Go looking down on me from the psych ward and seeing someone who could never change, seeing a life that could never change, and from that, believing nothing or nobody ever got any better, that life would always be the same shitty way it always was.

So I became Atausiq. And when Go let me onto the third floor to visit, on his fifth day in there, and we played ping-pong in the activities room, I told him it was now official—I was becoming Atausiq.

He looked at me with part suspicion, part shock, before deflecting his stare to the wall behind me and scratching at the back of his neck.

I said, "Nothing is permanent, man. That's why I did it."

I told him it wasn't because of our bet, but because I now believed nothing lasted forever.

I said, "It's the never same-same conspiracy."

He almost smiled right then, holding the paddle and ball, getting ready to serve. But he was far from okay. It took all of his energy to be around anybody, to be anywhere but alone in his room. If allowed, he would've sat on his window ledge all day, looking through the angled blinds and out the window, with the TV's dialogue indiscernible somewhere behind him, down a distant hall. He'd look at the busy city—the office complexes and clusters of housing developments climbing the foothills—and he'd remember Valerie's hands, how her slender thumbs were more wrinkled than her other fingers. How her nails seemed too thin. How alive he felt when those hands touched his. And Go would know that he'd never forget the way those hands looked while holding a pen, or a coffee mug, or an ulu, or resting idle on the arm of a chair, or even steering his boat upriver.

Go flipped the ping-pong paddle over and over in his hands. He said, "But that's not same-same."

I ended up spending over two weeks in the city while Go was in the hospital, learning this whole story, and learning about his past, and understanding that somehow, through it all, Go-boy's fantastic weird year had become my story too.

SISTERING

I walked into Go-boy's house and found Great-Uncle Stanley with a ten-gallon bucket of tools, trying to fix the hole that Go had cut in the living room floor five months earlier.

He said, "I think it isn't too safe," and he finished his sentence with a circular hand gesture. He'd removed my patchwork from the hole—an end table, which was on top of a woven rug, which was covering sheets of aluminum from a junked twin-engine airplane. Stanley laughed, said, "Maybe a real repair this time."

I'd beaten Go-boy back from Anchorage on the flight that morning. He was on standby and got bumped a day, but he didn't mind. He'd spent over three weeks in the Anchorage hospital, so he was nervous about coming home, nervous about reengaging with family and friends and the whole town, still mourning Valerie's death and his self-proclaimed role in causing that. I was surprised the hospital therapists didn't do more to convince Go it wasn't his fault.

"Maybe we need to redo the whole floor," Stanley said, kneeling on the carpet next to the damage, sizing the width of the hole with a tape measure—three feet. Stanley almost whispered when he talked, illustrating each point with his hands. His days were numbered and he was at an age when this was the first thing you noticed. But right here in the living room it sounded like he wanted me to ask him questions, like he wasn't sure how he would repair this. He was wading through his thoughts, weighing the suicide attempt that had caused the damage and that created a desire in him to fix this mess before Go-boy returned. He was waiting to come through it all with a solution as to how an old man like him could still be of value to his family.

"How are you gonna fix it?"

Stanley looked up, and under the extra skin and puffy white brows I saw a face that was once young. I saw his eyes had never changed. He was the oldest man I knew.

He said, "How good should it be?"

Stanley spun the tape measure a quarter turn, stretching it across the wider part of the oval, then set it down on the carpet. It looked like he wasn't sure where this project started.

I walked over and crouched next to him. Our knees were at the edge of the hole, lined along splintered wood and sawdust and frayed green carpet. Cold air poured into the house through the opening. I stuck my head down inside, saw the floor joists. I wasn't sure if these were the same on every house or building, but there seemed to be something important about the joists, about their invisibility, and I felt like I should know what it was. The long wooden I-beams disappeared into shadows. I'd never known anything about houses or electricity or plumbing, and not much more about cars, and I wondered how people could understand so much of this stuff. I wondered what Pop knew, or would ever know, and I wondered about Wicho, locked up, what he knew, whether he would ever learn anything about joists.

Stanley mimicked a sinking floor with his fingers, said, "I can't figure how it hasn't collapsed."

I agreed, but it wasn't very convincing.

"Two joists are cut," he said. "Everything right here should fall."

His frail kneecaps were just tiny bumps in his pant legs, like kids hiding behind curtains, and I was surprised he could stay sitting like this.

I asked, "Can you splice in a couple pieces?"

"Could," he said. "Probably shouldn't."

We stayed kneeling. Stanley rubbed his fingers along the edge of the plywood flooring where the chainsaw had ripped it open. Only skin as rough as his wouldn't get a forest of splinters. It looked like his hands still had fight left in them, but that was all; everything else in his body was shrinking and deteriorating, and it was the first time I'd ever witnessed this happening to anyone. By the expression on Stanley's face, I now understood that he knew what this repair would take but was hesitating because his body couldn't do it. He was considering shortcuts and compromises.

Stanley said, "I should've done this right away, after it happened."

"We'll get it fixed."

Stanley slid the yellow button on his tape measure, unlocking the tape, and it recoiled with a shattering sound and wound itself up from three feet to nothing. He dropped it back into the bucket. Years ago I'm sure Uncle Stanley was the guy who repaired and remodeled without writing out plans. At the peak of his game, he probably anticipated problems and breezed right through. And in his day I'm sure it was a lot harder to stay alive, to eat, to build houses and raise families and do anything. But right here, at the edge of the hole, he would have traded anything to have it back.

"What do you think?"

He said, "It's got to be done."

I told him okay and spent the next ten minutes listening to his ideas and commands. I left the house and hopped on his snowmachine and ran the errands he suggested. I started at the airport, asking the mechanic—an in-law of Stanley's—for a couple of large mechanical jacks. Then I went to the city garage, where I found the guy who plowed the roads and asked him for a cordless drill and Skilsaw. It was cold outside, so I hurried. I hit up the shop teacher at the school and showed him the list of wood Stanley needed, written out on an envelope. He laughed when he read, *Scraps will do*. He said, "That's all there is." I also stopped by the post office and asked the postmaster—a weekend construction guy—for two boxes of galvanized nails. I told everyone that Uncle Stanley was fixing Go-boy's house, and no one hesitated or held back. I even got some advice for quick and reliable methods, things I was supposed to pass along to Stanley but couldn't seem to remember. And I was back at Go's place an hour later, towing a trailer filled with almost twice the supplies needed.

"You'll have to do this for me," Stanley said with a heavy breath. He was staring at the hole, rubbing his hands up and down on the thighs of his pants. It was obvious he'd been thinking about ways he could work on the floor while I was gone. Now he knew there was little he could do. He had to rely on me.

I said, "Okay." I was taken by the idea of understanding how to fix a floor. At that moment there were hundreds of things I wished I already knew. Hundreds of things I couldn't wait to know.

"You'll have to listen to what I say."

We started the job, and for most of the afternoon I had no idea what was happening. Stanley told me this and that. He used hand motions more than words. I set the jacks and raised them to the foundation, lifting the floor, one corner of the house at a time. I placed car jacks on either side of the hole and raised the existing floor. I was cold, but that was easy to ignore while working with Stanley. I cut two-by-six boards in six-foot sections, and he showed me how to build floor trusses. Like a small wall, the new joists were twelve inches tall, six feet long, with a vertical board every foot or so. And as I worked, I felt like a vessel, like an extension of Uncle Stanley. We worked into the night. I became hungry and tired after a few hours, but we kept going. A couple people stopped by to help. Everyone came to check. The airport mechanic. The postmaster. The city worker. Kiana. My mom. Even the shop teacher stopped by around suppertime with a few of his old students. The postmaster hopped in his car to retrieve more nails. I watched our progress through their eyes. By nine o'clock we were almost done, but not quite, and Stanley suggested we start early the next day to finish the job. I'm sure he wanted it fixed before Go-boy came home.

When we had started the project, Uncle Stanley told me what we were doing was called sistering. He said sistering floor joists was done to saggy or bouncy floors, not floors with three-foot holes cut from them. Stanley told me we'd use the old section of wood flooring and we'd sister the joists together. But what I didn't catch while we worked was that sistering was technical-speak for splicing, or rigging. By sistering, it was possible to make the floor as strong as it was before by adding a few chunks of new wood alongside the old. And the way we did the job, with me under the house, cutting sections of wood, drawing lines with pencils, and driving in screws with the city worker's drill, I was learning how to sister without knowing what it was. And I would walk away replaying every step of the job in my head, replaying every hint and nod of advice I received from Stanley and his hands, because I would forever know how to repair a floor.

The next day Stanley stood on the repaired floor. It was finished. He bounced, his knees flexing, his arms straight out at his sides. I joined him on the repaired hole and jumped along. It felt solid. And it looked like it was supposed to be here—a circle cut from the carpet—a type of decoration or design.

Stanley laughed and looked at his feet. "We need to find the cutout section of rug so we can hide it."

I stepped back and looked at the circle of repaired flooring. The cut made by the chainsaw left a gap about as wide as a wedding band—the old piece didn't fill the hole all the way. The plywood was gray, but where the chainsaw had torn out splinters the wood was a fresh gold color. I stepped back farther. The ring, with its sporadic tears, looked like a child's drawing of the sun. It was in the middle of the living room.

I said, "Maybe we should leave it uncovered so Go-boy can see how we did it."

FOR WHAT WE WANT NOW

It took a full week for Kiana and me to break up.

It was late June. The sun was barely setting these days, maybe dipping under the northern hills for a couple hours each night, which meant no darkness, just a back-to-back dusk and dawn before the sun burned down on us again. School was done for the year. Kiana and I had both graduated in an anticlimactic week of ceremonies and parties. We broke up when Unalakleet had a citywide beach and street cleaning. Kiana signed us on.

The first night we worked Airport Road, carrying black trash bags, wearing leather gloves. When Kiana picked up an old rope that was frayed at both ends, she told me she had gotten everything completed for her college financial aid.

I asked, "Have you even been to Colorado before?"

"No," she said, scratching her nose with her forearm.

I found a rusted truck rim, halfway buried by sand and sticks, and I told Kiana that there were a lot of things I had been thinking about.

I said, "There's some stuff I've been meaning to tell you."

I had felt our breakup building. The closer we grew and the more time we spent together, the more I thought about the gang rape. It was like it had its own voice. I had to tell her, but couldn't.

After Go's second hospital visit, the three of us were always together. Kiana spent most of her time at our house because she was worried about her brother. Go-boy had again become a shut-in. He never left his room. He feared seeing any of Valerie's friends or family. In such a small town he couldn't run anywhere without bumping into someone who knew her or was related to her. Go was still convinced he was the reason for Valerie's death. So our house had been getting messier the longer he stayed in. Go would open the door to his room and stink would fill the hall. Everywhere the curtains seemed glued shut. The kitchen and bathroom sinks were swamped with dishes. Kiana came over to help clean and cook, and she and I would lure Go into the living room to play card games like snerts or three-way war, or we'd play trivia games or Uno. Anything to get Go back on track.

And as Go-boy started feeling better and was spending time with us, he and I began feeling more like family than friends. Family is who forces a deck of cards or a plate of spaghetti in your face when you feel like shit. Family is who is always around, doing laundry or leaving laundry. That was me and Go-boy. And that was Kiana too. We were always around each other. All of us. And at the start of summer, with no school during the day, it was even worse. We weren't three friends. We were three cousins. We weren't a boyfriend and girlfriend and her brother, we were three siblings. We were our own nuclear family.

After the first night of city cleanup, Kiana and me were in her old room. I started right in with my reasons for ending what we had.

She was leaving town in two months, going to an engineering school on a scholarship, and I told her I didn't want things to end bad. I said maybe I was even a little scared. I knew she'd have boyfriends the minute she got there. I told her that part of me felt like I hadn't been available to help Go-boy when times got rough for him. We were at a point in our relationship where I could be honest, and it sounded like I was, and yet I wasn't. She agreed with everything, even told me she'd been thinking some of the same things, but we were both lying. It was something else. Another reason that we didn't dare mention. We were both feeling the same—we were step-cousins—we were family. After everything that had happened this past year, and after the way it had all happened, she and I could never feel like we were just friends, or companions.

She said, "Okay, then. We're broken up."

We sat around a bit longer.

Kiana had a contented smile that made me comfortable being with her. She looked at home in her old bedroom. Her green bedroom. After a full year of me living here, the room was still the same. I knew she wanted it to be her room again, her only room. Even after becoming such good friends with my mom, I knew she wished her dad would get out of jail so she could come back here, sleep in her old bed, and wake up and make sourdough pancakes for Sean and her dad and Go-boy every Saturday morning.

Still, even while she was smiling, her eyes sliced the bedroom into threads. If you only looked at her black eyes and cropped out her tall cheeks and smirking mouth, you would think those eyes were contemplating issues so important and disturbing, even painful, that you would feel ignorant. You would feel little.

Still smiling, she said, "Will you follow me?"

"Where? Math school? No way."

She laughed, said, "Why not?"

But she knew I'd been following her for the past year. Chasing even. That was what I thought the smile was for. She knew that even though I was breaking things off between us, even though there was this weird familial thing we were aware of, I would always be following her. Or more so—every girl I dated from then on out would be following Kiana.

"I don't like math."

She said, "What about now?" and she leaned into me and kissed me.

In spite of everything, we had sex that night. We would have sex every night for the rest of cleanup week, as we broke off our relationship. It was that impossible gray area—the cloud that clogs the mind— a blur between what a person believes and what that person is living.

When it was over, she said, "Okay, *friend*." She laughed. I was glad she hadn't said cousin. Through our whole relationship the sex had never lasted long enough for her, not until this night. I can't say it had anything to do with me. For whatever reason, we were clicking. Maybe she wasn't so stressed. Maybe she didn't feel the need to convince me of anything. Or maybe now that we weren't dating, I felt okay that Kiana didn't know everything about my past.

I pulled a t-shirt over my head. She was still in bed and had let the covers slip off, with no thought of her exposed nakedness, or maybe with plenty of thought.

I walked home after our second night of trash cleanup, feeling the tingle of recent sex. I felt exposed. It seemed adults were looking at me different, like they could sense something, like people could just tell. But this was the first time I'd had sex and didn't feel a lit-tle gross afterward. Maybe because I hadn't initiated it or tried to get it. And this time, I wasn't embarrassed or proud either. This was new.

I ran into a group of kids on my way back to Go-boy's. There were about thirty total, and they were blocking Main Road, with sweatshirts and bikes scattered everywhere, playing an old Eskimo game called Manamanaa.

"Hey, Atausiq!" a few yelled.

There were two teams, separated by twenty yards, and they were running around trying to tag each other. Each team's base was marked with a circle scratched in the gravel. This was right in front of the windowless Igloo Store, which had high school kids sitting on the front steps and watching their younger siblings. I noticed Kiana's little brother was in the street too, running around, kicking up dust with the rest.

"Car!" someone yelled and the game stopped as all the kids cleared off the road.

They asked me if I would play, and at first I didn't. I sat on the ground, leaned back against a telephone pole, and watched. Each team had a jail. And somehow, by tagging an opponent, they would send that person to prison. But all the kids in the jail could be res-cued if they held hands, stretched out in a long line, and touched a free member of their own team.

When Kiana's little brother took a spill and cut up his hands in the dirt, I waited to see if he'd cry and come over to me. The game stopped and a couple older kids helped him off the ground, checked his scrapes, and dusted his pants. Bum One jumped up and helped Sean wash off the little smears of blood, talking and distracting him from crying.

It was then that I understood something about this place, and about Go-boy.

I joined the game later. It took a little while for me to figure it out, and by the time I did, they were ready to play something else. Red rover. Freeze tag. Games I'd played hundreds of times.

Everyone branched off toward home just before midnight. I walked with three kids. The clouds above us were way up in the sky, like they were in space, and I could just barely see a bunch of seagulls—black dots against the gray. I'd never seen those birds fly so high, but I was sure they were seagulls—flying in their apparent chaos. I had once heard that these birds spent their whole day up-river, looking for dead fish, cleaning the shores, and at night every single one migrated back to the ocean. They ended each day grouping back together along the beach.

Two of these kids were brothers, and the other was their older cousin. The three were laughing and sharing funny stories about their family—like adults did, and like how Kiana and my mom did—except these guys told stories about their dads that involved dead animals or long boat rides. These three were just like most of the kids in Unk—from big families where kids helped raise other kids—a cycle—cousins, sisters, brothers.

"Where's Go-boy?" one of them asked.

He was probably at home right then, doing nothing, hiding, sleeping, bumming out. But I said I didn't know.

Kiana and I would pick a section of road to clean, or a section of beach along the slough or ocean. Each night was low tide and we combed up and down the sand, observing what the high water had left behind. The ocean side sometimes stank, with something rotting. This was the time of year when dead sea animals washed ashore. Dead seals, ugruks, walruses with the tusks already removed. Lots of fish. Sometimes a whale. But we also found gillies, put them in our pockets, and later gave them to Go-boy.

The river side of town stank too, but with more of a temporary smell from the fish guts people left after cleaning their catches. This was where we found the most trash. Broken bottles. Chunks of old porcelain dishes revealed from under the sand. Shirts. Sometimes baseball caps. Once we filled three trash bags.

Every night we walked past an abandoned semitrailer that was parked just off Airport Road. Behind that was the graveyard, and hills, and behind those was a burnt sky catching the manic sun, which rested a bit before it returned the next day and gave itself for another twenty-two hours. The semitrailer was white with bits of old graffiti tagged in faded black paint—*UP YOURS!* and *AC DC*. Each night it glared orange from the sunset. Centered on the trailer, one of Go-boy's signs still hung—*#68: SOMETIMES WE'RE ALWAYS REAL SAME-SAME*. It was the last sign remaining in town, and I wondered how long it would stay there.

· · ·

You sure that's not a dog's?" I said.

Kiana held a tooth out in front of her, squinting one eye like she was aiming it. We were standing on the wet riverbank.

"Haven't you ever lost a tooth?" she said. "This is an adult molar."

The tide was low and the sandbars that were normally hidden beneath the water were now visible, exposed like small brown continents up and down the river. She dropped her arm to her side. I was waiting for her to toss the tooth into the river or into the garbage bag.

She said, "Who leaves a molar on the beach?"

Kiana had been telling me all night about how much she disliked living in town and how bad she wanted to leave. *Needed* was how she put it. Kiana couldn't wait.

I now asked, "How long have you been planning to move?"

"I've been thinking about leaving the village, and even Alaska, since I was a sophomore."

"I thought you liked it here."

"I love it here," she said, dropping the tooth and turning back in the direction we'd come from. "But I need to leave."

I took this personal, and I'm not sure why. I said, "How can you want both?"

Kiana was stepping in her old footprints. I walked beside her. Our garbage bags were pretty empty. Someone must have cleaned this shoreline already.

She said, "I don't know. It's just something I have to do."

"That doesn't make sense."

She took a heavy breath and walked faster. She was frustrated that I wouldn't talk about anything else. We stepped over a busted tree that stretched out of the water and onto the bank.

Then she said something I wouldn't forget. She said, "Don't you know that what people want right now, and what people want in life, is always two different things?"

I had to think about that.

I said, "Not if right now is all you want."

She stopped walking, smirked, and said, "What we want is never right now."

.   .   .

left Kiana and walked home. Our argument had ended the night. On my way back to Go's I heard a couple jumping jacks and then the hiss of a bottle rocket arcing through the air, followed by its pop. It was two weeks before the Fourth of July.

I started to think about what Kiana had said—*What we want right now is never the same as what we want in life.* It made me think about Go-boy's theories from the summer before.

Like his conspiracy idea—how he had believed that all the rich and powerful and famous people in the world were conspiring to make a heaven on earth for everyone. When he first told me, I thought it was a joke. I didn't believe him. I didn't think a person could suspect that some of the most corrupt people and corrupt systems were really working for the benefit of the world. I remember telling Go, "Maybe in a remote village like this one, people could do that. But not everywhere."

As I walked home—a year after he'd first preached the stuff—it started to seem like a good angle on things. It seemed like a good argument against Kiana's pessimistic outlook. Why wouldn't we want heaven?

Go had said the immediate moment is where everyone is equal—where we are all connected, where we are all the same. If we could just see each other in the now, without judgment, then we could see that everyone hopes for a similar joy and meaning—a similar heaven. And when we see that, we will begin to free ourselves, here on earth.

Kiana said what we want in life is never the same as what we want right now. Go-boy had argued that heaven isn't perfection but the perfect perspective.

Somehow, the two seemed opposite.

I walked through town, down Main Road. The north sky was all orange and there were no kids playing out. Even though Kiana and I had just argued and were broken up, I had that good summer feeling—the invincibility—the energy—like the feeling of getting a new kick-ass haircut. And with all this summer sun, it was hard to believe that Unk ever had a winter with freezing temps and darkness. It was hard to believe the sun wouldn't keep on spinning around the sky, giving us its undivided favor, forever.

COFFEEPOT

We are in the middle of the Coffeepot Race—two miles upriver in Go-boy's boat, filling our pot with river water—when I know I'm not leaving this little town . . . at least, not for a while.

The sun is right there on top of us, on top of the late afternoon and all over the ripe green flats and hills; the sun is penetrating tundra, growing berries and fireweed, illuminating the ocean, prompting the salmon to return to their spawning grounds. Unk is alive. Go-boy turns the boat around in a single dipping motion and I drag the pot full of water. We then face our village—a treeless silhouette of single-and double-story buildings syncopated by telephone poles, stretching along the horizon maybe a half mile, left to right. Behind that is the ocean.

Fourth of July. Stage one of the Coffeepot. We are chasing water and I've made the decision that I will stay here, in this secluded place, even though I'd already been staying.

The race goes like this: two people on each team. One boat, with a motor no larger than fifty horses. One coffeepot. All teams race upriver a few miles to Nuthluk Hill, fill their pots, race back to the Bering Sea, collect driftwood from the beach, then race to the shores along town, build a fire, and boil water. The first team with a hot cup of coffee wins. I didn't used to like the stuff until I started living with Go, when all I could find in the house to eat or drink some days was coffee and frozen French fries. Now I drink a cup or two a day. But I guess that isn't the point of the race.

Go-boy says, "Nice," as I pull the full pot into the boat without spilling.

Go has been drinking coffee for a few years, ever since he started college, but today he won't touch the stuff. Today the only thing he is hoping to drink is a can of Pepsi. He claims he hasn't had an ounce of pop in two months because doctors told him caffeine wouldn't mix well with his medication. But I know he quit drinking soda when Valerie died—it was some connection between them. So today is his day to drink a pop and end his fast.

He again looks at the pot of water between us and yells, "Yeah, man. Nice."

Go turns the boat out of the main channel. We are heading back to town, toward the ocean. Go aims at a shortcut through some shallow water, and the village silhouette disappears behind an island of willows and tall grass. I don't know if we are in the lead at this point.

Cellophane sticks out from Go-boy's sweatshirt sleeve, the film flapping in the wind as he holds the wheel. He finally got his forearm tattoo just a few days earlier, and it's still healing. I'd been asking him to roll up his sleeve almost every twenty minutes so I could see it. It's not that I like the tattoo, just the sight of that fresh black ink, raised a little off his brown skin. With the same arm, he turns up the volume on a battery-powered stereo sitting on the floor of his Lund. I'm not sure what the song is, but he cranks it, and the tinny sound of rural AM pop music fights with the hum of motor and wind. Go stands to see the water's depth, with the steering wheel at his waist and the cellophane flapping around his right wrist.

I yell, "Hey, Cousin. Let me see it."

We must be in the lead. I don't notice any other boats around.

The girl who inked the tattoo on his arm gave Go-boy, besides a perfect rendition of his drawing, a real jump start. He needed someone like her, a stranger, to reassure him that the world wasn't laughing.

She said, "This design is absolutely fascinating."

We were in Anchorage a week before the Coffeepot Race. I had urged Go-boy to get this thing put on his arm, for real. Go hadn't been talking about his heaven-on-earth theories or his tattoo anymore, and anytime I mentioned either of them, he shrugged, like those things were embarrassing now, something foolish from his past. But I'd found myself starting to catch on. I'd found myself thinking and writing philosophical ideas.

I told him, "We need to get lost." I was quoting what he'd said months earlier—right before he tried to hang himself. I said, "We need to get out of this place for a while."

After breaking up with Kiana I was seeing and thinking from a different perspective. I realized that from a new angle, everything could look like something else. From a new angle, everything could be questioned. Turn a situation upside down, backward, inverted, and the whole thing changed. So this put me in a spot where I wanted the deep-thinking version of Go-boy back. I convinced Go that we needed to fly out of town, to anywhere, but probably to Anchorage. And then I suggested it was a good time to get his tattoo.

The girl with the ink needle worked her way up and down Go's forearm that day, spending almost five hours poking skin and dabbing at the beads of blood with tissue.

"Fascinating," she repeated.

She had very few of her own tattoos showing. There was a purple-and-red flower covering her elbow and some type of vine that peeked out of her t-shirt collar.

She said, "I've never heard of an Eskimo Jesus."

"It's a woman," Go added.

"It's perfect."

I could see on his face, for the first time in almost a year, that he believed in this tattoo again.

I left the shop and walked around downtown Anchorage with a list of things I needed to get for myself and for the whole family. I had a sandwich at Snow City Café, stopped at the Army-Navy Store for some rubber boots for Sean, stopped at an office-supply store and picked up paper and pens for Kiana and Mom. While I gathered stuff and crossed items from my list, I stopped in a drum shop. There were new sets crowded throughout the small store, assembled with cymbals and stands and everything. I had never seen so many. There was a small aisle weaving in and out and around. Bordering the room were stacks of drums not yet set up, and in the farthest corner were used drums. Most of the kits, even the old ones, were too expensive, except one. It was ancient. It was a beat-up and scratched maroon color—just a bass, a snare, and two toms. The pocked drumheads were yellowing. Its one cymbal was spackled with rust, like a rock star had spit a mouthful of water on it years earlier. And I knew then, if I had this set—my own set—in Go's house—if I dropped the rest of my fish-tower money on these drums—I could stay in Unk.

The Eskimo Jesus, after only a couple hours, was looking just how Go wanted it to look. Now that he'd been in the shop a while, he was more relaxed. The girl had already asked Go where he was from. He had already answered, telling her about Unalakleet. He'd already asked her how she'd gotten into tattooing. Back in Houston she had a brother who used to let her tattoo his legs with a home-made contraption fashioned from a guitar string and an ink pen. She asked him where he'd found such a unique image. He told her he did it himself. "You draw?" she asked. She was impressed.

They were now talking about Alaskan politicians and the oil industry.

She said, "Bureaucratic shit, all behind closed doors, with no ear to the public. It was the same in Houston."

"But it's not all evil," Go said. "Corporations still listen to stock-holders. Stockholders are approachable groups and individuals who—" He trailed off. He had that glow again. He enjoyed this.

Later—"That part was inspired by a song lyric."

Later—"I ship organic vegetables up from Washington. I order t-shirts from LA. We also have a store in town."

Later—"Rain is made of individual drops. After death we're the ocean, we're the clouds, we all blend into one. On earth we're indi-viduals who originated in unity, we desire unity. We need it."

It seemed to have worked—this trip to Anchorage—this tat-too—this plan.

Go steers our boat through that shortcut, and about halfway, the silhouette of town reappears from behind the island. The village seems twice as big. And it isn't a silhouette anymore now that we are closer. Now we can see the different house colors and the glare from windows and the flicker of aluminum boats lining the shore.

We're leading the Coffeepot Race. I am sure of this now. Go and I watch the village, anticipating the first sight of a couple hundred fellow townspeople along the water, waiting for us to pass, to pick up driftwood, then return and, in front of them, build a fire, boil water, and win the race. There hadn't been many people at the start—probably all still watching one of the other Fourth of July events, like the fish-cutting contest or the target shoot—but we know that hordes of people will be there for the end. Hordes of people will be cheering. And more than that, hordes will be rooting for Go-boy. This race is the town's favorite. I'm excited, yet nervous too, as I always am around groups of grown-ups I don't know. I look at Go. He seems to be feeling the same, but opposite—terrified by this group of people he does know.

That's when the motor hesitates and the prop stutters, jerking the boat, and everything drags to a stop, beaching us.

I look over the sidewall. We're stuck on a sandbar. The sound of waves cutting up the shore circles us, and we hear boats trailing behind on the main river.

"This is a shortcut?" I joke.

Then I say, "Man, we've got to stop beaching boats."

Go has a strange look on his face, like maybe he tried to get us stuck. Like maybe he knew it was too shallow through this area.

When Go and I flew back to Unk from our Anchorage trip, I loaded my drums into his AMC. Go said he needed to walk, and he left me with his car. The cellophane peeked out from his sweatshirt sleeve. He was still nervous about being in public around the village, especially alone, and especially with this tattoo, even though the tattoo girl had given him a spark. I could see it in his slow walk and his wandering eyes.

I packed the drums into the wagon and drove home.

"Let me see it again," I said, rolling down the driver's-side window as I pulled up next to Go.

He slid his sleeve up and pulled back a layer of gauze. His skin was tender and shiny, and I noticed Go-boy smile a little as we looked at it.

When I got home there was a group of kids—seven- to thirteen-year-olds—waiting for Go-boy on the front step. All spring they'd continued to stop by and force Go to hang out with them. And during his whole funk, since hospital visit number two, these kids hadn't let Go hide himself away.

"Could I use Go's bike for the Fourth of July race?"

I asked when that was, joking, and each kid reminded me that the town has a whole day of games and contests on the Fourth of July.

"So could I?"

I said, "I don't know, man. You got to ask Go."

One of the events was the Coffeepot Race. It sounded all right to me, like a good idea for getting Go-boy to do something again. And as the week went on and Go became even more of a shut-in, I knew I had to come up with something. I thought Fourth of July would be a good distraction, and of all the races, there were only three team events—a four-person paddling race, the Coffeepot, and a raft race. Since he'd done the raft thing with Valerie the year before, I got a schedule, tagged it to our refrigerator, and circled *COFFEEPOT.*

. . .

Go says, "I thought it was deep enough through here, man. It's still high tide."

"Put up the motor," I say. "I'll push us over there."

"Man, we should just turn around."

I say, "Put up the motor."

I'm ankle-deep in the water and I'm very aware that we're in the lead. Now I want to win.

I push the boat off the sandbar. Go is sitting behind the wheel, waiting to start the motor. He's repositioning a piece of tape so the cellophane over his tattoo doesn't fly off. Next to him, on the floor, the coffeepot of river water sits, still full.

Go says, "There's something I've always wanted to ask you."

"Okay," I say, rushed, pulling myself back into the boat. My shoes and socks are soaked, now three times as heavy as they were before.

"Do you think Wicho really did it—shot those kids? Do you think he's really guilty?"

I sit next to him, stunned. I forget about the race. I forget about everything because I don't know. I don't answer right away. I watch a group of seagulls fight over some fish guts on the shore next to us. One seagull dives into the water and resurfaces with intestines or fish eyes or something, and the rest pounce on the bird. I'm amazed by how much a seagull can swallow.

"Man," I say.

Wicho has always seemed guilty to me because I know how he was living at the time. I know he was running with gangs. I'd heard him talk about those kids, saying they were going to get what they had coming. I know he was capable of taking stupid risks—he was always a bold person. But hearing that question from Go-boy makes me feel different.

I say, "No, he's always just been a brother to me."

Mom had told me I could've used the money I'd spent on the drums to go back to LA and visit Wicho. My brother had been transferred from LAC state prison to someplace else, and he'd been calling a lot more since being transferred. But I figured we wouldn't hear from him once he got settled into this new place, made some new friends. Mom said he'd been asking about me. She said the transfer had nothing to do with his sentence—he was still locked up for life, with no chance of parole in the next twenty years. She always liked to remind me of that.

She said, "He wants to see you. Or at least talk to you."

She told me this the same day I came back from Anchorage, when I already had the drums. And even if I hadn't bought them I doubt that I would've tried to visit Wicho. He'd been in prison for six years, almost seven, including the time during his trial. If I visited him it would be like sitting with a stranger, and he'd still have to stay in there after I left. That was the thing. It was ideal to say we'd always be brothers—that blood is the thickest—but he was in prison for life. He was no longer a brother or a son or even a person. He was a subject of that place. A name on paper. Visiting him would only be to revisit the people we used to be. We could no longer share in each other's lives. His brothers were his cellmates, prisonmates, and shit, even the guards. Not me. Not anymore. And never again.

"You should at least talk on the phone," Mom said.

I knew he wouldn't call again. It was so rare. He wouldn't write, either. And the journals he'd told me he was sending would never come.

The problem with what Mom said was that I felt like I couldn't visit Wicho ever again. Of course I wanted to. I wanted to see him, to tell him everything about Alaska and my year here, about Kiana and Go-boy. Of course I needed that. But what I now knew and had known for six or seven years was a loss of everything else. Interactions had to be scheduled and planned. Phone calls were timed, maybe even monitored. And the one time he had sent a short letter, everything was backward because Wicho was a high school dropout and wrote at a seventh grade level, and witnessing this was worse than anything, worse than the time away from him, worse than not really knowing him anymore. At some point in my life, I had surpassed my older brother. I had become smarter than him without even noticing. He was stuck in that place. Stuck in a time. Stuck in a mentality, in an atmosphere where everyone was stuck. His idea of respect and honor seemed so distant from what I now knew. If I someday came through like I had always planned and went to college and became the governor to get Wicho out of prison, he would probably be the same stupid kid who'd landed himself in there, with the same stupid ideas about life and the same stupid ideas about what he wanted. He would probably leave prison still thinking those fifteen-year-olds kids had deserved to be shot.

Go starts the motor and points the boat back toward town, back toward the race and the finish line. Now I wish I could rephrase my answer about Wicho. I wish I could say, *He's guilty of ditching us. . . . He's guilty of forgetting about me. . . . He's guilty of being a dumb kid with adult problems and adult capabilities.*

Instead I say, "I don't think he feels guilty about it at all."

Go nods. "Really?"

"I know he doesn't."

I tell Go that's the shame of it. When people like his dad go to jail alongside people like Wicho. But what I don't say, and wish I could say, is that I'm one of those people like Wicho who deserves to be locked up. I'm one of those gangbangers. One of those rapists. One of those criminals who lucked out and can hide his ugly past from the world. I'm one of those guys who can pretend he's just like everyone else.

I say, "Man, your dad doesn't need to be in jail. Everyone knows that."

Go-boy says, "Nobody ever *needs* to be in jail."

"Some people deserve it."

"Sure," Go says. "But they don't need it. They need money or rehab or some type of renewed perspective. Not imprisonment."

Go then tells me that time is never a substitute for understanding.

The boat's off the sandbar and we're back in the main river, back in the race, and it looks like we've fallen to fourth place, but Go's boat is fast and we pass a team on speed alone. A headwind blows off the ocean, and the boat thumps on each wave.

Then we're in third, inching up on the town.

Two boats are ahead of us. One is already parked inside the mouth of the river, the racers are out, running up the beach for firewood. The other team is almost there.

People line the town side of the river, to our right. They wave and cheer as we pass—some for the excitement, some to create excitement. Kids run around, weaving through the adults, skipping rocks. Somebody's dog is swimming, chasing the humpies that jump and cut their backs out of the water. Others sit in trucks and on four-wheelers, men talking about crab pots, women talking about kids.

"I don't think I want to win," Go says. He eyes the crowd. He still looks nervous, like he did when we came back from Anchorage. All these people are waiting along the shore, and they are all people he knows well, and who know him well, and who haven't seen him in months but have been talking about him anyway.

I say, "I doubt we still can. What's the prize?"

"Five hundred bucks," he says.

"Five hundred!"

"Well, five hundred bucks of free cargo shipping."

"Still."

He turns and looks at me longer than a person should while driving something. There are no words, just the sounds of motor and wind and the boat slapping water. Go's waiting for me to convince him again, to assure him that whatever he's thinking isn't real.

He says, "We can still win if you want to."

"It's five hundred bucks, man."

The boat is nearing the beach where we are supposed to collect driftwood. The team in first place has a few bundles in their arms. Beyond that, the water stretches out over the ocean, forever in front of us.

"You want to win?" he says.

I nod.

Go hits the throttle harder. We approach a steep bank that looks almost vertical and is closer to us than the spot where the other teams have docked.

I say, "What are you doing?"

We close in on the shore—forty yards, twenty—and Go hasn't dropped our speed. I lean back on the bench and push my wet feet hard into the floor. At the last minute, right before we hit the sand, Go spins the boat at a slight angle and shuts the engine off. We slam into the bank and pitch up the beach, just high enough for the boat to hold and not float away. The force throws me to the floor.

"Shit," I say.

Go's laughing. A real laugh. It's the first time I've heard him do that in months. It's nice, and I almost forget to collect wood.

Go says, "Throw that stuff in here."

The other two teams up the coast look at us. The guy and girl in first place get back to their boat—one person inside, organizing the wood, and the other shoving them off the shore.

"Throw it!" Go says. "The bark too."

I toss about eight pieces of wood, some small, some large, fifteen feet down the steep bank and into the boat. Go pushes off the wet sand with an oar and fires up the motor as I hop in, and we're back in the river, alongside the first-place boat, aimed for town, now ready to win.

Go says, "I told you, man. I told you we could still do it."

We inch past the first-place team. And at that moment Go-boy's little fifty-horse motor seems like an airplane engine, like the engines on the NAC jet rattling every windowpane in town. And Go-boy seems right there too, just as powerful.

"Show me your tattoo," I say.

He doesn't raise his sleeve this time, but I know he can hear me.

Right before the Coffeepot Race, Kiana met Go-boy along the shore of the river. Go was alone, inspecting the boat motor, checking the oil and the gas jugs. Kiana hopped into the front and sat on the bow. She hadn't yet seen his arm. She'd only heard about it.

"Where's your Nanook of Jerusalem tattoo?" she said and laughed.

Go stopped working and slid up his sleeve. He held his arm out straight.

She said, "Wow. It's real . . . huge."

"What do you think?" Go scratched behind his ear with his other hand.

She moved closer, rotated the driver's seat so it faced the back of the boat, sat in it, and looked Go's arm up and down. Kiana then looked at her brother. She wiped a smudge of grease from his chin. She could tell he was nervous. She could tell he wanted her approval.

She said, "Go-boy, it's really weird."

Go smiled. He knew she liked it.

Kiana had been busy, and Go and I hadn't seen her in a while. After we broke up, she began watching Sean around the clock, giving my mom a needed break. Even though Mom was more than happy to have a chance at raising a little boy in Unalakleet, she got worn out at times and needed rest. And Kiana loved taking care of him. I could tell she needed Sean to need her. It was important for Kiana—important in helping her feel like the family was together again.

"I think you should get another tattoo," she said, still in the boat.

"Why?"

"To balance out Jesus. You need another tattoo on your other arm."

Go said, "Man, I think I'm good with this for a while."

Kiana hesitated. She smoothed the cellophane on his forearm. Then she said, "You're right. One is good enough for now."

I know I'm staying in this town when Go drives the boat through a bend in the river and we race to a shoreline filled with people—the village. Colorful homes stretch left to right, and beyond that miles of hills and trees and nothing else. Everyone is right here, watching.

I know Go-boy is ready to run this boat up the shore—in front of all these people—and win the race because he's rolled his sleeves to his elbows.

I say, "You don't need that cellophane anymore."

He shrugs but keeps it wrapped around his arm.

We scratch onto the sand in between rows of small fishing boats, hop out, and hurry up the shore and into the people, Go with the wood, me with the full coffeepot. Go-boy crouches in the sand and starts a fire with bark and kindling, then builds a wood frame to support the water. He adds more sticks, puts his face near the fire, and blows.

Most of the crowd circles us. The boat in second place has just landed and the man and woman run up the beach to a spot near us. The race is close now. I've helped get us this far, but I don't know how to start a fire, or get the hottest flame, so Go will be on his own from here.

But now on shore, in town, I don't care about winning anymore. I don't care about the five hundred bucks.

"I'd rather have a pop," I say.

Go-boy looks up from the fire, smiles.

I say, "I think I'll get us some Pepsi."

I weave my way through all the people in town, rubbing against shoulders and bumping into hips. I look to see if any of these people are Kiana. There are a hundred faces. There's a chin with thin, inch-long black hair. Another is freshly shaved. There are a set of bifocals with a staple woven and twisted through the screw hole, holding the glasses together. A hood pulled tight. A hoop earring. A camera to someone's eye. I recognize only a few people. There are crooked teeth. Crooked noses. Perfect teeth. Crooked ball caps. Bangs freshly cut tabletop-flat across thick eyebrows. Double extra-large smiles. A dime-sized mole on someone's temple. A woman's long black hair with wise-looking gray streaks. Sideburns. Skinny necks. Deep-pored cheeks. Some ivory–smooth like they are brand new. Some wrinkled brown skin that has all of its years right here in Unalakleet. Bandanas. Round earlobes. Bowed legs. Rubber boots. Nylon coats with metal snaps. V-neck t-shirts. Some of the people are clapping hands. All of the people are circled around Go-boy. And I leave him there with everyone, on the beach, to finish the race alone. Yet, in reality, I'm not leaving Go-boy this time—like I've always been try-ing to do. I'm joining him. This is, after all, part of a plan. Part of the plan. This town, these people, this day. Something is starting every minute in every place, and here we all are, standing on the same ground. And here we all are, standing on this ground. Sure, none of these people have ever participated in a gang rape. None of them have ever seen anything so ugly. But in a way, they have. In a way, every person here has raped someone. Every person in the world has raped someone. Be-hind each of these faces there is plenty of ugly to focus on and pay at-tention to. Plenty of ugly to see. Plenty of ugly to hate. We can notice it because we all know it, and because we all have it. But in another way, none of us has participated in a gang rape or anything ugly. In this way we are all here, right now, standing on the same ground. And in this way, none of us has any ugly or knows any ugly or sees any ugly. We are all someone's son, or sister, or cousin, or mother, or uncle. We are all watching and cheering for Go-boy. We are all part of this village, and not part of someplace else. We are all going to be okay.

M y plan is to leave Go-boy along the shore, walk a block to AC Store, and buy two cans of soda—one for me, one for him. I'll then head back, slip into the crowd, and watch the outcome of the race along with everyone else. I'm not worried Go will quit trying to make that fire or boil that water. I'm not worried he'll disappear again. He'll still be there, squatting by the flame, with everyone watching to see if he can pull it off. I know he'll do like he'd said— try to take the race back, try to win.

I'll walk up and hand him that cold pop. He'll open it, drink a little. He'll think of Valerie. Hopefully some of the people standing around him will think of her as well.

And even if Go-boy does quit the race before he can brew coffee, even if he quits before the water starts to boil, I know he'll at least wait for me to get back there, to see what I am planning to do that night, after the race. Maybe we'll walk down Main Road, maybe we'll play some Eskimo games with the kids or softball with the adults. Maybe we'll take his car and ride around town, ride out on the road. And again I will ask him to show me his tattoo, even though his sleeves are rolled up and it's in plain view. And I will ask him three or four more times later that night. And then I'll ask him again, maybe one more time, the next night.

ACKNOWLEDGMENTS

This project would have been impossible without the strength and support of my wife, Tera Cunningham.

Thank you to my family—Donna and Ray Roesch, grandparents, sister Mandy, Dave and Annabelle, brother Reuben, Willa and Gary, and the whole Towarak crew; thanks to the village of Unalakleet, Luis Garcia-Lezama—we've come a long way, Stéphanie Abou for your agenting skills, Greg Michalson and Caitlin Hamilton Summie and everyone at Unbridled Books, Connie Oehring, Dale Gregory Anderson for showing me the way, Sigrid Nunez, Jerod Santek and The Loft, Nick Flynn, David Treuer, Warren Wilson MFA program staff and students, Stacey D'Erasmo, Sven Birkerts, Dave Eggers and the BANR committee, Evelyn Rogers,

Tom Jenks and Carol Edgarian, Megan Savage, Abdel Shakur, James Scott, Colleen Donfield, Tim McKee, Sarah Stone, Corey Everhard for the tough questions, Mark Sandberg for the tough ideas; and thanks to all the writers who volunteered their time to read this novel (or parts) when it was still limping—Eric Braun, Jeremy Weizel, Scott Wrobel, Michelle Freeland, Heather Goodman, Ali Gharavi, Stephanie Johnson, Ayme Almanderaz, Joshua Carlson, May Lee, Eireann Lorsung, April Lott, Molly Quinn, Vanessa Ramos, Brenna Rausch.

And I especially thank you—the reader—for inviting Go-boy and Cesar and Kiana into your life.

A NOTE ABOUT TYPE

The text of this book was set in Adobe Garamond Pro.
The display type in this book is set in a font called Device.

This book was designed by Claire Vaccaro.